The Parrot's Beak

It was late afternoon when Master Sergeant Anthony B. Fetterman caught the first faint whiff of an odor he'd smelled many times before in war.

Tyme moved over to Fetterman and asked quietly, "You smell it?"

"I think we might have found the patrol," Fetterman answered.

Through the gaps in the trees they saw the remains of the ARVN ranger patrol they'd been sent to look for. There were about a dozen men lying on the trail. The man closest to them seemed to have a black face, and for an instant Fetterman wondered if there had been any Americans with the South Vietnamese patrol. But as they approached, he could see that the body was alive with flies, each fighting the other to get into the man's mouth or nose or eyes.

Another man had both hands locked on his abdomen, in a desperate and dying attempt to keep his intestines from snaking out the huge hole in his stomach. His eyelids were open, but again the eyes were obscured by flies.

Fetterman shrugged. This was Vietnam.

VIETNAM: GROUND ZERO

ERIC HELM

A GOLD EAGLE BOOK FROM
W☉RLDWIDE

TORONTO · NEW YORK · LONDON · PARIS
AMSTERDAM · STOCKHOLM · HAMBURG
ATHENS · MILAN · TOKYO · SYDNEY

First edition August 1986

ISBN 0-373-62701-7

Printed in Canada

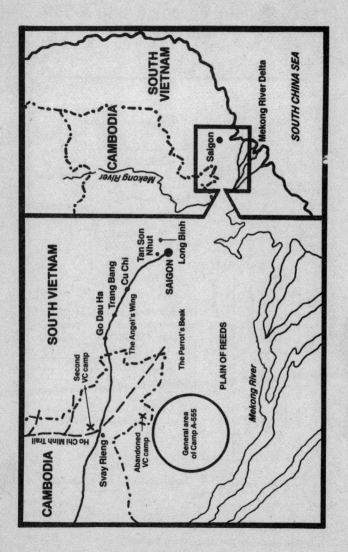

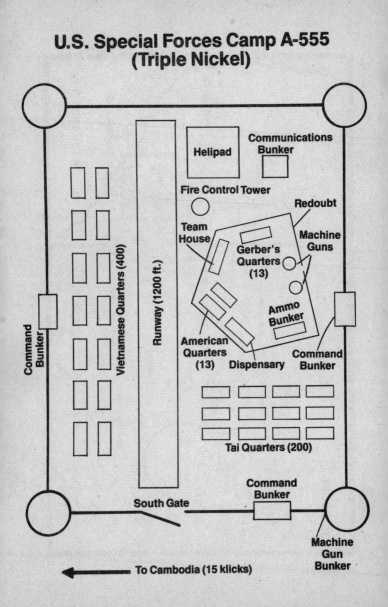

U.S. Special Forces Camp A-555
(Triple Nickel)

Helipad

Communications Bunker

Fire Control Tower

Redoubt

Team House

Machine Guns

Gerber's Quarters (13)

Ammo Bunker

American Quarters (13)

Dispensary

Command Bunker

Vietnamese Quarters (400)

Runway (1200 ft.)

Command Bunker

Tai Quarters (200)

Command Bunker

South Gate

Machine Gun Bunker

To Cambodia (15 klicks)

VIETNAM: GROUND ZERO

PROLOGUE

**MEKONG RIVER REGION
SOUTH OF THE
PARROT'S BEAK,
REPUBLIC OF VIETNAM**

Lieutenant Chuyen Tri Lam had been in the Vietnamese army for all of his short adult life. His family was well connected so he had received favorable assignments, including the one to the rangers. That didn't mean that he wasn't a good soldier, only that he had some opportunities that weren't available to his colleagues.

The patrol into the former heart of VC territory was one such opportunity. The Americans at the Special Forces camp had driven most of the VC across the border into Cambodia. They only returned in small groups to lob a couple of mortar shells at the camp or to briefly terrorize the villagers.

The patrol should be routine and would look good on Lam's service record. As leader of the expedition, any glory would be reflected on him and would enhance his reputation with the men who never ventured from Saigon. And, if there were no glory to be found, he had still taken his men into the heart of VC territory.

Lam didn't expect trouble. Charlie was gone. Charlie was on the run. It was Charlie that was now afraid.

Lam had just completed these comforting reflections when there was a deafening explosion at the side of the trail. Lam's first thought was that one of his men, falling out into the jungle to answer a call of nature, had stepped on a booby trap. As he turned to stare, the world seemed to explode around him. To his right he saw the muzzle flashes as the enemy raked the trail with devastating fire from AK-47s and SKSs. Lam's elite rangers were dropping fast, trying to unsling their weapons, trying to load and return fire or trying just to get down out of the way. Trying to stay alive for a few more seconds.

As the intensity of the shooting increased, Lam tried to draw the handsome pistol his father had given him at his commissioning. As the pistol cleared his holster, he took a hit in the shoulder. The force of the impact spun him around, ripping the pistol from his nerveless fingers to fall among the wounded and dying ARVN on the trail.

Another round tore into his guts, blossoming out his back in a crimson jet of blood. Lam never felt the pain. He just fell, rolled to his side and was angry because his general had told him the VC were all gone. As his vision failed, his last sight was of his platoon lying shattered on the jungle floor while the VC ambushers pumped round after round into the bodies. They wanted no prisoners.

THE CHINESE OFFICER in tactical command of the VC stood up, carefully staying behind the firing line, and shouted, "Cease fire! Cease fire!"

When it was finally quiet, he took a few minutes to study the massacre. The ARVN had walked into the ambush and never fired a shot. Their unit discipline was nonexistent, their noise discipline lax and their response under fire predictable. They had been bunched together, without a real point, no flankers and no rear guard. Obviously, these dead men were not from the Special Forces camp. They had been too poorly trained, and they wore the uniforms of the Saigon puppet soldiers.

The officer signaled his men out of their ambush positions to check the bodies, pick up the weapons, which included a couple of the new American M-16s, and look for documents. He didn't try to stop them from swarming onto the trail to strip the watches, rings, boots and equipment from the dead—the Vietnamese believed it was their right to these spoils.

As the Chinese stood over the body of the foolish young ARVN officer, he noticed the fancy pistol lying near the dead man's outstretched arm. It was a legal trophy. A legitimate spoil of war. And it wasn't beneath the dignity of the Chinese officer to take it. Such a fine weapon should belong to someone who would appreciate it. He picked it up, checked the magazine and the safety and tucked it into his pocket. He then signaled his men, sent the point out and started his indirect retreat to Cambodia. He knew that even if the Americans at the nearby Special Forces camp knew the patrol had been ambushed, they would not have had time to react. There would be no pursuit of his unit and no reason for haste. He would continue his mission, swinging more or less toward Cambodia, and hope that he would find more easy pickings.

1

U.S. SPECIAL FORCES CAMP A-555 IN THE PARROT'S BEAK REGION NEAR THE CAMBODIAN BORDER

Radio watch during the day wasn't a very important task if there were no patrols out, and for the first time in a month, there were none out. Army Special Forces Staff Sergeant Galvin Bocker didn't mind sitting in the fairly cool, dimly lighted communications bunker, his feet propped up on the scarred plywood of the makeshift counter, waiting for radio messages. It beat working in the sun, filling sandbags and stacking them around a newly constructed antimortar bunker.

A sudden burst of static drew Bocker's attention to the radio. He dropped his feet to the dusty plywood floor and reached over to turn the gain knob on the olive drab UHF radio. He picked up the mike, acknowledged and slid a pencil from the top pocket of his sweat-stained jungle fatigues. It might be cool in the commo bunker, but the humidity of the afternoon—the unseen enemy in Vietnam—seemed to invade everywhere, even the sandbagged, Z-shaped entrance of the bunker.

"Zulu Ops, this is Big Green Ops. Prepare to copy," said the voice over the radio.

"Roger, Big Green. Ready," Bocker replied.

"Advise Zulu Six that Big Green Six has received inquiries from higher-ups regarding the failure to report of an all-indigenous patrol in your AO. Please ask Zulu Six to investigate and report soonest."

Bocker stared at the message pad, reading over the light pencil scribbles to make sure he'd gotten it all. "Roger," he said, "investigate and advise."

"Roger. Out."

As the radio lapsed into silence and Bocker ripped the top page off his pad, he wondered briefly what the ARVN had gotten themselves into and how the Special Forces team was supposed to find them with no information to go on. He hoped the captain knew something that he hadn't told them. Bocker turned to make sure that his Vietnamese counterpart, Sergeant Xuyen, was handy. Xuyen had been recently elevated from the ranks to work with Bocker, and the young and eager Vietnamese had shown a real interest in radios and seemed to have a knack for working with them. "You stay and listen carefully," Bocker said. "Something important happens, you let me know. I'll be with Captain Gerber."

Outside the bunker Bocker blinked in the bright afternoon sun. If the humidity inside the commo center was bad, outside it was worse. The first jolt seemed to send the lungs into shock, making it hard to breathe. Just another June day in paradise, Bocker thought as he started for the team house over near the runway. He slid to a sudden stop. Off to the right near the helipad, which was marked by four dark-green rubberized sandbags that held down the large black mat painted with a bright-yellow H, he saw two other team members helping a helicopter crew unload a UH-1D slick, a Huey. Captain Mack Gerber was sifting through the boxes of C-rations, piles of web gear and new knapsacks, crates of ammo and bayonets for the M-14s, checking the contents of each before he signed for it.

"Say, Captain," said Bocker as he walked over. "Got a message here that you need to take a look at."

Gerber stood, wiped a sleeve across his forehead to soak up the sweat and then rubbed a grimy hand against the front of his stained jungle fatigues before he took the paper from

Bocker. He scanned it quickly. "Well, shit," he muttered, shaking his head. "That's all we need. Anything else?"

"No, sir. That's it. You want me to take out a patrol? It's my turn."

For a moment Gerber didn't say anything. He just stared at the message, remembering what he had been told about the Vietnamese patrol. The information had come from Saigon, but had been sketchy because the Vietnamese had been afraid it would be compromised before the patrol could hit the field. Gerber had said nothing about it to his team; they didn't need to know. When Gerber had queried Lieutenant Colonel Alan Bates, his commanding officer at B-Team Headquarters, Bates had told him not to worry about it. It was an all-Vietnamese show.

Leaving Bocker's question unanswered, Gerber said, "Tell Sergeant Fetterman to meet me in my hootch in a couple of minutes. We'll decide what to do after we've had a chance to look over the maps."

Gerber watched his commo sergeant stride across the compound. A career officer who had just celebrated his thirtieth birthday, Gerber was six feet tall with brown hair, which was longer than regulations said it should be, and blue eyes. At two hundred pounds, he was carrying a little more weight than he had as a rookie, but he kept in good shape and the pounds were solid. He had been in the Special Forces for most of his Army career because he believed the Special Forces had the best soldiers in the world. But he was getting tired of having to fight everyone at American headquarters in Saigon for everything he needed, including food, weapons and uniforms. Saigon seemed to think that the masses of supplies being sent from the United States were to be stockpiled and counted, but not used by the men in the field. They seemed to get upset if anyone actually wanted to *use* the supplies.

It wasn't just the supplies, either. This new request from Big Green, which translated into Brigadier General Billy Joe Crinshaw, was just one more example of the haphazard way things were being done. Saigon felt the Vietnamese needed a more active role out here near Cambodia so they sent out a patrol that was probably made up of city boys and officers with commissions bought from the government. When they got into trouble, Gerber was tasked to find them, but had to operate in a vacuum. They were out here "somewhere near the Mekong River, south of the camp." That's all he knew. It was a typical Army bullshit assignment, but if he didn't find them quickly, Crinshaw could call him to Saigon for an ass chewing, never mentioning the fact that Gerber had had no concrete information.

Shaking his head as he thought the situation over, Gerber reached for a clipboard and scribbled his signature on the various forms, acknowledging receipt of the supplies. That done, he tossed it into the cargo compartment of the helicopter for the crew chief to store. Finally, without another word to anyone there, he turned and walked to his hootch.

Gerber's home in Vietnam was a small structure located next to the team house inside the redoubt. It was U.S. Army standard issue all the way. Sandbags were stacked about waist high around the walls, the belief being that in a mortar attack the occupant would either be on the floor trying to avoid flying shrapnel or in the fire control tower directing the counter-mortar fire. Inside, Gerber sat on a metal cot covered with a paper-thin mattress and leaned against the wall of plywood and bamboo matting. Beside the cot was a nightstand made from an old ammo box, and on it was a bottle of Beam's Choice. Gerber winked at his green-label "Pepsi" and resisted the temptation to reach for it.

He looked over at his desk, one that he had made himself from discarded wood torn from old ammo boxes and pieces of bamboo, and his eyes took in a pile of papers, most of them Army forms he was required to fill out that seemed to have no useful purpose. Reports on the number of hours of rifle instruction given to each of the strikers in the Vietnamese companies and how often they were able to hit the bull's-eye. Did the Vietnamese prefer the standard U.S. Army target of a rectangle with a notch cut out or did they want something else? Reports on how often the Vietnamese washed their uniforms and what kind of soap they used. Some of the reports demanded information that should have been classified, others were instructions on how to deal with the Vietnamese and the Tai, or advice on how to organize his companies and ordnance. The advice and the instructions always seemed to contradict each other and were usually written by staff officers who never got into the field or, even worse, by civilians who understood nothing about war.

The tap at his open door broke into Gerber's reflections. Looking up, he saw the small dark team sergeant standing in the rectangle of light. Master Sergeant Anthony B. Fetterman was the veteran of three wars and countless conflicts and was probably the toughest man Gerber had ever met. Yet Fetterman didn't look anything like a combat soldier. He looked as if he should be selling pots and pans door-to-door. He was someone you wouldn't notice if you walked past him on the street. Unless you saw his eyes. There was a hardness behind them that suggested Fetterman was a man who meant what he said and could back it up. He was friendly enough when you got to know him, but reserved until he learned whether you measured up or not.

"You wanted to see me, Captain."

"Yes, Master Sergeant. Come in and grab a chair. We've got a minor problem to solve." When Fetterman was sitting in one of the two lawn chairs that Gerber had imported from Saigon for conferences in his hootch, Gerber continued. "Seems some of our allies may have stepped into some shit. Saigon says they've lost a patrol out here somewhere."

"I see," said Fetterman, nodding. "And you want me to go out to find it."

"If it wouldn't be too much trouble."

"Know where they are?"

Gerber got up and moved to his desk, where he pulled a map from under the pile of papers. He turned to face Fetterman and pointed to an area nearly fifteen kilometers, or klicks, south-southeast of the camp, in the maze of rivers that belonged to the Mekong and near the village of Ap An Minh. "From what I've been told, they were down here somewhere. Can't really tell you more. Saigon kept everything under wraps so that Charlie wouldn't learn about it and ambush them."

"Uh-huh," said Fetterman. "I'm just supposed to go wander around out there and find these guys."

"Shouldn't be that difficult."

Fetterman snorted. "Knowing the Vietnamese, and I assume from what you've said they are Vietnamese, we'll be able to hear them from a couple of miles away."

"Who do you want to take with you?"

"I suppose Sergeant Tyme and two squads of the Tai. Maybe Sergeant Krung as senior Tai NCO. That would give me about twenty-five people."

Gerber looked at his watch. "It's getting pretty late in the day to begin something like this."

"No problem, sir. Shouldn't take more than an hour to get ready. We could move out at dusk, walk a couple of klicks and settle in for an ambush. Or, I suppose I should say, set up an ambush for the practice it will give our people on how to do it. Tomorrow we can sweep through the trees south of the Song Vam Co Tay and see what we can find."

"Okay. Remember, we're going to send out Bocker and Washington tomorrow on that civic action mission to Moc Phong. They're going to provide a little medical aid to the villagers, but they shouldn't cross your path. Just be aware of them."

"Anything else, Captain?"

"That's it. I'll see you at the gate before you move out."

THE SOUTH GATE WAS NEAR the center of the south wall of the camp. The approach was controlled by large sandbagged bunkers flanking each side, along with .50 caliber machine guns backed up by four M-60s. Six rows of concertina wire protected the wall, and the path through them was irregular and concealed.

As Gerber approached, he saw Fetterman and his choice of second American on the patrol, Sergeant First Class and light weapons specialist Justin Tyme, a bright kid destined to spend the rest of his life living down his parents' sense of humor. Sergeant Krung and the Tai who would make up the two squads were off to the right of the gate getting their gear in order.

Gerber stood to one side, still sweating in the heat of the evening. The red ball of the sun had nearly disappeared behind the dark, distant hills across the border in Cambodia, and in the failing light he watched Fetterman and Tyme checking the packs carried by the Tai. Gerber knew the Tai tended to throw away things that were sometimes needed because they couldn't see the point in carrying them. Clean socks, a poncho liner and the like were things the Tai felt they could do without. Fetterman would want to make sure they had everything they would need, as well as extra food, which was little more than packets containing rice and fish heads, and extra ammo. The 7.62 rounds for the M-14s that some of them carried were heavier than the .30 caliber ammunition the rest had for their M-1 carbines. With the Tai done, Fetterman and Tyme checked one another's packs, and then Fetterman came over to speak to Gerber.

"Anything else I should know about this boondoggle, Captain?"

Gerber gave his shoulders a little shrug. "You know as much about it as I do. I don't even know the recognition codes the ARVN were using, or if they were given any. They should have had them, but Saigon didn't tell me about them, and now no one there seems to know a thing about it. I would hope that they will be careful before they start shooting, but I doubt that, too."

"Yes, sir," said Fetterman, "I guess that means I better spot them before they spot me."

Gerber grinned at the seasoned sergeant. "I guess that's exactly what it means."

"We'll try to get back in two days—by Thursday. If we don't find anything and we haven't had any problems, we might stay out another day. We'll call if we plan to do that."

Gerber glanced to the right and left and saw that the Vietnamese guards on the walls and in the bunkers were all at their stations, too far away to eavesdrop. He leaned closer to Fetterman and said, "Normal check-in times. Break squelch twice if everything is okay, once if you need help.'' It was a standard procedure that only the Americans on the camp knew about. At midnight and at noon Fetterman would key the mike button on his PRC-25 twice so that Bocker or whoever was on radio watch would know that Fetterman and his patrol were safe. It was a way of passing information by radio without really transmitting it.

"Anything else, Captain?"

"Just good luck and good hunting."

"Thank you, sir." Fetterman turned, pointed at Tyme and then toward a clump of trees about five hundred meters away.

Tyme nodded his understanding, opened the flimsy wire gate and escorted two of the Tai out to set up a point, even though they hadn't yet cleared the perimeter wire. Then Sergeant Krung led the main body of the patrol out. Fetterman and two Tai brought up the rear.

From a position near the command bunker on the south wall, the largest and best armed of the bunkers and the one that had the field phone so that the officer in charge there could relay information to the fire control tower, Gerber watched the patrol disappear into the elephant grass several hundred meters from the south side of the camp. When he lost sight of them, he headed back to the commo bunker so he could study the maps tacked to a piece of plywood that hung there.

ONCE CLEAR OF THE CAMP, out of sight of the men in the bunkers and the twenty-five-foot-high fire control tower, Fetterman turned to the east. He was paralleling an old trail probably made by farmers on their way to the rice fields on the west side of the camp, figuring that the lost Vietnamese patrol would be east of camp near the river. The Mekong River, with its wide tributaries winding out of Cambodia, made it the best route of travel. In riverboats, the Vietnamese patrol would have had access to a large area. Much of it was open paddy, and since there were no reports of the patrol, they must have stuck to the swamps and jungles south and southeast of the camp. Fetterman decided that it was the most logical place to begin his search.

An hour out of camp Fetterman ordered his men to take up ambush positions. Then, when it was fully dark, he moved them quietly nearly a klick to the east in case someone had seen them deploying in the light. By moving, he hoped to break up any attempt to attack the ambush from the rear. He wasn't yet out of mortar range of the camp so if he were attacked from the rear, he could call for artillery support.

When they were settled again, he had the men take turns eating and then told half of them to try to get some sleep. At midnight the other half got a turn to sleep, and at two everyone went on full alert. Fetterman believed that most of the action, if they ran into trouble, would happen between two and three in the morning. It was the time of the day when everything was at the lowest ebb, and even if he had spent years working the graveyard shift, three o'clock in the morning would see him at his least prepared. It happened to everyone.

Two o'clock, then three, came and went and nothing happened. At four o'clock, an hour before sunup but with false dawn on the horizon, Fetterman reduced the alert, leaving only a couple of men awake while the others caught up on their sleep. At seven they all ate a breakfast from the C-rations menu. Today's special was cold scrambled eggs that tasted more like processed pulp from a paper-box plant. Adding salt made the eggs taste a little better. But not much. When the meal was finished, the men buried the remains of cans and wrappings. Tyme mumbled a few words, as if giving last rights at a grave site.

Fetterman hoped they could make good progress before the sun rose high enough in the sky to bake the ground and turn the jungle into a sauna. Without the sunlight beating on them, the humidity that never quite allowed the sweat to dry was at least bearable. With the sun, it drew the strength out of a man like a giant syringe, turning the strongest man into a weakling who staggered through the jungle and elephant grass praying for a chance to sit down, not caring whether the enemy was close or not. Within half an hour Fetterman had his team up and marching, paralleling the Mekong, but staying in the trees out of easy sight of anyone on the river.

Neither Fetterman nor Tyme had any real search plan. Without some guidance from Saigon, Fetterman could only guess what the Vietnamese leader would do, and knowing most of the Vietnamese in Saigon, Fetterman believed the man would take the path of least resistance. That meant he wouldn't get too far from the river and would stick to the trails and paths in the jungle. He was also searching for some clue of the ARVN passing. The ARVN would not concern themselves with trying to conceal their route. They would chop their way through the jungle and leave the remains of their meals on the ground. They might kick out their fires, but the burned wood would be left in plain sight for all to see. The VC, on the other hand, had learned how to move through the land without leaving a trace. Fetterman had learned a lot from them.

At noon they took a one-hour break. Again they ate a cold meal. Fetterman had the boned turkey. He used as much salt on it as he could stand because of the heat and humidity. Besides, the salt made the food edible if not palatable. When he finished the meal, he drained the last of his water from one of the three canteens he carried and then rested. Although they had been crossing fairly level terrain, Fetterman felt as if he had been running up and down hills all morning. Sweat had soaked his uniform so that it was dark green. There were rings of salt under his arms and down his back. The Tai, who had grown up in a similar environment, didn't seem to be holding up very well, either. Three of them lay sprawled on the ground, breathing rapidly as if they couldn't get enough air.

After an hour of rest, Fetterman changed the direction of the march and now headed his patrol due west toward the Cambodian border at a point where a tributary of the Mekong crossed into South Vietnam. By late afternoon Fetterman was convinced he wouldn't have any luck finding the patrol and decided he wouldn't be surprised to learn that the whole platoon of South Vietnamese rangers either had defected to the other side or had gone to Cambodia to find sanctuary. That sort of thing was not uncommon among ARVN troops.

It was about that time he caught the first faint whiff of an odor that he had smelled only a day and a half after he landed in France in 1944. Checking the wind, which was just a light breeze from the southwest, Fetterman altered his direction again so he was moving directly into it.

When Tyme finally smelled it, he moved over to Fetterman and asked quietly, "You smell it?"

"I think we might have found the patrol," Fetterman answered.

Staying off the trail, using the trees and bushes for cover, the unit moved forward. Fetterman took the point with Krung. They knew they were close to their destination when they heard the buzz-saw racket of a hundred thousand flies. Then, through a series of gaps in the trees and bushes, they saw the remains of the South Vietnamese patrol. There were ten or twelve men lying on the trail, their bodies shattered by the bullets that had been pumped into them. Fetterman knew what he would see when they got closer because he had seen similar things before. The man closest to them seemed to have a black face, and for an instant Fetterman wondered if there had been any Americans with the South Vietnamese patrol. But as they approached, Fetterman could see that the body was covered with flies, each fighting the other to get into the man's mouth or nose or eyes.

Fetterman tied a handkerchief around his head, covering his nose and mouth, before he stepped onto the trail. The stench from the dead seemed to rise from the trail in an almost visible fog. One of the Tai troopers turned away from the carnage and threw up violently, the remains of his lunch splattering the man standing next to him. Others stood at the edge of the trail, staring down at the broken, bloated bodies. There were severed limbs lying next to some of the dead. The ground was a strange rusty color, as were the uniforms of the dead men. Dried blood was everywhere, and sticky pools of it puddled near a couple of the bodies. Huge black flies sucked at the crimson pools.

Fetterman crouched near one of the bodies and saw that the man had taken seven or eight hits in the chest. He could see the neat, rounded bullet holes of the entrance wounds. He could also see the jagged wounds of the exit holes. These were nearly fist sized, with bits of bone and shriveled internal organs protruding. Another man had both hands locked on his abdomen in a dying and desperate attempt to keep his intestines from snaking out of the huge holes in his stomach. His eyelids were wide open, but his eyes were obscured by flies.

Slowly he moved from one body to the next. The number and type of wounds changed, but there was always the same fatal result. This man was missing his face, left hand and both his legs. The next had no head; there was a huge pool of blood where it should have been. Lying facedown a few feet away was another man. He was missing both arms and most of one leg. Still another had been cut nearly in two, the intestines piled almost on his thighs.

Tyme approached, having set up security. He had placed two men at opposite ends of the ambush site and then sent flankers into the trees to watch for enemy movements.

"How long ago did this happen?" Tyme asked.

"It's hard to tell in this environment. The heat and humidity accelerate the decay, but I wouldn't think it was much more than forty-eight hours ago," Fetterman replied.

"So what do we do now?"

Fetterman stood up and stepped over a couple of bodies to the side of the trail. He had noticed that there were no weapons, no watches, no rings and no boots on any of the dead. Some wore parts of uniforms, but those were the pieces that were so badly shot up or bloodstained that no one would want them.

He pulled out his map, which was covered by plastic so the humidity or rain wouldn't ruin the paper, and studied it quietly for a few minutes. It wasn't far to Cambodia, only a matter of ten or fifteen klicks. To the north were hundreds of paddies—open ground that would leave a VC raiding party vulnerable to air attack or artillery fire. To the south was the Mekong River—impossible to cross without help. To the east were more rice fields and swamp. The only open route to

Cambodia with sufficient cover was a meandering course that would easily triple or quadruple the distance.

"Near as I can tell," said Fetterman, "the guys who did this should still be in South Vietnam."

"So what?" asked Tyme. "We've finished our mission."

Fetterman glanced at his second in command and then stepped past him to the bodies on the trail. Sure, the South Vietnamese were soldiers and they had walked into an ambush that had killed them, but it seemed somehow excessive to put fifteen or twenty rounds into each man. There was something indefinable about it, almost as if the VC had been shooting helpless men. Something cold and cruel about it. Fetterman wasn't sure what it was he felt. He knew he could easily pull the trigger in an ambush and kill the enemy trapped in it. He could sneak up behind a sentry and cut his throat, but he didn't think he could stand over an unconscious wounded soldier, put a pistol to the man's head and coldly pull the trigger. It seemed inhuman. More inhuman than fighting a war because you had reduced it to a level where you were murdering people.

He looked back at Tyme and asked, "Wouldn't you like to get the guys who did this?"

Now it was Tyme's turn to look again at the ambush site. He had been sickened by what he had seen; it was hard to look at mutilated human bodies and not feel something. He nodded once and almost whispered, "Yeah, I would. But they've got to be long gone by now."

"Not necessarily," responded Fetterman. "We've got two things going for us. One is the terrain. They can't move all that rapidly because they'll be spotted. Hell, we've got airplanes and helicopters all over the place, and they're always looking for the enemy. That has got to slow them down. Means they only travel at night."

"But they've got a two-day head start," interrupted Tyme.

"May not matter because of point two. They'll think they're out of this free and clear. No survivors to point the way. No survivors to run to us for help. They move only at night because they feel no pressure to run. They follow the trees and the jungle and avoid the open ground. That gives us a chance to catch up because we don't have to do either. We only have to travel ten or twelve klicks to their fifty or sixty."

"We've completed our mission," repeated Tyme.

"This was a very well-coordinated ambush," said Fetterman. "Well executed. There is no evidence of any return fire or any enemy casualties. In the last year we've run into this kind of operation again and again. It might be the same guy running each of these shows. I think that we should try to get into a position so that we can ambush him."

"Ambush who? You're guessing about something with no evidence at all. The captain's not going to like this. He'll want us to report back immediately to evaluate the data."

"But there's a chance we can catch them and eliminate them before they can get back to Cambodia!" Fetterman insisted.

Tyme shrugged and glanced at his watch. "We've only got a few hours of daylight left."

Fetterman folded his map and stuffed it into the pocket of his fatigues. "We have an opportunity here we may not get again. We can guess, with a fair degree of accuracy, where that VC patrol is going to be. And I think we can get them."

"It's your show," said Tyme reluctantly. "You can do what you want."

WITH THE EXACT COORDINATES of the ambush site noted so they could be given to the Vietnamese in Saigon, Fetterman and the rest of his men moved off to the west. Leaving the trees, they entered an area of paddies, where the men walked on the dikes, small walls of dirt only eighteen or twenty inches high that kept the muddy water in the paddy. He didn't like using the dikes—the VC might have booby-trapped them—but he didn't have time to avoid them. Besides, the accepted method for walking through a rice field was to step on the plants so you didn't sink in the mud and that angered the farmers. This way kept the farmers happy and allowed them to cover three or four klicks an hour.

Although Fetterman tried to keep the men moving rapidly, the heat and humidity of the late afternoon sucked their strength. Everyone was covered with sweat, their uniforms darkened by it. Fetterman found it necessary to take frequent breaks, scattering the men around the paddies to try for some sort of security. But the open ground made it difficult, and no one wanted to sit in the water. It might have been cooler to do that, but the method of fertilization made the idea repulsive. The human waste dumped in the paddies gave the water a stench that stuck with you like a second skin.

At dusk they were less than a klick from the Cambodian border, south of the Parrot's Beak and slightly north of the Mekong River. Here the jungle tapered until it was only a couple of hundred meters wide, and although there were other places to cross the border, this seemed to offer the best protection. Fetterman stationed his men in the trees, separating them by fifty meters where the jungle was thin and fifteen meters where the underbrush and trees were thick. He had them eat another cold meal, and although they didn't complain about it, he knew they were getting sick of the cold C-rations. A little heat and a lot of salt helped. The franks and beans he had taken were fairly good even cold. When he buried the empty cans, he realized that his pack was now three or four pounds lighter for getting rid of the heavy C-rations.

They went to half alert after they ate, but at midnight they returned to full alert. Fetterman crept around the perimeter, checking on the Tai to make sure none of them slept.

It was just after four-thirty, with the sky beginning to lighten in the east, when Fetterman heard the splash of someone falling into water. At night, sound traveled a long way. Fetterman couldn't be sure where the noise originated, but he took it as a sign that the enemy was close. Quietly he passed the word for the unit to pull together and form an L-shaped ambush on one side of the tree line, facing into the jungle.

For ten minutes Fetterman crouched near a huge palm, his eyes on the horizon, trying to use the expanding light of the rising sun to see the enemy soldiers. He was sure it was too early for a farmer because the farmer would be afraid of being shot as an enemy in the night. Everyone knew only two types of people ventured into the dark in Vietnam: the Americans and the VC.

Finally, in the early light of the dawn as it filtered through the trees and the ground mist, Fetterman thought he saw movement. As he concentrated his vision, a shape darted around a tree and disappeared behind a bush. He waited patiently, hoping that Krung and his Tai would also be patient, ready for the enemy when they got closer.

Slowly, quietly, the enemy slipped through the trees, weaving in and out to avoid thorny bushes and fallen trunks. They were nearly in Cambodia, yet even with the safety of the close border, they maintained their unit integrity and noise discipline.

Fetterman let the single point man walk by, and as he disappeared into the undergrowth, Fetterman rose to his knees and tossed two hand grenades into the middle of the VC unit. They exploded with a crack and a roar in the stillness of the jungle, followed by an instant of absolute quiet, as if everyone and everything were trying to figure it out. Then the jungle erupted with noise. Fetterman and his men opened fire with small arms and a single M-60 machine gun. The ruby tracers of the American-made rifles laced through the jungle alone for a second, then were joined by the green tracers used by the enemy. In front of him Fetterman could see the flash of grenades as they detonated in fountains of sparks. The monkeys and birds, jolted awake by the sudden impact of the weapons, added their voices to the din, and the jungle was transformed.

Suddenly all the firing seemed to be outgoing. Only red tracers and the distinctive bangs of the American M-14s and M-1s could be seen and heard. Nothing came from the other side. Nothing from the AKs.

"Cease fire," ordered Fetterman. "Cease fire!"

For a moment Fetterman waited, trying to detect the sounds of men among the noise of a thousand birds and animals. Carefully he got to his feet and inched toward the enemy position.

He ordered Krung to take half the Tai force and sweep to the left, away from the ambush site. Tyme swept to the right with the rest of the patrol.

Fetterman soon stumbled on the bodies of two NVA soldiers. He stopped only long enough to claim their weapons and then hurried toward the edge of the tree line. When he was joined by a couple of Tai from Tyme's group, he handed them the AKs and raised his binoculars to his eyes. He thought he could see the enemy fleeing in the distance, less distinct now that the sun was rising and creating more ground mist.

The Tai soldiers dropped to their knees and opened fire, their red tracers lancing forward and then dancing skyward as they ricocheted off the ground.

Fetterman scanned the area, seeing some of the enemy as they dived for cover, then got up again and dodged toward Cambodia. He kept searching until he saw a flash of khaki-colored uniform. He swept by it with his binoculars and came back, but it was gone. The growing light helped, but he couldn't locate the target again.

The enemy was four hundred meters away and spinning to return fire. They were nearly to the border, if not already across it, and they seemed to slow down, knowing that the Americans couldn't and wouldn't follow them.

Again Fetterman found the khaki uniform, but could only see the man's back. He kept his attention focused there, watching the enemy soldier as he ran for the protection of the border. Fetterman mentally begged him to turn around, to allow him a single glimpse of the face, but the rifle fire from the Tai and the proximity of Cambodia conspired to keep the man's face turned away.

Suddenly Fetterman realized he was letting the man escape. He had wanted to be sure, but there was no way to do it. He shoved the binoculars into their case and pulled his weapon, making sure that a round was chambered before sighting carefully on the enemy's back. With each second the distance increased. Fetterman began to slowly squeeze the trigger, telling himself not to rush the shot. To let the weapon fire itself. When he felt the satisfying recoil of the rifle, his target had disappeared. He could no longer see him, and Fetterman knew he had missed.

As Fetterman took in the situation, he realized most of the enemy had gotten away, across the border into Cambodia. Not far away. Not more than a klick, if that much. But the border made it impossible to follow.

Tyme approached, his M-14 rifle in his hand, and said, "Let's get out of here."

At first it was as if Fetterman hadn't heard. He was going to tell Tyme that they had to get that guy, that he was too dangerous to leave alive. They had to kill him, no matter what the cost. Then he realized all the cards now belonged to the VC. Fetterman and his men were almost in Cambodia. They were out of useful range of the American artillery in the fire support bases. And they had already been in the field for the time allotted them. They would be out of food and supplies by nightfall. Reluctantly he agreed with Tyme. "Okay," he said, still staring into the distance where he had seen the khaki-clad officer disappear. He was sure, for no good reason, that his target was a Chinese. Fetterman hadn't seen the face, and the NVA did wear khaki uniforms, but Fetterman knew.

"I'll get you yet, you lucky bastard," he promised the empty jungle.

2

U.S. SPECIAL FORCES
CAMP A-555

While Master Sergeant Anthony B. Fetterman was searching for the lost Vietnamese patrol, his commanding officer, Mack Gerber, was in the commo bunker listening to Big Green demand his presence in Saigon. Although it was hard to get anyone upset about going to Saigon, Crinshaw had managed it because Crinshaw summoned a person to Saigon for one reason only—to rake him over the coals.

Gerber remembered the other times Brigadier General Billy Joe Crinshaw had made similar demands. None of the meetings had been pleasant. Crinshaw was a general of the old school who believed that wars were won by massed firepower and infantry support. He didn't believe the Special Forces had a place in a real army. He considered the Green Berets an elitist bunch of troublemakers who were good in barroom fights but who should be thrown out of the Army.

Crinshaw also believed in the old ways—if he gave an order, it should have been anticipated so that he could have the result immediately. He tolerated the enlisted men only because someone had to do the work that was beneath the dignity of the officers. Bates had once described General Crinshaw as "a man of the century—the nineteenth century."

Having received his instructions over the radio from Crinshaw himself, Gerber slowly walked from the commo bunker to his hootch so he could pack for an overnight stay in Saigon.

He spied the nearly empty bottle of Beam's sitting on his nightstand, picked it up, pulled the cork and took a deep drink, trying hard to set his throat and stomach on fire. He drained the bottle, and then he carefully corked it.

A moment later Bocker knocked and stuck his head in. "Chopper radioed, Captain. Said he was about five minutes out."

"Okay," said Gerber, staring at the empty bottle. "Find Lieutenant Bromhead and have him report to me. What's Sully doing?"

"Think he's trying to place those new claymores we got in this morning."

"Find him and have him get over here, too. Make it snappy. I don't want to keep that chopper on the ground any longer than I have to."

"Yes, sir."

A minute later Bromhead knocked and stepped in. He saw Gerber stuffing a change of clothes into a knapsack and said, "You wanted to see me, Captain?"

"Yeah. Sit down. I'm off to Saigon to see General Crinshaw about something. You'll have the camp for tonight. Intel says there's nothing building around here just now, so it should be quiet. But you might want to check with Kepler anyway."

"Why do I suddenly have a feeling of déjà vu?" asked the young first lieutenant.

Gerber drew the straps tight on his knapsack. He grinned and said, "I give up. Why?"

"Seems that every time you're called to Saigon, the shit hits the fan here."

Gerber shrugged. "I don't think you've got anything to worry about, other than Fetterman's patrol."

Gerber dropped his pack on the makeshift desk and sat in the chair behind it. He studied the young officer standing in front of him. Johnny Bromhead was not yet twenty-four. In the past few months he had developed a knack for handling the men, both the American NCOs and the Vietnamese strikers. Everyone respected him now, and Gerber had come to rely on

Bromhead, certain he would be able to take care of anything that happened.

There was another knock on the door, and Sully Smith, the senior demolitions sergeant, entered the room. "You wanted to see me, Captain?"

"Just to say that I'll be out of the camp tonight. His Royal Highness has called for an audience." Gerber immediately regretted his words. He might not respect Crinshaw, he might not like him personally, but he shouldn't say anything to communicate those feelings to the men under him.

"At any rate," he continued, "while I'm in Saigon and Fetterman is out with his patrol, I'll want you to fill in as the team sergeant, assisting Lieutenant Bromhead tonight.

"As I told Lieutenant Bromhead, your only problem is Fetterman's patrol. If he steps in some shit and you're required to lend support, remember that we now have fire bases around here for artillery support, fighters based at Tan Son Nhut and Bien Hoa, and we can even get some infantry help from Cu Chi. Just think things through."

Bromhead nodded and then said, "No problem, Captain."

From outside they could hear the rotor throb of an approaching helicopter. Gerber stood and reached for his knapsack and M-14. "That's my ride," he said. "See you tomorrow."

AS THE AIRCRAFT TURNED to the north, Gerber looked out the open cargo-compartment door. Ten months ago the land spread out beneath him had been a sea of elephant grass broken only by the rice fields of a hundred local farmers. Now in the center of the large plain and on top of a slight hill stood Camp A-555, or Triple Nickel as the men called it. The camp was rectangular with a short runway on the western side. Just off the eastern edge of the runway was the redoubt, oval-shaped and not more than seventy-five meters across. The redoubt was just an earthen breastwork that was five feet tall and had only one tiny entrance on the east side, which was protected by three .30 caliber machine guns.

Six strands of concertina surrounded the whole camp. Scattered among the rows of wire were claymore antiperson- nel mines, barrels of foogas, trip flares and booby traps. The nearest cover for an attacking force was a clump of trees al- most five hundred meters away on the south side of the camp.

The helicopter broke away from the camp after climbing to altitude by the standard procedure of circling. In the event of an engine failure, they would then be in a position to autoro- tate back into the safety of the camp and wouldn't have to land in the paddies or elephant grass. Gerber kept searching the ground below him as if he were on a reconnaissance flight rather than a routine ride into Saigon. He couldn't talk to the flight crew because of the turbine roar and the ever-present popping of the rotor blades. All the crewmen wore helmets to allow them to communicate among themselves, and without one all Gerber could do was sit back and look out the doors as the wet green of the rice fields slipped beneath him. Breaking the monotony was an occasional village—just a few hootches with corrugated tin roofs that flashed in the sun to betray their location in the clusters of palm trees.

Highway 1 from Go Dau Ha to Trang Bang flashed by. It was a two-lane paved road with light traffic made up of lambret- tas, ox carts and military trucks and jeeps. The trees had been cut back so that there was open land for fifty meters on each side of the thoroughfare to prevent ambush. The only places where the trees came close to the road were near the tiny vil- lages.

Gerber let his mind roam. If he didn't, he would think of Crinshaw, and there would be enough time for that when he got to Saigon. He had no idea what Crinshaw wanted. But he was tired of being pulled out of the field to take Crinshaw's all- too-frequent abuse. He knew that it was partially his fault; he had done things in the past that had made Crinshaw look bad. He and Bates had conspired to put Triple Nickel in the heart of VC territory when Crinshaw had wanted it closer to Tay Ninh. They had used General Hull's authority to get it done. Crinshaw had lost face when he lost the fight. That hadn't been the only thing, either. Both he and Bates had worked the supply system to foil Crinshaw, and that hadn't helped the situation. Gerber knew that Crinshaw was just looking for an excuse to nail him, and he didn't like walking a tightrope between Crinshaw and the enemy.

Gerber was momentarily surprised when the helicopter suddenly seemed to drop out from under him. Through the cargo-compartment door he could see they were now only three or four feet above the ground, racing toward a huge gap in a tree line half a klick in front of them. Helicopters were required to fly under the approach path to Tan Son Nhut airport. Once through the trees they would pop up to five or six hundred feet to be cleared into Hotel Three, the helipad at the airfield.

They turned left and Gerber could see the runways, hangars and sandbagged bunkers of the Air Force complex at Tan Son Nhut. They gained a little more altitude and then lost it all, coming to a hovering stop a couple of feet off the ground. A second later they touched down, and before the pilots had time to shut off the engines, Gerber, his knapsack and M-14 in hand, was running in a crouched position across the grass of the helipad.

He was almost to the terminal, an unpainted wooden structure under the tower, when a dark-haired NCO in freshly starched fatigues approached him. The man came to rigid attention in front of Gerber, saluted and asked, "Are you Captain Gerber?"

Gerber nodded in reply, and the NCO continued talking. "I have a jeep. General Crinshaw asked that I meet you here and escort you immediately to his new office complex." The sergeant reached out and tried to take Gerber's knapsack.

"That's all right," said Gerber. "I can manage. You been waiting long?"

"Not all that long. The pilot radioed the tower when he was twenty minutes out."

The jeep ride took Gerber past the world's largest PX, a post exchange that would rival any of the department stores in the States. Gerber had only been in it once, but that was enough for him to know he could buy anything he wanted there except a woman, and if he wanted that, he needed only to step through one of the many gates leading out of the air base.

The sergeant stopped his jeep in front of a new two-story building that had recently received a coat of light-blue paint. A boardwalk led to double entrance doors directly in front of him. Off to his right a flagpole sprouted from a bed of brightly colored flowers, but there was no flag on it.

As Gerber retrieved his knapsack from the back of the jeep, the NCO said, "General Crinshaw's office is on the second floor. There's a sign on the door."

Gerber nodded his thanks and wondered how the sergeant kept his uniform looking so crisp in the humidity of Saigon. Gerber felt as if he had just stepped out of a sauna.

Upstairs in Crinshaw's outer office sat the same tight-lipped master sergeant that Gerber had seen on all his other trips to see Big Green. The office and the furniture—just a desk and chair for the sergeant and a couch for visitors—might be new, but Crinshaw's aide definitely was not.

When Gerber entered, the sergeant picked up a field phone, spun the crank and said quietly, "Captain Gerber is here."

As he placed the handset of the phone on the cradle, he said, "You may go in now, sir. I'll watch your weapon."

Stepping into Crinshaw's inner sanctum was like walking into a refrigerator. It couldn't have been more than sixty degrees in the room. The new office was large, paneled in rich mahogany, carpeted with thick broadloom and lined with bookcases. Captured weapons, mounted on plaques like game fish, hung on a wall near a single curtained window. It seemed as if General Crinshaw were trying to freeze everything in sight with a gigantic, brand-new air conditioner.

Inside were two other American officers, one of them Lieutenant Colonel Bates, Gerber's immediate superior, the other a major Gerber didn't know. Sitting in a large leather chair was a Vietnamese general. Standing behind him were three Vietnamese officers.

As Crinshaw impatiently waved him forward, he said in a voice that barely concealed his sarcasm, "What the hell is going on out there, boy?"

Shit, thought Gerber. Here we go again. Just what the hell was going on, and why were all these others standing around collecting dust? He thought of all the things he wanted to say, but settled for, "I'm afraid that I don't follow, sir."

Crinshaw seemed not to hear as he stormed on. "There's a Vietnamese ranger unit missing out there. What are you doing to find it?"

Suddenly Gerber understood. This had nothing to do with Gerber or his camp. It was being done to placate the Vietnamese general. "We've got a large patrol scouring the countryside for the missing men," Gerber said. "We're standing by, prepared to lend whatever support they may need."

"A single patrol?" Crinshaw asked, incredulous.

"I felt that deploying more men in that area would be counterproductive, General."

"You let *me* be the judge of that, Captain," Crinshaw said in a hard, sharp tone as he pushed a piece of paper across the highly polished surface of his mahogany desk. The Special Forces captain read the words ordering him to go to the field and to do anything and everything necessary to find the missing Vietnamese. "Do you understand that?"

"Yes, sir."

Crinshaw motioned to the Vietnamese officer and said, "General Vo, do you have any questions for this officer?"

General Nuyen Van Vo of the Army of the Republic of Vietnam stood, his hands behind his back. He took two steps forward and looked at Gerber with stern disapproval. "How long has your patrol been out?" he asked.

"Since late yesterday," replied Gerber.

Vo turned and translated the response for the others. There was a hurried conversation in Vietnamese, but Gerber, who had learned a lot of the language in the past few months, couldn't catch much of it. It was too fast for him.

Vo now ignored Gerber and looked at Crinshaw. "I think, General, that you should dispatch more men into the patrol zone. I also think you should find someone who is a little more capable to run your base there. I will be waiting for some word about my missing men."

Crinshaw got up and came around his large ornate desk, holding out his hand. "You may be assured, General, that we will resolve this matter to the satisfaction of everyone."

"I would hope so," Vo said as he shook Crinshaw's hand. Then he turned, nodded to Bates and the major and left. He was followed by the other Vietnamese officers.

Just before the door closed, Crinshaw shouted, "Damn it, Captain, how long am I going to have to cover for your stupid mistakes!"

Twenty minutes later Alan Bates escorted Gerber out of Crinshaw's office.

Downstairs, as they walked to the front door, Bates said, "Don't let all that crap get to you. Crinshaw has to keep our allies happy. That was mainly to let them know that we're as concerned about their men as we are about our own."

"Yeah, well, Crinshaw could have told me all that himself. I figured out what was happening, but it would be nice if the General would take the time to explain it. And the comments by the Vietnamese general were totally unwarranted."

"Of course they were," agreed Bates. "Crinshaw is playing a political game with our allies, and you got caught in the middle."

"I don't suppose that Crinshaw is about ready to DE-ROS," said Gerber.

"Generals don't have year-long tours like the rest of us, so I'm afraid that you can't hope for that."

Gerber stepped forward and pushed open the door so Bates could exit first. "Yeah, I know. But it would still be nice."

Outside, under the bright, starry night, Bates tried to change the subject. "How are things between you and that flight nurse?"

"You mean Karen Morrow?"

"That's the one."

"Not good. Besides, she rotated home two weeks ago and was mad that I couldn't get to Nha Trang to say goodbye."

Bates climbed into the driver's seat of the jeep he had checked out of the motor pool earlier in the day. He unlocked the steering wheel and dropped the padlock and chain to the floor. "We could have worked something out," he said.

"I know. But I think she was almost happier to have it that way. Now she can go home mad at me. Maybe she'll write, but somehow I doubt it."

Bates shot a glance at Gerber, who seemed to have taken a sudden interest in the surrounding territory. Gerber hid his emotions well, and if it hadn't been for a knot of muscles bunched at Gerber's jaw, Bates might have believed that Morrow meant next to nothing to Gerber.

"You want to eat at the club?" said Bates as he started the jeep. "I'll buy the steaks."

For a moment longer Gerber was quiet. Then he smiled and said, "I never turn down a free meal."

JUST INSIDE THE FRONT DOOR of the Tan Son Nhut officers' club was a sign instructing incoming personnel to deposit their weapons in one of the boxes provided. Gerber didn't like the idea, but while Bates stood by and watched, Gerber slid his M-14 into the box farthest from the door.

Bates pushed open the second door that led into the club proper. Inside, the large room was hazy with cigarette and cigar smoke and packed with two or three hundred people. One wall was dominated by a gigantic bar and to the left of it was a door with a sign over it that read, General Officers Only. Gerber couldn't figure out why anyone would *want* to enter a room that contained only generals.

"You want to eat in the main room or the bar?" asked Bates.

"The bar," said Gerber. "We'll be able to get a drink faster in there."

Bates turned to look at Gerber once again, wondering what was going on below the surface. Gerber seemed to be in control, but he also seemed about to explode. Something had to give, and in a combat environment it would give very soon. Bates couldn't have a man in the field who had his mind clouded with a lot of other problems.

They found a corner table away from the bandstand and the ring of huge speakers. Both men knew that the band, now in the process of setting up, would soon be blasting rock and roll at the crowd.

Almost as soon as they sat, they were approached by a Vietnamese waitress in a tiny black skirt and a tight red blouse that was open almost to her navel. Her jet-black hair hung to the middle of her back and was damp with sweat. The skin between her breasts glistened. It was goddamned hot in the bar.

Bates ordered the steaks for both of them, T-bones, medium rare, with baked potatoes, and a bottle of red wine. While they were waiting for the meal to arrive, they went through half the bottle without much conversation.

As they ate their meal, the band started playing at a level that drowned out even the sound of the jets taking off from the nearby airfield. By the time they finished eating, the band had quit for a break. Bates, holding the wine bottle—having just poured another glass for each of them—used it to point at the bar.

"Thought you said that your nurse friend had rotated home."

Gerber turned in his chair and looked back over his shoulder. He saw a blond woman, fairly tall, standing at the bar with her back to him. The hair looked lighter than it should have been, but there was no mistaking the pose, the shoulders and the shape, even through the loose-fitting fatigues.

Gerber turned back and shrugged. "I thought she had. I don't understand."

"You going to talk to her?"

Gerber smiled sheepishly. He pushed back his chair and stood. "Of course," he said. Then more quietly, almost as if he didn't believe Morrow was still in Vietnam, he said again, "Of course."

Slowly Gerber approached the bar. The blonde was talking to a young pilot, and Gerber waited until there was a break in the conversation before putting a hand on her shoulder.

"Karen," he began as the woman turned. He looked into her green eyes, saw the blond hair that hung in bangs to her eyebrows and stopped speaking. The woman was almost a dead ringer for Karen. Same size and build and looked enough like her to almost be a twin.

For a moment she met Gerber's incredulous stare and said, "You must be Mack Gerber."

"Yeah, that's right," Gerber said. "Have we met?"

"No," she replied, grinning.

Now Gerber was thoroughly confused. He took a step backward and looked at the woman in front of him for a moment. "You look enough like a woman I know to be her twin sister," he said.

The woman smiled again and laughed lightly. "You must mean Karen."

"Yeah," Gerber replied, nodding his head. "But how did you know?"

Finally she let out a deep, throaty laugh and then reached out, touching Gerber on the arm. "I'm sorry, I shouldn't do this to you. Karen is my sister. She told me all about you, showed me a picture and asked me to keep my eyes open for you."

"I didn't know Karen had a sister," Gerber said, still staring.

"I'll bet you didn't know she had a husband, either," the blonde said, her laugh subsiding to a wry smile.

Gerber felt a cold, clammy hand twist his stomach. "You're joking," he finally said.

"Hey, don't take it so hard. It's the same thing you guys do all the time. Lead some poor girl on and then run back home to the wife." The woman's tone was almost flip, taunting.

Gerber shook his head. He didn't know whether to laugh, get angry or get drunk. Maybe all three. He wanted to say something to the woman, but he didn't know what. Finally he turned and without a word headed back to the table where Bates was sitting, drinking wine and trying not to notice what had happened.

Gerber dropped into his chair, poured a healthy shot of the wine, downed it and then searched wildly for the waitress. "Damn it," he growled. "I want something with a little more kick."

"Everything okay, Mack?" asked Bates.

"Yeah, everything is fine. Just fucking wonderful."

"That wasn't Karen," said Bates, pushing slightly.

"No, that wasn't Karen. That was her sister. Karen is home with her husband."

A dozen responses ran through Bates's mind, but all he could come up with was, "Oh."

"Yeah. Oh. Now can we get something real to drink?"

Karen's sister walked up to the table and stared into Gerber's eyes.

"Look, Captain, I think that I may have misread the situation between you and my sister. If I have, I'm sorry about what I said."

Gerber didn't say a word, and as she turned to go, Bates stood and said, "Can we buy you a drink, ah..."

"Morrow. Robin Morrow. And yes, you can."

Bates flagged down the harried waitress and ordered Beam's Choice all around. When the drinks arrived, Morrow turned her attention to Gerber and said, "I didn't know how you felt about my sister. I'm sorry that I was so callous about it."

Gerber picked up his bourbon and stared at the dark liquid. "Don't worry about it," he said coldly. Gerber was brooding and he knew he was brooding. And to make it worse he was sure that Bates knew it, too.

As if from a great distance he heard Bates say, "So, Robin, what do you do here in Saigon?"

FOURTEEN HOURS LATER, after Gerber had made a C-123 flight to Dau Tieng, a Huey flight into his camp and had been briefed by Fetterman on his mission and the discovery of the remains of the Vietnamese patrol, he was on another Army helicopter heading back to Saigon. Isolated from the crew by the whine of the turbine and the popping of the rotor blades, Gerber had little to do other than reflect upon the massacre that Fetterman had described and the plan that he had evolved.

They had been sitting in Gerber's hootch, a bottle of Beam's between them, while Fetterman detailed his chase of the enemy unit to the Cambodian border.

"I had to break contact at the border, Captain," said Fetterman. "It was getting late, and I couldn't follow him without jeopardizing the patrol. I'd still like to take a squad out to get him, though."

Gerber held up his hand as if to halt an infantry squad. "Get him?" he asked. "You've jumped over something here."

"I saw him. I had him in my sights and he got away. He got away again."

There was suddenly something else in the tiny room. Something other than the heat and humidity and red dust that tried to bury everything. Gerber, not fully understanding it, reached for the bottle of Beam's, jerked the cork free and took a healthy swig.

"You're not making sense, Tony."

"It was the Chinese officer. You know the one I mean. Kepler and his intelligence boys have heard rumors about him for months. We've seen him on a couple of operations. Always in the distance. Always in the background, advising the VC and the North Vietnamese."

"And you're sure it's the same guy," said Gerber. "How can you tell?"

Fetterman reached across the desk and took the bottle from Gerber's hand. Before drinking, he said, "It has to be. Every time we've run into him, it's with enemy units that understand what they're doing. Well trained, well disciplined. It's almost like his signature. His signature was all over that ambush. The man is a military wizard."

"Okay, Tony, suppose you're right. He's still a Chinese national, and he's in a neutral country as long as he's in Cambodia. There's not a lot we can do about him under those circumstances. For us to cross the border could cause an international incident—if we were caught. It's a move neither of us has the authority to make. I assume that you are suggesting that we cross the border."

"The CIA has been running cross-border ops for a couple of years, and there's been no international repercussions. Besides, everyone knows the VC and NVA have bases in Cambodia," said Fetterman.

"Don't be naive, Tony. You know that we can't do it. When we get close to Cambodia, we have to explain our every movement, and we have to report our position to Saigon almost every hour. Makes no difference that the VC can run across the border like they're stepping over a crack in a sidewalk. We don't have that luxury."

"But we have to do something to kill that man, Captain. He's too dangerous."

At that moment Bromhead stepped through the door and looked at Gerber.

The captain waved him forward. "Come in, Johnny. You might want to listen to this."

"Did I hear Tony suggest that we smoke someone?"

Fetterman hesitated before replying. He was wondering if he had said too much already.

"I want to go after that Chinese officer who has been causing us so much grief," he said abruptly.

"We didn't learn that tactic at the Point," said Bromhead, moving toward the cot so that he could sit down. He reached for the bottle of Beam's, hesitated and let his hand drop away without touching it.

"No, sir," said Fetterman. "But I didn't think you were one of those ringknocker types."

"But kill him? Just plan his death like plotting a murder?"

"Oh, come on, Lieutenant," Fetterman snapped. "Let's stop beating around the bush. That's what this is all about. We go out hunting the enemy, setting up ambushes to increase the body count. We talk about rules of engagement and land warfare, but it all comes down to one thing: killing the other guys. I'm merely suggesting that we, for this once, don't rely on random factors to determine the targets. I suggest that we go out and kill that Chinese officer."

Gerber stood up and walked to the door and shut it. As he sat down again, he said, "I don't know."

Fetterman shifted his attention to Gerber. "We plan missions to eliminate specific units. We learn that a VC hard-core regiment is working our AO, so we devise a mission to destroy it. All I'm saying is, we're doing the same thing on a much smaller scale."

"Tony, you don't have to convince me," said Gerber. "But I can understand Johnny's point of view, too. Somehow this just doesn't seem right. Targeting one man. It reduces this whole thing to a personal confrontation."

"So what, Captain? That's how war used to be fought. Each knight, wearing distinctive colors, fighting knights in other colors. Each man identifiable to the others. The Chinese officer is the same. Distinctive."

Gerber remained quiet, staring at Fetterman's boots, which had been recently shined. Gerber never ceased to be amazed at the master sergeant. He was always in a clean uniform with polished boots. Not necessarily spit shined, but polished. He went by the book most of the time. Why was he now advocating such a rogue action?

"This isn't right," said Bromhead. "What you're saying makes sense, but it still sounds like we're sanctioning an assassination."

"Think of it as going out to destroy a specific unit," Fetterman replied.

"It's still plotting a murder, no matter how we dress it up," said Bromhead.

And the hell of it was that Bromhead was right, Gerber thought. It was plotting a murder. A murder of a foreign national in a neutral country. Gerber couldn't just nod his head and tell his men to go out and do it. He had to tell someone that he was planning such an action, and that was why he was in the helicopter heading back to Saigon. While neither Bates nor Crinshaw would give approval for an assassination, Gerber had another contact that might see the value of such a mission. As many of the Special Forces officers in Vietnam, Gerber had a case officer who haunted the dark, cold, lower reaches of the MACV headquarters. Sometimes the CIA needed help with a mission, and they sent someone out to a

Special Forces camp. Sometimes it was the other way around. This was one of the times it was the other way around.

At Hotel Three Gerber avoided the terminal building and walked to the gate. There he found a taxi, and as he got into the back, he told the driver to take him to the MACV compound on the other side of town. Upon arrival, he paid the driver with a handful of MPC, the military script issued for use in the local economy to prevent black-marketing, and headed inside. The American MPs at the gate didn't even blink as Gerber approached. He was obviously an American.

Gerber pushed open the first of the large glass doors, entered, went through another set of doors and into the nearly uncomfortable air-conditioning of the headquarters building. He walked along the tiled floors, avoiding speaking to the men and women he encountered until he reached a stairway. At the bottom he was stopped by a guard standing in front of a gate of iron bars that ran from ceiling to floor. He asked Gerber to produce an ID card, then used a field phone sitting on a small desk to verify that someone inside knew Gerber and would meet him.

Once through the iron gate Gerber turned down another corridor lined with cinder-block walls that were damp with condensation. Rust spots where metal chairs, tables or cabinets had been set and later removed stained the tiled floor. Gerber halted in front of a dark wooden door and knocked.

The man who opened the door was short. He had dark hair and dark eyes and a sunburned complexion. He wore a white suit that was wrinkled and stained. His thin black tie was pulled down and the collar was open. He held a big hand out, not so Gerber could shake it but so he could pull the Special Forces officer out of the hall.

Inside, one wall was lined with a series of gray four-drawer filing cabinets. The one in the corner was massive with a combination lock on the second drawer. A battleship-gray metal desk, the top littered with papers and manila file folders, was shoved into the far corner. Four empty Coke cans were lined up against the edge closest to the wall. A small chair was near the desk and a larger one sat next to it. A single picture, showing cavalrymen fighting Sioux Indians and labeled The Wagon Box Fight, was hanging on the wall. The office, because it was below ground and had no windows, was entirely artificially lit. The super-cooled air from upstairs did not reach down to this level, but it was still cooler than it was outside the building.

"Mack Gerber," said the man, "have a seat and tell me what you have on your mind."

"Just like that, Jerry," said Gerber. "No 'how are you?' No 'how are things at the camp?' Just 'have a seat and tell me what's on your mind'?"

"Okay." Jerry Maxwell smiled as he sat behind his desk. "How are you? How are things out at that camp of yours?"

"I'm fine, thank you. And things aren't all that great out at the camp. That's why I came down here." Now Gerber smiled. "See how nicely that works?"

"Don't get cute, Mack," said Jerry. "Just because you have a paper saying you're an officer and a gentleman, it doesn't mean you can give etiquette lessons."

"I believe that Congress only commissions us as officers now. That gentleman crap went out a long time ago."

"You win. You want a Coke or something?"

"No, thanks. I'd like to get straight to a problem I have and see what we can do about it."

"Okay," said Maxwell, pushing a stack of paper out of his way so that he could lean an elbow on his desk. Several reports with cover sheets stamped Secret were revealed.

For the next thirty minutes Gerber detailed the confrontations his patrols had had with the Chinese officer, concluding with the most recent attack on the ARVN rangers. He told the CIA man all that he knew and all that he suspected, explaining that the role of the Chinese soldier seemed to be as an adviser and tactical commander. Gerber also told the case officer that the Chinese had good military training, that he rarely missed opportunities to ambush ARVN and American patrols and that dozens had been killed by units led by him.

Maxwell finally held up a hand to stop Gerber and said, "So you want to go hunting, right? You want to target this guy?"

"We want to eliminate him, yes," said Gerber. "Gains us two things. First, we kill the one man in our AO who seems capable. Without him, we'll be fighting the same kind of rabble operating in the rest of South Vietnam. This guy is very good. And second, we show the VC that we can go anywhere. They are not safe in their own camps if we decide to eliminate them."

"This guy's base is in South Vietnam?" asked Maxwell.

Gerber scratched his forehead and stared at the floor for a moment. Then he said, "We think he's operating from a base about twenty klicks inside Cambodia."

"Uh-huh. And you want to go chasing after him, across the border, even with a hundred military and Congressional directives prohibiting cross-border operations."

Now Gerber grinned as if he had just heard something funny. His only response was, "Yeah."

"Okay, Mack," said Maxwell, idly flipping through the papers on his desktop. "I'll let you in on the big picture. Something new has been added. The folks at home are not pleased with our involvement over here. So far, it's mainly college kids of draft age who aren't thrilled with the prospect of winning an all-expenses-paid vacation to the dream spot of Southeast Asia, but that dissatisfaction is spreading. The President wants us to do something to help get us out of here."

"That's interesting, Jerry, but what has it to do with my problem?"

"I'm coming to that. The DCI, along with some of the intelligence people here, have decided that a war of attrition is not the answer. Hell, MacArthur said that fifteen years ago. Stay out of a ground war in Asia, and here we are, right in the middle of one.

"Anyway," continued Maxwell, "the DCI and the others have decided that we should go directly after the enemy leader. Cut off the head and the snake dies. In the last month—and I warn you, this is all top secret—but in the last month we've sent out a half dozen sniper teams to eliminate a number of high-ranking enemy political and military leaders."

Gerber stared at his friend for a moment, wondering if he were being kidded, and then saw there was no humor in what he was being told. Assassination teams had been dispatched to kill enemy civilians. Assassination was being sanctioned by the highest levels of the American government. For some reason that surprised Gerber even though he, along with Fetterman and Bromhead, had discussed the same thing only hours earlier.

"This is sort of a pacification-by-assassination plan," said Maxwell quietly as if someone might overhear. "There's no written directive sanctioning it, and it doesn't even have an official code name, although someone has suggested we call it Phoenix. You know, the new government rising from the ashes of the old."

"I take it," said Gerber, choosing his words carefully, "that you are telling me to go ahead with the plan."

"Not in so many words. In fact, if you get into trouble, I will deny that this discussion ever took place. But if you think this Chinese is a big problem and his death will shorten the war, then by all means go after him."

"Into Cambodia and smoke a foreign national?"

"Captain, I will not give you permission to violate the military instructions and regulations under which you operate, nor will I tell you to violate the neutrality of a foreign government. I will tell you that a successful mission will not be questioned."

"And by successful you mean . . . ?" Gerber asked.

"I mean that no one hears about it and your target is quietly eliminated."

3

Gerber stood in the terminal building of Hotel Three near the corner window where he could watch the helicopters operating from the field. Six large cement squares marked the official landing pads, and a wide grass strip paralleled a chain-link fence on the far side, about a hundred meters away. The helicopters that were haphazardly scheduled, the ones that flew in from the outlying camps without distinguished visitors, were required to land on the grass. The one that Gerber waited for would have to land there.

While he waited, he considered the assignment he had been given. He smiled to himself, remembering that there really wasn't an assignment at all. Just a civilian who worked for the CIA telling him that no one would squawk if his men entered Cambodia secretly, found the Red Chinese officer and shot him. If they got in and out without anyone noticing, then it was a successful operation.

Outside a Huey came to a hover, turned toward the tower momentarily and then settled to the ground, its rotor still spinning and its engine running. A large white hornet was painted on the front, identifying it as a helicopter from the 116th Assault Helicopter Company. Without waiting for the clerk behind the thin plywood counter to call his name, Gerber grabbed his knapsack and weapon and ran out the door.

Dodging a couple of Army privates and one massive sergeant, Gerber hurried to the helicopter. He stepped up on the skid so that he could look in the aircraft commander's window and shouted over the turbine noise, "Catch a ride with you to Triple Nickel?"

The pilot, a young warrant officer who looked as if he belonged in high school, nodded and said, "I'm on my way to Tay Ninh. We can drop you off."

Gerber held a thumb up and grinned at the young pilot. "Thanks," he shouted.

When the helicopter took off again and they reached altitude, away from the staggering heat and crushing humidity of the ground, Gerber realized he was spending too much time in Saigon. He had been there two nights in a row. This time he had taken a room in the Bien Hoa BOQ so he would be away from Saigon. He had used the field phone system to route a call through Cu Chi, Dau Tieng, Song Be and Tay Ninh to the switchboard at his camp, if switchboard was the right word for it.

He told Bromhead he'd been summoned to Saigon for another briefing about the disposition of enemy troops in the AO and not to worry. It was a routine briefing and he'd be back by noon the following day.

Then he'd gone to one of the many officers' clubs around Bien Hoa, had another steak dinner and watched as a group of Vietnamese strippers took off their clothes while bored men sat around and drank heavily.

In the morning it had been easy to catch a ride back to Saigon and then discover who had aircraft coming in. He waited until he saw one with insignia he recognized. As many who had been in Vietnam for several months, he knew he could get anywhere in-country by waiting around the airfields.

At A-555 the helicopter landed in a billowing cloud of purple smoke from a marker grenade Bocker had thrown so that the aircraft would have a landing point and an idea about wind direction. The pilot had alerted the Special Forces sergeant that they were inbound, and he had decided to meet the aircraft at the pad himself. Gerber leaped out of the cargo compartment and waved his thanks as the aircraft lifted to a hover, sucking red dust up from the ground and blowing it into a fog that obscured everything until the chopper cleared the wires and was climbing out rapidly.

As the helicopter disappeared, Bocker, who had been standing at the edge of the pad, approached. He didn't salute—none of them ever did. It wasn't a good idea to salute in the field because it pinpointed the officers for the enemy, not that they expected any VC to be close enough at the moment to see them.

Shouldering his knapsack, his rifle in his left hand, Gerber said, "Morning, Galvin. Is Fetterman around?"

"When I last saw him, he was in the team house eating breakfast," Bocker replied.

After Gerber had dropped his knapsack in his hootch, he made his way next door to the team house. Fetterman sat at one of the tables, a cup of coffee in front of him, reading a week-old copy of *Stars and Stripes*.

Gerber poured himself a cup of coffee from a pot standing on a small table next to the door and then sat down opposite Fetterman. "Morning, Tony," he said.

Fetterman carefully folded his paper and set it down. He grinned and asked, "What's the good word?"

Gerber shot a glance at the Vietnamese woman who stood behind the counter that separated the tiny kitchen from the rest of the team house. He lowered his voice, keeping his eye on the woman, and said, "I want to meet with you, Lieutenant Bromhead and anyone else you want with you on this. Say my hootch in twenty minutes."

"Meaning?" asked Fetterman.

"Meaning your trip to the west," answered Gerber.

Gerber was sitting on his cot when the others arrived. Fetterman took one of the lawn chairs to the side of the desk. Bromhead grabbed the metal folding one behind it, letting Tyme have the third and last. Gerber watched the three men for a moment, wondering what was going on in their minds.

None of them knew he had been to Saigon to meet with the CIA case officer. In fact, only Fetterman knew there was a CIA case officer.

"Gentlemen," said Gerber, "this is a general planning session for our mission to the west. Given the nature of this mission, I don't think it's a good idea to take notes. The fewer written documents we have, the fewer problems we'll have."

All three of the men looked confused. Gerber said, "Sergeant Fetterman has made a suggestion that we dust the Chinese officer. I think that the idea has some merit and want to discuss it."

"As I said before, Captain—" Bromhead began.

Gerber cut him off. "You misunderstand Johnny. We're not here to discuss whether or not to go on the mission, we're here to plan it."

"Yes, sir."

Now Fetterman spoke up. "I've been thinking about this for some time, Captain. We know the Chinese officer operates from a base in Cambodia, not more than thirty klicks from here. He's been running patrols and ambushes in our AO for a couple of months, and if he were farther away, we wouldn't have seen him so often. We also have an idea of the location of the enemy camps from the aerial recon the Air Force has flown for MACV and Army Intelligence."

"All right," nodded Gerber. "We've all had the same briefings about that in Nha Trang. What's your point?"

"I think we can limit the search area quite a bit by using that information. Maybe Sergeant Kepler can get us some more by going to Nha Trang personally. Hell, he's the intel specialist with the team, he should be able to get us something."

"Let's get to the logistics of this," ordered Gerber.

"Easy enough, sir," replied Fetterman. "Since this is a cross-border op, we'll want to take sterile equipment. There are enough weapons in our captured arms store to outfit a company if we want. Sergeant Tyme has checked most of them out and can pull enough for us."

"That's right," agreed Tyme. Tyme was a tall, sandy-haired man in his midtwenties. He seemed to have no real passions in life other than weapons. He lived, breathed and dreamed small arms. There were only a few light weapons made in the world that Tyme could not identify, break down, clean and repair. "Some of the rifles have suffered battle damage, shrapnel into the stock or bullets into the magazine, that sort of thing, but quite a few of them are in mint condition."

"I assume," said Gerber, "that you'll be using one of them to make the kill."

"Oh, no, sir," said Tyme. "I'll be taking a specially adapted M-14 with an automatic ranging sniperscope mounted on it. I'll file the numbers off so that it can't be traced directly to us, but I'm afraid that everyone will know that it was manufactured in the U.S., if it comes to that."

"That reminds me," said Fetterman. "We'll be wearing standard fatigues, but with no U.S. markings or patches. Again, if the enemy should get their hands on any of it, they'll know the source, but not the who."

"Except for the soldiers," said Gerber.

Fetterman smiled slyly. "Well, maybe not. I'll want to take Krung and five or six of the Tai. Their ethnic makeup is remarkably like that of the Cambodes. If they don't speak, I don't think anyone is going to be able to positively identify them."

Fetterman stood and gestured at himself. He was a small man with a dark complexion. Sometimes, when he had been drinking, he joked about an Aztec heritage, and his facial structure, with the long hooked nose, did suggest he had ancestors in Mexico.

"I can pass as a Hispanic if I'm not required to speak Spanish in front of anyone from South America or Mexico."

Wiping some sweat from his forehead, Gerber said, "You're obviously planning to take Tyme with you."

"Yes, sir. I know that he stands out like a sore thumb, but he's our best marksman. I thought we could dye his hair and stain his skin to make him a little less identifiable. His Nordic features are a problem."

"You know," said Tyme, "you all make it sound as if we're not going to make it."

"Just covering the bases," said Gerber. "Have you thought about the rest of this, Tony? Mission specifics?"

"Yes, sir. The mission specifics," repeated Fetterman. "Providing Sergeant Kepler can get confirmation on the enemy base location, either through the intel network he has set up or from the classified sources available in Nha Trang, we'll leave the camp in about a day and a half at 1700 hours. We'll patrol to the south, then turn west to the border, crossing at one of three locations. Once inside Cambodia we'll halt for a day or so, set up an advance base before we move deeper to the NVA camp.

"Once we've located that, Sergeants Tyme, Krung and I will find concealment so that we can observe the enemy. Ideally, we will be able to identify our target and make the kill at about dusk. That will give us all night to evade back toward our advance base if possible, or provide an opportunity to lose anyone tracking us if we can't get back to our advance base."

Bromhead let out a low, quiet whistle. "Damn! I don't like the sound of this."

"You have a real problem with that, Johnny?" Gerber snapped.

"No, sir. Not at all. I just don't like the sound of it."

"With luck," continued Fetterman, "the enemy won't realize what has happened for a while and give us an even better head start."

"Why wouldn't they?" asked Bromhead.

"Well, sir, we're going to make the shot from about a klick if the conditions are right. That's why we need to take the M-14 instead of one of the weapons from our captured stock. The single report could be lost in the distance. If the man is alone, it might be several minutes, maybe twenty or thirty, before someone finds him. Long-range sniping produces some weird results because it's the last thing the enemy is going to suspect."

"And if your man is out on patrol?"

"We're prepared to stay put for a couple of days observing. Give us a chance to learn the routine of the camp, but if the target presents itself earlier, we won't pass up the opportunity," answered Fetterman.

Gerber stood up and moved toward the front of his hootch. "A couple of days after you've deployed, I'll mount a large patrol and move to the region of the border. Tony, I'll get together with you a little later and outline a specific route so that you'll be able to locate us. That way, if you're being pursued, we'll be in a better position to lend a hand."

"So what's the code word?" asked Bromhead.

"We wanted something that would be confusing to anyone who picked it up and that would not possibly be used by anyone else. Something unique," Fetterman said.

"Fine," said Bromhead. "The code?"

Fetterman smiled. "I will report that we have sighted Crinshaw's body."

SIXTEEN HOURS LATER the project became more complicated. Gerber, who was eating a cold breakfast of Cheerios from a single-serving box—the cereal covered in cool milk he had made earlier with lukewarm water and powder—heard the noise of approaching helicopters and picked up his glass of reconstituted orange juice. Since the only scheduled flight had come and gone, he stepped to the team house door and saw that a formation of five Huey helicopters was obviously on approach to the camp. He glanced toward the commo bunker in time to see Bocker exit it and run for the helipad.

Bocker slid to a halt and tossed a smoke grenade onto the center of the pad. He retreated as soon as he saw it begin to burn, the purple smoke blowing leisurely toward the northeast. Gerber caught Bocker's attention, and the commo sergeant changed direction and headed for the team house.

As Bocker approached, Gerber asked, "Who the hell is that?"

"Don't know for sure. Call sign was Crusader One-Two. That's a unit from Tay Ninh according to the SOI, but the pilot refused to provide any more information."

Gerber reached into the team house so that he could set his empty juice glass on the table that held the coffeepot. He grabbed his beret from the hook next to the door and said, "Okay, let's not fool around. I don't like this at all."

"It's probably just some kind of search-and-destroy mission that wants to use our camp as a temporary base," Bocker said as the two men started forward.

"They should have coordinated it with me first," said Gerber, his eyes on the inbound chopper. "Let's get some people around the pads and have Lieutenant Bromhead swing one of the machine guns in the northeast corner of the camp so that it's aimed at the pad. We'll give them a welcome they don't expect."

As Bocker trotted off, Gerber ran to his hootch, grabbed his M-14 and two grenades and headed to the helipads. There he met Fetterman, who was holding an M-3. Fetterman pointed to the fire control tower, and Gerber turned to see Tyme scrambling up the ladder.

The helicopters crossed the outer wire, settling toward the ground. Gerber sent Fetterman to a stack of sandbags to cover the lead ship. Bocker had gone back to the commo bunker, picked up his weapon and was now crouched in the Z-shaped entrance. Bromhead and two of the Tai had lifted one of the .30 caliber machine guns and turned it and its tripod so that they had an unobstructed field of fire that could rake the entire helipad and a long section of the runway.

As soon as the helicopters were on the ground, men started piling out of them. The crew chief of the lead chopper leaped to the ground from his position in the gun well, a long cord from his helmet still connected to the radio jack and a small black button in his hand. He opened the copilot's door, and when the crew chief jumped back out of the way, the pilot stepped down, pulling the flight helmet from his head.

Brigadier General Billy Joe Crinshaw stood squinting in the morning sun. Gerber made no move to come forward. Crinshaw stood in the cloud of swirling red dust and handed his flight helmet to the crew chief. Then, ignoring the rotor blades, he stepped close to Gerber.

For an instant, as the whine of the Huey turbines quieted, Gerber considered what he was going to say. He didn't like people appearing on the horizon without announcing their plans, and although the VC and the NVA didn't have Huey helicopters, he thought it was a stupid move. Over the sound of the dying engines, Gerber shouted, "I could have shot your ass out of the sky."

Crinshaw momentarily stiffened at the hostility of the remark, let alone that it was a junior officer who had made it. He stood there silently, waiting for Gerber to say more.

"Next time you come in here, you tell us who you are. There's no need to drop out of the sky like some demented bird of prey."

"Watch what you're saying, Captain," Crinshaw cautioned him.

"General Crinshaw," said Gerber, "there are some very real military considerations here. I have to know who is approaching the camp and why they are coming in. An unidentified flight of helicopters cannot be tolerated. If the lead pilot had not made the request for smoke on the pad, we would have had no idea who you were."

"The pilot was acting on my orders. You do not question my orders, Captain. Never question them."

"The point here is—" started Gerber.

"The point is," interrupted Crinshaw, "that I wanted to look over your operation. And I see it's pretty weak. You make big talk about shooting us out of the sky, but you only have a single rifle."

Gerber was going to tell him about the machine gun crew covering them and point out Bocker, Fetterman and Tyme, but decided it would prove nothing. Rather than prolong the debate, he said, "What's going on here?"

He could see men who had arrived on the helicopters unloading supplies. Cardboard boxes of C-rations, crates of ammo, extra weapons, M-60 machine guns and even a couple of 60 mm mortars.

"Let's watch those smart-alecky tones, Captain," said Crinshaw. "I brought these boys out for some first-hand training and experience in the field."

A major who had arrived on one of the choppers approached from the rear and stood waiting. He looked like a regular Saigon commando. He wore a camouflaged uniform, but it had been starched so that it held a knifelike crease even in humidity high enough to wilt concrete. He had highly polished insignia on his collar that flashed in the sunlight and even wore spit shined boots. He was a stocky man, not more than five-foot-seven, with a bulky jaw and soft, pale eyes. His face was a pasty white, as if he didn't get out in the tropical sun very often.

Crinshaw stared at Gerber for a moment longer and then turned to the major. "Get your equipment together and prepare to move it out of here."

Although no one told the major where to take his equipment, he spun and began ordering his men to gather it so they could get it away from the helipad.

"The aircraft, General," Gerber reminded him. "We can't let them sit here all day."

Crinshaw looked irritated and then said, "Yes, of course." He held a thumb up, telling the lead pilot he was released and could take off.

Gerber waved Fetterman over and said to him, "Take the major and his men and find a place for them."

Two hours later Gerber was back at the helipad waiting on another flight of choppers, this group carrying a Vietnamese general who was bringing in men to recover the bodies of the dead rangers. As he and Bocker waited, he leaned close and asked, "Kepler get away?"

"Got the morning resupply chopper. He shouldn't have trouble with the connections to Nha Trang."

When they could see the helicopters clearly, Bocker tossed a yellow smoke grenade onto the center of the pad.

Just as the helicopters touched down, Crinshaw arrived to watch. He stood with one hand on his head, holding down his baseball-type fatigue cap as the rotor blades tried to lift everything into the swirling wind they created.

The Vietnamese general, obvious in his tailored uniform and rows of brightly colored ribbons, stepped down from the cargo

compartment. He then turned and held his hand out so that
the woman traveling with him could exit. As she entered the
bright light from the shadows in the cargo compartment,
Gerber recognized her immediately.

Crinshaw stared in disbelief and demanded, ''Who in the
hell authorized that woman to be out here?''

She pulled a folded piece of paper out of the top pocket of
the khaki bush jacket she wore and handed it to Crinshaw.
''You did, General. You signed it yourself a couple of days ago
and General Vo was kind enough to give me a lift.''

Crinshaw grabbed the paper from her, stared at it, saw his
signature scrawled at the bottom and knew he had been had.
It had been a request that Morrow, R., be allowed to report
on the activities at Special Forces Camp A-555.

Crinshaw recovered nicely. He handed the paper back to
Morrow and said to Gerber, ''You see that she gets everything
she wants. Everything.''

Morrow turned and grinned at Gerber, acting as if she had
never seen him before.

When Fetterman arrived moments later, Gerber said,
''You'll have to find a place for Miss Morrow.''

''That's the least of our problems, Captain,'' he said, mo-
tioning to the helipad.

Gerber took a moment to look at the new group of men, the
two generals standing near each other, talking quietly, the
seven helicopters sitting on the pad, their rotors spinning
slowly, and the new piles of ammunition and explosives. He
was thinking about the mission that Fetterman had planned
for that night—providing Kepler could confirm enemy camp
locations—and how they were going to operate with everyone
falling all over everyone else. Finding quarters for Morrow was
definitely the least of their problems.

He turned back to Fetterman and said, ''Let's get these
people out of here and get their equipment stored.''

''Everything still on for tonight?''

''I don't know. Let's hang loose, wait to hear from Kepler
and then see how the situation breaks.''

4

FIFTH SPECIAL FORCES HEADQUARTERS, NHA TRANG, REPUBLIC OF VIETNAM

Sergeant First Class Derek Kepler sat in the anteroom of the Fifth Special Forces Intelligence Officer watching the ceiling fan revolve slowly as it fought a losing battle to stir up a breeze. Plywood paneling stained a dirty brown covered the office walls from the floor to the midpoint, where screen hidden behind louvered one by sixes climbed the rest of the way to the ceiling. That was to let in any breeze that might be blowing, in a futile effort to keep the inside comfortable. The canopy from a parachute flare was suspended under the rafters.

Kepler was the intel specialist for Mack Gerber's A-Team and had been with Gerber's group since they had deployed to Vietnam. His job was to learn all he could about the enemy's troop movements, locations, the local population, the climatic conditions they might face and anything else that could be helpful. He also had a network of agents spread through the villages and hamlets near the camp. They were supposed to tell him of anything unusual, such as VC recruiting trips or reprisals that took place. Most of the agents were people who wanted to do something to help the Americans or who hated the VC.

It was his own agents who had first alerted him to the VC-NVA base camp just over the Cambodian border, and they had given him a good idea about its location. Recon photos from the Air Force had helped him pinpoint it, although it was information that had done him little good until now. Since the captain had asked him to verify the site of the camp, he found his knowledge helpful. He hoped he could get more recent recon photos from the intelligence officer and possibly determine if the camp had been moved. The VC didn't like to stay in one place too long.

After nearly thirty minutes of sitting in the outer office on an old wrought-iron settee with gaudy green fabric and a dozen rips that had been patched with electrical tape, the clerk typist, who had been ignoring him, stood. He moved to the door that was closed, knocked once and looked inside. He turned, glanced at Kepler and said, "The major will see you now."

Kepler got to his feet and stepped past the clerk. The office he entered had an air conditioner humming in one corner, trying hard to keep up with the heat and humidity outside, but slowly losing the battle. It was cooler in the office, but not much.

The major stood and came around a scarred metal desk stuck in one corner. He was a tall, thin man with prematurely graying hair and bushy black eyebrows that were in stark contrast to his sharp, fine features. His brown eyes had laugh lines radiating from them, and his mouth carried an amused grin. He had his hand out, meaning he didn't expect a salute from Kepler. "Welcome to Nha Trang, Sergeant—or maybe I should say Derek," he said. "How have you been?"

Kepler shook the major's hand. "Just fine, lately. I trust that my reports have been getting here satisfactorily."

The major sat on the corner of his desk and pushed a nameplate with a major's oak leaf stuck into a blue field and the name Houston inscribed to one side on it. "Everything has been coming in just fine. I appreciate those updates on the VC movements. Helps us coordinate the activities for the other teams in your general AO."

"Yes, sir. Just trying to do my job. I do have a bit of a problem, though, and thought you might be able to help."

"Anything you need," said Houston.

"I wondered if you had any new aerial recon of the Parrot's Beak region. I need to look at things along the Cambodian border. Charlie seems to be building up there somewhere."

Houston scratched his chin and said, "I don't recall seeing anything about that in any of the new classified. You have anything more specific?"

"No, sir. That's why I thought looking up the latest recon photos might help. I can compare them with what I've seen before and spot the trend."

"All right," said Houston. "I'll pull the stuff out of the safe. Parrot's Beak region?"

"Yes, sir. About fifteen or twenty klicks on either side of the border."

Houston stood and moved to the door. "Wait here and I'll see what I can find."

When the major was gone, Kepler took the opportunity to examine the office closely. On the wall next to the door were the obligatory captured weapons. Houston had an RPG-7 mounted on an oak plaque and an AK-47 with a small brass plate attached to the stock claiming both weapons were captured on August 17, 1964, in the Plei Me area.

A scarred conference table surrounded by four chairs sat at one end of the office. The finish was dull and cracked, the varnish burned where lit cigarettes had fallen. The chairs weren't in any better shape.

Just as Kepler sat down in one of the chairs, the door opened and Houston reappeared carrying a folder that was stamped Secret top and bottom, front and back. Before Kepler could stand, Houston slipped into one of the other chairs and slid the file toward the Special Forces intel officer.

Kepler took the photos from the folder. Each one was also stamped Secret in red letters. He used the map that was enclosed in the file to orient the pictures so he could recognize some of the major terrain features, such as the point where the Mekong River crossed the border and the Moc Hoa canal.

Once he had the pictures laid out in order, he began to study them. The black-and-white photos, shot from over thirty thousand feet, didn't contain much obvious detail for the untrained eye.

Using the magnifying glass that Houston took from the middle drawer of his desk, Kepler carefully examined the area where he believed the enemy camp to be. At first he saw nothing except the tops of the palms that formed the upper level of the triple-canopy jungle. Slowly he began to see things that didn't seem to belong—symmetrical shadows that betrayed the presence of a low building, and a point of light where the corrugated tin of a roof caught and reflected the sun. Kepler spread a piece of clear plastic on the photo and then traced the shadows and reflections with a grease pencil. By erasing and changing the lines, he had soon drawn the portrait of the enemy camp. It was an oval, containing fifteen or twenty buildings as well as a dozen small structures that could be sheds. He even found what he thought was the outline of a truck hidden under the trees, but the resolution of the photo wasn't quite good enough for him to be sure.

All this time Houston sat across from him, smoking cigarette after cigarette until the atmosphere in the room took on the hazy blue of a nightclub. He said nothing as he watched Kepler work through the photos.

Having confirmed the location of the VC base, Kepler went back over the photos looking for other evidence of VC activity. He found a place on one picture that might have been a snatch of the Ho Chi Minh Trail and an enlarged area near it that might have been one of the rumored rest stops along it. He located a number of single structures, little more than hootches, that probably belonged to rice farmers. He checked the coordinates of them all, memorizing them because he knew that Houston would not let him carry the information out in writing. To do that, he would need permission from nearly a dozen sources, including the Air Force and the CIA.

He was about to quit when something caught his eye. Studying it under the magnifying glass, he became convinced that he had found another base—smaller than the first and hidden better, but an enemy camp all the same. Then, as he searched through the blacks and whites of the trees in the photo, he felt his excitement grow. He sat back, stared at the ceiling in disbelief and then turned back to the picture.

"What is it?" asked Houston, puzzled.

"I don't think I believe it," said Kepler, unable to keep the surprise out of his voice.

Houston stood and came around the table so he could get a close look at the photo.

Kepler held the magnifying glass and pointed with his free hand. "Right here," he said, circling an area with his index finger. "If you look closely, you'll see what appear to be bleachers sitting in the shadow thrown by that large tree."

"Yes. So?"

"Look very carefully now." Kepler put a finger on the photo at the side of the bleachers. "This," he said, "is the instructor. Right here are the students. It's a picture of a damned VC class!"

For a moment Houston didn't say anything. Then he laughed out loud and said, "My God! I think you're right."

"Of course I'm right. The fucking VC sitting around in a fucking class."

After making a series of quick measurements to determine distances and directions from the first camp to the second, Kepler scooped up the photos, tapped the edges on the table to align them and stuffed them back into the file folder. He stood and said, "I guess that does it, sir. I've seen what I need to see."

"Anything else?" asked Houston.

"No, sir. That should do it."

Houston picked up the folder and said, "I'll get this back in the safe. You need anything else, let me know."

Kepler left the intel office and turned up the corridor, heading toward the radio room, where he could use the lima lima to make a call to the camp, providing they could get the routing to work. The phone system the Army was building in South Vietnam was not the efficient operation that Ma Bell had in the World. It was a haphazard conglomeration of switchboards and commo wire that was down more often than it was up. But Kepler wanted to stay away from using the radio if he could. Fewer people could listen in on the land line.

The switchboard operator, a Spec Four in sweat-stained fatigues who looked as if he were fifteen years old, said he didn't think he would have any luck because things were acting up all over. He could not define what things were acting up, but he sat in a folding metal chair and cranked the handle that rang phones on other switchboards anyway. He pulled wires from some slots and jammed them into others, asking operators to route him on farther to the west. Finally, with a jury-rigged line that ran from Nha Trang to Phan Rang to Phouc Binh to Dau Tieng to Saigon to Tay Ninh, he was able to ring the switchboard in the commo bunker at Camp A-555.

Bocker picked up the phone on the second ring, listened for a moment and then handed it to Fetterman, who was checking the radio equipment he'd take with him on the mission.

Fetterman took the receiver of the field phone and said simply, "Go."

"I have confirmed the location," said Kepler.

"Understood," said Fetterman.

"Be advised that I have also discovered a second prime location fourteen klicks to the southwest."

"Understand a second location fourteen klicks to the southwest."

"Roger that."

AS SOON AS HE HUNG UP, Fetterman grabbed one of the maps from the chart table and plotted the information. He examined the terrain, looking for hills and valleys, rivers and ravines and swamps and jungle that could make the patrol impossible. There was nothing on the maps to indicate he couldn't get from one camp to the other if he had to.

That done, Fetterman left the commo bunker, stepping into the late-afternoon heat. He put a hand to his forehead to shade his eyes and went looking for Gerber.

He found Gerber in his hootch, working on a report that Crinshaw had demanded. It was a listing of the supplies used in the past two weeks to establish a new antimortar bunker, and a description of the ammo requirements of the perimeter defense weapons—meaning the .50 and .30 caliber machine guns located in the bunkers on the four walls. The report was a make-work project that would be of no benefit to anyone.

Gerber stopped working when a shadow fell across the floor in front of his desk. He then waved Fetterman in, capped his pen and said, "What can I do for you?"

"Kepler reported in. He confirmed the location of the base camp and said he'd found another several klicks away."

"That cause you a problem, Tony?"

"Only if it turns out that the VC have moved."

"Then you're still planning to go tonight?"

"Well, sir, that's the real problem. Seems odd, doesn't it? We're about to embark on this mission and both the Vietnamese and the American high command decide to show up with a series of excuses about why they're here."

Gerber turned so that he could stare at the master sergeant. "Are you suggesting a leak somewhere?"

"I'm merely calling attention to an amazing coincidence."

"This whole thing was your idea, Tony. We're under no time constraints. We can postpone it if that would make you feel better." Gerber hadn't told Fetterman that the CIA was interested in the mission. The CIA wanted to see it accomplished, but had put no time restrictions on it.

Fetterman wiped a hand across his forehead. "No, sir. As I say, I'm merely pointing out a coincidence. Besides, we're supposed to be running patrols."

Gerber sat back and locked his fingers behind his head. "Crinshaw and his boys could cause us some real trouble if they learned where you are going."

"No reason they should, Captain," said Fetterman. He thought for a moment, his eyes on the dusty plywood floor. "Unless you think we should delay until the generals are out of camp, I would say that we go ahead."

"How soon do you want to jump off?"

"About an hour before dusk. Give us a chance to get away from here before we lose all the light."

FETTERMAN STOOD in the early evening light near the gate in the center of the south wall of the camp. He was looking at the crowd of men who loitered around it. Not only were Tyme, Krung and the five Tai of his patrol there, but there were also fifteen other Americans brought by Crinshaw and almost fifty Vietnamese brought by Vo. All were suddenly preparing to leave the camp on their various patrols. Crinshaw and a half dozen members of his staff were nearby, watching everything that was going on.

Leaning close to Gerber, Fetterman said, "How in the hell am I supposed to get out of here with nine-tenths of the American and Vietnamese population in the camp watching?"

"Just follow the normal patrol route. Once you're outside the wire, I doubt anyone will pay attention to you." Gerber then noticed the collection of American-made weapons carried by Fetterman's men. "I thought you said this was going to be a sterile mission?"

"I did, Captain. But with Crinshaw standing here to ask questions, I figured we'd better carry the American stuff. Besides, the M-1s are nearly as good as sterile. So many have been given to so many foreign countries, they shouldn't raise eyebrows. Hell, the VC carry them."

At that moment Tyme came over to report. "The Tai equipment checks out. I've been through their packs to make sure that they have everything they're supposed to."

"And you?" said Fetterman.

Tyme nodded. "The scope's in the bottom of my pack, protected by clean socks and a poncho liner. I've also cushioned it in mosquito netting."

"I take it you're all ready, then," Gerber said.

"Yes, sir," replied Fetterman.

Gerber held out his hand to his master sergeant. "Good luck and good hunting. We'll be listening for your first check-in. I'll go over to Crinshaw and see what I can do to hold up his people and give you a chance to fade into the night."

"Sounds great," said Fetterman as he pushed open the flimsy gate. Everyone figured that if the VC got to the gate, it would make no difference if it were sturdy or not. The enemy had to be stopped before it penetrated that deeply into the camp's defenses.

As Gerber engaged Crinshaw and his patrol leader—the major who hadn't been into the field—in conversation, Fetterman and his men worked their way through the perimeter. They entered the elephant grass, trying to avoid the pathways they had made on earlier trips. Fetterman was breaking the trail, being careful because, during the dry season, the grass could cut through cloth fatigues like a razor.

He looped to the south, toward the clump of trees they all too often used as a staging point once outside the camp. He halted under the trees and spread his men out in a circle so that they could guard all approaches. He watched the camp and soon saw the other patrol following the trail that Fetterman had made.

That in itself was not sinister. It might not mean anything other than that the patrol leader was inexperienced. Elephant grass was hard to walk through, and until you learned the trick of twisting the foot as you stepped on it, it was very tiring to break a trail. The major was following the path of least resistance.

Although Fetterman didn't think the other American patrol would be following him, he didn't trust Crinshaw. In the past the general had done things to hurt camp operations, like refusing to issue the new M-16s because the old M-14s were still serviceable, and ordering people to Saigon at critical moments. That hurt operations. It wasn't outside the realm of possibility that Crinshaw had told his men to follow Gerber's. Rather than heading to Cambodia, Fetterman turned farther to the south, keeping the clump of trees between him and the other American patrol. Just as they were leaving the trees, Fetterman turned back long enough to see that General Vo's patrol had now joined what was turning into a parade.

As the last of the light began to fade, Fetterman halted again. He set his men in an L-shaped ambush, pairing them up so that everyone had a buddy. Once that was done, he crawled along the rear of the ambush and found himself a place to hide. He picked a position where he could see the trail they had just followed.

He heard them long before he could see them. Their equipment rattled, they were talking and, unbelievably, two of the men in the rear were smoking. Fetterman crawled back to his ambush and told his men to fall back, away from the trail. He grouped them together, hiding under bushes and behind fallen palms. They lay there quietly and watched the other American patrol stumble by, oblivious to everything around them.

When Crinshaw's men were out of sight and Fetterman could no longer hear them, he silently moved among his men. He tapped each on the shoulder to alert him and then pointed west toward Cambodia. The point man, Sergeant Krung, took his compass out, checked the luminous dial and sighted on a light-colored palm trunk in the distance. He used a long stick to feel the ground in front of him so that he didn't fall into hidden holes or walk into trees he might not see in the dark.

They kept moving through the night, the pace slow but steady. They rested more often than usual because there was something about the night that made travel more difficult. A man had to use all his senses to the maximum. He had to stare into the inky black trying to see things that might be in the way. He had to listen so intently that it seemed the ears moved like radar antenna. Fetterman could actually feel his ears twitch as he heard the sounds of the nocturnal jungle animals in the distance. Although it wasn't nearly as hot as the daytime and he didn't have the sun baking his skin, Fetterman was covered with sweat. Sometimes he thought he preferred patrolling in the daylight.

About two o'clock, just as they stopped for a short break, the rain started. For a few seconds it was no more than a drizzle that didn't reach through the thick jungle growth to the ground. But then the clouds opened up and the rain poured down in sheets, rattling through the triple-canopy jungle, bouncing off the leaves until it reached Fetterman and his men.

For thirty minutes it rained hard, the sounds of the jungle drowned in the roar of the precipitation. Fetterman wanted to move, knowing the VC wouldn't be out in the lousy weather, but he was afraid his patrol would become separated. The only thing he could do was sit tight, wish he were dry and wait for the rain to end.

It was nearly three before the weather had cleared enough that Fetterman could resume the patrol. Again Krung took the point and slowly led them closer to Cambodia. As the sun came up, they were still fifteen klicks from the border, but all alone in the jungle. There was no sign of Crinshaw's men. Not far away, only a klick or so according to the map, was open ground where paddies bordered a swamp. It would be easier to travel over that type of terrain, but Fetterman wanted the protection of the jungle. He kept his patrol moving through the dense, wet jungle avoiding pathways, crawling around fallen trees and jungle undergrowth when they had to.

At nine in the morning, as the sun was beginning to heat the jungle and the steam was rising from the earth, Fetterman decided it was time to halt. The men had to get the wet socks off their feet, and they needed a chance to rest after marching all night. Besides, there was no point in getting too close to Cambodia in the daylight.

Fetterman rotated the duty so that everyone had a chance to sleep and eat a cold meal. By late afternoon they were ready to break camp.

Fetterman made sure each of the men drank a lot of water and took salt tablets, although the crushing heat of the day had passed. He also made sure each man drained the canteen he was drinking from because he didn't want the water of a partially filled one sloshing around. As always, each man carried three or four canteens to be sure the patrol had sufficient water. Given the territory, just north of the Mekong, there were plenty of places to fill canteens, and Fetterman had a large supply of halazone tablets to purify water.

As it started to get dark, they neared the Cambodian border. Fetterman took a number of final compass readings, plotted them on his map and then pointed it all out to Tyme and Krung.

"We'll cross the border about an hour from now, in total darkness," he said. "I want to travel about ten or twelve klicks after that. Give us some distance from the border and put us fairly close to the VC camp.''

Tyme took the point, leading them nearly due west. The others in the tiny patrol followed closely, with only a meter separating each man from the soldier in front of him. Fetterman brought up the rear and could only see the man directly in front of him.

Fetterman wasn't sure of the exact moment they crossed into Cambodia. There was no change in the terrain; the jungle was as heavy as before. There was no physical obstacle they had to climb and no guard posts to avoid. Just the seemingly endless jungle filled with the sounds of the creatures of the night and the buzz of the mosquitoes as they searched for victims.

They continued moving slowly, feeling their way through the jungle with their walking sticks. Clouds moved in to obscure the moon, making travel even more difficult.

About four in the morning, Fetterman began searching for a campsite, but it was nearly nine before he found what he wanted. One with good cover and many ways in and out. There was low brush around it so he could see anyone approaching and, by staying down, escape. He established a rotating guard, keeping half the men awake and watching while the other half slept or ate. And then the patrol settled in to wait for nightfall.

MACK GERBER SAT in the team house drinking coffee spiked with Beam's and relaxing. He had spent most of the previous day trying to convince Crinshaw that nothing unusual was happening and that the patrol he was running was normal. In addition to that, General Vo was wandering around, talking to the Vietnamese in the strike companies, ignoring the Tai.

Gerber had just finished his coffee when Crinshaw entered. Without a word Crinshaw walked to the coffeepot, poured himself a cup and then sat down on the other side of the table.

''What's going on out there, boy?'' he demanded.

''What's going on out where, General?'' asked Gerber.

"Let's stop dancing around," said Crinshaw. "Where is your patrol? I've talked to my people, and they say that your people disappeared."

Taking his time, Gerber stood, moved to the coffeepot and refilled his cup. He turned, sipped and said, "You mean that your people were following mine?"

"I said to stop the dancing. My people say that they watched yours head into the jungle and disappear. Now where the hell did they go?"

"The itinerary was not rigidly established. Sergeant Fetterman was told to play it by ear. He had a general patrol zone, which I'll be happy to show you, but I don't know his exact location."

"I'm not buying that, Captain. You have to know his location. Otherwise, you couldn't give support if he needed it."

"You know that I can tell you a general location, but if the sergeant needs help, he'll have to call for it."

"Okay, boy, I'll let you get away with that. Now, why did he work so hard to lose my people?"

"Then you're saying that they were out there to follow my men?"

"Just answer the question."

Gerber moved to the table and sat down, wishing he could pour a couple of fingers of the Beam's into the coffee now, but he knew Crinshaw wouldn't approve. "They were not trying to lose your people. I would imagine that Sergeant Fetterman was following standard field procedures, and if your people couldn't keep up, or lost sight of them, then I would think it is their fault and not Fetterman's. Not to mention the fact that it isn't good policy to throw that many patrols into the field following each other. Gives the enemy too much notice of who's going where. Besides, my men weren't advised to maintain contact with yours, so they had no reason for doing so."

For a moment Crinshaw didn't say anything. He stared at Gerber, trying to force him into saying something more, but when Gerber didn't fall into that trap, he said, "I'm going to stay here for a couple of days and watch your operation. I think there are things happening here I should know about.''

Gerber drained his coffee, set the cup down and stood. ''That's fine, General. You stay as long as you want. Now, if you don't mind, I'm going to check our defenses.''

FETTERMAN WAITED FOR DARK before he broke camp. It was nearly 2300 hours when they moved out again, heading for the large VC camp Kepler had identified for them. They moved through thinning jungle, crossed dozens of open rice fields, sometimes staying on the dikes to keep from making noise in the water, other times moving through them because the farmer had already drained them. They had to circle a couple of farm hootches, and once when they saw a light bobbing through the trees in front of them, they had to take cover, but the light never came close and soon disappeared. They heard no noise from the area and never did figure out what it was.

Overhead they heard a number of airplanes, most of them small propeller craft. Once or twice there were jets, but they never saw any lights from them. Fetterman thought they might be from bases in Thailand, heading to missions in South Vietnam.

The patrol kept up a steady pace, stopping for rest every hour. Fetterman let Tyme keep the point, sure that the young NCO would be able to handle the job. Leading a patrol through foreign territory at night was no easy task, especially when it was the enemy's territory. But Tyme didn't seem to have a problem. He avoided the pitfalls with what seemed to be a psychic ability. He kept them marching in as much of a straight line as the jungle would allow.

Tyme halted at about quarter to three, and Fetterman crawled forward, past the Tai who had dropped into hiding places as soon as Tyme had stopped moving.

He found the young sergeant lying prone, facing north. He put his mouth next to Tyme's ear and asked, ''Why have you stopped?''

Tyme pointed ahead and said, ''We're here!''

5

VIETCONG BASE CAMP, NORTH OF KOMPONG RAU, CAMBODIA

As the sun came up, Fetterman realized the camp was deserted. The camp was oval in shape, with short guard towers every fifty or sixty feet along the perimeter. Unlike the American bases in South Vietnam, there were no open killing fields outside the wire. The bush and jungle had been cut back so that the guards could see into the trees, but there was no open ground. But now the guard towers were deserted, and the fences were falling down. From his position, slightly above the VC camp, Fetterman could see a half dozen buildings that resembled barracks, long, low buildings with corrugated tin roofs and a row of small windows just under the eaves.

Near the center of the camp was a shed that might have housed a generator, and near it was a low, squat building that looked as if it were made of cement blocks and could have been the armory. There was a larger two-story stone building with steps leading up to it that might have been the headquarters, and a half dozen other small wooden structures.

Near the larger stone building were the remains of two trucks. One of them looked as if the back end had burned. Weeds and bushes had grown up around the vehicles and buildings, hiding some of the doorways, the ground and the walkways.

"Looks like they're gone," said Fetterman.

"Now what?" asked Tyme.

"I want Krung and the Tai to split into two squads of three men each and keep to the trees to cover us. Then you and I will enter the camp."

When the Tai were in place, Fetterman and Tyme began to work their way down the hillside, keeping to the cover of trees and bushes, dodging from hole to bush and back to hole as much as possible. While one of them moved, the other guarded, reversing their positions every thirty meters or so. When they were near the wire, they got down to crawl forward. Although he was worried about it, Fetterman had discovered no evidence of land mines or booby traps as they approached the fence. They found cover under a large flowering bush where they could study the inside of the base. There was still no sign of movement.

Finally sure there was no one left on the inside, Fetterman whispered, "We'll split up. We're looking for anything that might tell us about the VC, especially any documents that might be useful to Intel when we get back. If you find any useful military material, move it outside. We'll either take it back with us or destroy it before we move on."

They moved to the wire, found a large hole in it and avoided it. Fetterman figured that they could get through anywhere they wanted to, and if Charlie were going to booby-trap the camp, he would do it in the most likely spots. A hole in the wire, providing easy access, was a likely spot.

They separated, each moving along the wire for fifty meters. Fetterman cut the wire near one of the guard towers and entered underneath it. Once inside Fetterman carefully climbed the short wooden ladder so that he could search the guard tower, but there was nothing in it. When he looked back, he saw Tyme was already inside, heading toward the camp's center.

Tyme moved carefully through the compound, watching for trip wires, depressions in the ground and places where the leaves of the weeds were tied back, all things that indicated booby traps. He passed the generator shed, noting the oil stains on the hard packed ground.

Near the center of the compound, he came to the large stone headquarters building. The wood of the porch was partially burned away. The doors in the front were missing, and except for a few panes that showed evidence of bullet holes, all of the glass in the windows had been removed. Inside, the walls had been stripped of everything that might have been useful. There was no furniture left in it. No light fixtures. No wire. No papers. Nothing.

Tyme went out the back door toward the two trucks. One of them was an American Dodge and the other a Soviet Zil. They looked almost the same, as if the builders of one had copied the other.

Neither had tires. Slowly Tyme opened the hood of the Dodge, being careful when he lifted it. Inside, he found almost nothing. Every piece that could be easily removed from the engine was gone. There was no battery, no wires, no spark plugs and no hoses.

He walked around the outside of the vehicle, opened one door of the cab and looked in. The seats had been taken out. The steering wheel, the gauges, even the door for the glove compartment, had been removed. The truck bed had been burned, but the gas tank had not exploded. He was looking at the skeleton of the truck.

The Zil was in a little better shape. It hadn't caught fire. The only interesting thing in it was a plaque, inscribed in Russian, that probably detailed the operating instructions. For a moment Tyme thought about trying to pry it loose and then decided against it. It was that kind of trophy hunting that got people killed.

Across the camp Fetterman was having no better luck. He had found the officers' quarters in a small building near the long barracks. It had once been divided into individual rooms, but the partitioning walls were gone now, and only the stud marks remained on the floor. He searched carefully, knowing that things sometimes slipped from sight, and those in a hurry to leave an area sometimes overlooked those things in their haste.

All he found was a color photograph of an undressed blonde. Fetterman recognized the picture. He had seen it a couple of months earlier in a *Playboy* magazine. The magazine itself was over a year old so that alone didn't provide any clues about how recently the VC had been in the camp.

Back outside Fetterman worked his way to the long barracks. The first one contained nothing but stripped walls and empty space. The floor was worn in the center, and there were squares of fresher-looking wood where the cots or lockers had stood. The windows were small and let in only a little light. With no breeze it was hot and humid inside.

Fetterman walked slowly through the building, spotting nothing of value. Debris from outside, mostly palm leaves and dirt, littered the floor. In one corner he found an empty U.S. Army C-ration can. That and the picture of the naked blonde indicated the VC from the camp had raided an American outpost at some point.

As Fetterman left the building, he realized they would find nothing they could use in the camp. The VC were gone and had taken everything with them. To continue to search the camp would just waste time, time that could be used heading to the new base that Kepler had spotted on the aerial recon photos.

Tyme had just finished searching his sector of the camp when Fetterman approached. Without exchanging a word they worked their way back through the base to the wire, and then each exited, using the hole that Fetterman had cut.

AT CAMP A-555 Gerber was talking to his counterpart, Captain Minh, in the commo bunker. Gerber had briefed the Vietnamese officer about the mission because, technically, Minh was the camp commander. Besides, Gerber trusted him as much as he trusted any of the men on his team. Sergeant Bocker stood to one side, keeping a watch on both the doorway and the radio.

"You may have to take the company out tomorrow without me," warned Gerber. "I'm not sure exactly what Crinshaw has in mind. I don't know why he has picked now to make his visit, but he's going to make the patrol difficult. Make it hard to get a company out of here without having to answer a lot of awkward questions."

"I'm not sure that I can help you, old boy," responded Minh in his clipped British accent. "Genral Vo is causing as much trouble. It's almost as if someone has spilled the beans."

Gerber moved to the battle map that decorated one wall of the bunker. It showed the location of the camp, and a couple of sites that Intel suspected of being VC strongholds. Turning from it, Gerber said, "I could put Bromhead in operational control. He's quick enough to handle anything. I just don't want him leading the patrol that could blow up into an international incident."

"If either of us go out, we're liable to alert one of these rear-area louts," said Minh.

"Still, it's not fair to send Bromhead. He'd go happily and do a good job, but damn, he's so young."

"So what do you plan?"

"If I'm still having trouble with Crinshaw tomorrow, I'm going to send the company out under the control of either Sergeant Bocker or Sergeant Kepler. Then, first chance I get, I'll go out with another patrol and link up with them."

"What do you want me to do, old boy?"

"I want you to find out what the hell is going on. Why do we suddenly have brass running all over the place? Then find out where the hell the leak is, if there is a leak, so that we can eliminate it."

"You think Vo or Crinshaw know what's going on?"

"I don't think Vo knows much. He's here to recover the bodies of the dead rangers. I doubt that Crinshaw knows exactly what's happening. But he suspects something. That's what has me worried."

A little later Gerber found Robin Morrow sitting alone in one corner of the team house. She had spread her notebooks and reference materials over one table and had a steaming cup of coffee sitting in the middle of the litter. She seemed to be concentrating on the coffee and ignoring everything else.

After pouring himself a cup that contained most of the grounds, Gerber walked to the table and sat down opposite the reporter. "I didn't get a chance to tell you how much I enjoyed your first meeting with General Crinshaw," he said.

Morrow looked up and smiled. "I'm afraid I don't understand."

"You did a number on him. Tricked him into letting you come out here. And you had the documentation to make it stick. Anything you need, you let me know and I'll see what I can do. You deserve it."

Bromhead entered the team house and came over. "Miss Morrow," he said, "I hope you found your accommodations to be satisfactory."

"Why so formal, Lieutenant?" she asked, smiling. "The accommodations, as you call them, suck. It's hot and muggy. The floor is dirty, the roof leaks and there are insects running all over the place."

"And we've given you the best we have," responded Gerber, getting up. "We even moved the rats into the latrine so you'd have more room. If you two will excuse me, I've got a couple of things I've got to do."

When Gerber was gone, Bromhead said, "Are you enjoying yourself out here?"

Morrow drained her coffee and said, "Of course I'm not enjoying myself. I'm out here to do a job."

Bromhead suddenly felt like a teenage boy in the presence of an older woman. Anything he said was going to be wrong or misunderstood. He had known when he asked his question that no one really enjoyed being hot and miserable ten thousand miles from home, but some people enjoyed their work and that compensated for the misery. He wondered what he could say to Morrow because he wanted a chance to talk to her.

"Of course," she said, softening, "I do enjoy my work."

Trying to cover his embarrassment, Bromhead reached for her cup and asked, "Would you like some more coffee?"

"What I would really like," responded Morrow, "is an ice-cold beer. Or a Coke. Anything cold."

Bromhead put the cup down and headed for an old refrigerator. "I'm afraid there might not be much of anything in here, and if there is, it might not be too cold."

"That's okay, Lieutenant. I'll consider anything under a hundred to be cold."

"Call me Johnny. Everyone does." And as he said it, he realized how young it made him sound. Men were called John or Jack. Boys were called Johnny. But it was too late to take it back.

"Okay, Johnny. You can call me Robin. Now what's a nice guy like you doing in a hole like this?"

"Well, it's a long story," he said as he pulled a couple of beers out of the icebox. "You're in luck, Robin. We've got a couple of Millers." He opened them using his P-38 and handed one to Morrow.

"Thanks." She smiled at him, staring into his eyes for a moment longer than necessary. "Now, I have all day. Why don't you tell me how you ended up here."

FETTERMAN HADN'T been too happy about the first camp being deserted. It meant he was going to have to move deeper into Cambodia. It meant he was farther from help if he needed it. It meant there could be more enemy soldiers between him and the border. But there was nothing that could be done. If he were going to complete the mission, he would have to accept the additional risks and move closer to Svay Rieng, where Kepler's information put the new camp.

The patrol spent the rest of the day chopping their way through jungle so thick with undergrowth that in places they were only making fifty meters an hour. They had to rotate point men every few minutes because the burden of cutting through the vines and bushes in the heat of the afternoon quickly sapped a man's energy. The men gulped their water at each rest break, downing it hastily. Fetterman was concerned about heatstroke, and he made sure that everyone took salt tablets.

An hour before dusk the point man stopped moving and Fetterman crawled forward through the clinging vines that grabbed at his uniform until he reached Krung kneeling near the split trunk of a palm. Before Krung said anything, Fetterman heard noise filtering through the trees. He listened, concentrating, and heard voices speaking Vietnamese and the rattling of metal equipment.

He looked back over his shoulder and waved the others to cover. Then, with Krung flanking him on one side and Tyme on the other, he crept slowly forward, carefully pushing the branches of the thorny bushes aside until they were closer to the source of the noise. Through gaps in the foliage, Fetterman could see soldiers moving. He caught glimpses of NVA uniforms and VC black pajamas. And he saw a couple of AK-47s slung on the shoulders of the soldiers. He looked right and left and then signaled for Krung and Tyme to back up so they could return to where the others waited.

With the Tai in a loose circle around Fetterman, Krung and Tyme for security, they held a hasty whispered conference. Fetterman started it, saying, "I think we're up against the Ho Chi Minh Trail. We're going to have to cross it."

"I don't like having a major enemy supply line behind us," commented Tyme.

"I don't, either, Boom-Boom, but to complete the mission there's no choice. The enemy camp is on the other side of it."

"So how do we get across the Trail without the VC knowing we're here?"

"That, my boy, is the problem. We'll have to cross in the dark, probably extremely early in the morning. Right now I suggest we take the opportunity to eat and get some sleep. I think we're going to have to put in some long hours during the next few days."

At 3:00 A.M., when there was little noise along the Trail, no sound from the jungle and everything was at a low ebb, Fetterman motioned Tyme, Krung and the Tai forward. They crawled carefully, quietly, edging their way toward the Ho Chi Minh Trail.

When they finally reached it, Fetterman was surprised. Although he'd heard about the Ho Chi Minh Trail since he'd arrived in Vietnam, he had thought it was something like a normal jungle trail. Maybe a little wider than most, better defined than most, but a trail nonetheless.

But what he was looking at was anything but a trail. From the edge of the jungle, where he now crouched, to the other side was nearly twenty meters. Looking up, he could see the jungle had been carved out under the triple canopy. The vegetation of the jungle came right to the edge of the Trail, but there it was cut back, as if the mowing machines used by the highway departments in the States had been used to retard the growth. There didn't seem to be a break in the cover, and everything on the ground must have been invisible from the air.

The surface of the Trail looked almost like concrete. He reached out and touched it and realized that it was compressed earth and pea gravel. And it was smooth. There were no potholes or roots sticking up through it. It was as well maintained and functional as some of the new interstate highways being built back in the World.

He sent Tyme to scout along the Trail to the north and Krung to the south. Then he inched forward so that he could survey more of the Trail. The section he could see was straight for a hundred meters in either direction. The only thing missing were the cars and the white lines down the center. This wasn't a trail. It was a goddamn highway.

Both Tyme and Krung returned quickly and reported that they had seen and heard nothing. That done, he had Krung and one of the Tai set up the light machine gun so that it could cover them as they ran across the Trail. Fetterman fell back and to the right to protect the machine gun's flank. When he was set, he signaled Tyme with a single short whistle.

Tyme stepped cautiously onto the Ho Chi Minh Trail. He heard the pea gravel crunch under his jungle boot. It sounded incredibly loud in the quiet of the night. He sprinted across the Trail, stopping short because he didn't want to dive into the jungle on the other side. He pushed the foliage out of the way, stepped over a rotting log and crouched, turning so he could watch as the Tai followed.

When they were in position, their light machine gun covering the Trail as Krung's had on the other side, Tyme whistled once, signaling Fetterman. Together with Krung and the remaining Tai, Fetterman crossed and then had them move into the jungle.

Fetterman kept them moving until it was nearly dawn. Then he began searching for a place to hole up. Again he tried to find a place that wasn't likely. He dismissed a cave that had a good source of water: if push came to shove, he didn't want to be trapped inside. He did, however, have each of the men fill their empty canteens from the cold, clear stream and add halazone tablets to purify the water.

A few minutes later he found a more suitable site. It lacked a source of water, but made up for it with a good view of the surrounding territory. Fetterman spread the men out so that they could get some rest and eat another cold meal. They rotated the security so that everyone had a chance for some uninterrupted sleep.

Fetterman, again tired of the cold meals that had no taste, opened the single flat tin of peanut butter and crackers that he had packed. The peanut butter was of the poorest quality. There was a layer of amber-colored oil on top of the peanut butter that was so hard he couldn't stir it up. If they hadn't been in Cambodia, he would have tried to heat it. Instead, he just ate the crackers and buried the tin.

They passed the heat of the afternoon lying quietly in the shade of the bushes and palms of the jungle. Even though they weren't exerting themselves, they were uncomfortable, sweating heavily. Late in the day clouds blew in, blotting out the sun. The clouds brought a breeze, making things a little more bearable.

When it had been dark for over an hour, they moved out again, walking slowly, listening to the sounds of the jungle around them. The normal sounds of the jungle at night. Animals scrambling through the underbrush or up the trees to avoid predators. Insects announcing the temperature with chirps or their presence with buzzing.

Near midnight a new sound penetrated the jungle. At first it was no more than a quiet hum that sounded like a persistent insect, but as they moved toward it, it became louder and steadier until it changed to the rhythm of machinery. Then, through the thick jungle trees, Fetterman saw a point of light. An electrical beacon that led him and his patrol straight to the enemy compound. Fetterman hoped they weren't going in like moths, blinded by the light and careless of the dark. Men died that way.

They circled the base slowly, staying a klick or more away from it, looking for the best place to set up and observe the activity inside camp. By five they had found exactly what they wanted, a place on a rise that was shielded by thick undergrowth for their protection, but gave Fetterman and Tyme an unobstructed view. Krung and the Tai were now scattered around the jungle, protecting the position taken by Fetterman and Tyme.

As the sun broke through the low-hanging clouds, Fetterman and Tyme saw a huge, almost circular compound that boasted six long barracks at the northern edge. Ten or twelve smaller buildings, possibly officers' quarters, were near them. Nearby were the motor pool, a generator shed and the mess hall. What Fetterman took to be the headquarters stood in the center.

He glanced at Tyme as the younger man shrugged off his knapsack and began unwrapping the automatic ranging sniperscope, which he had almost lovingly packed. Tyme set it carefully on top of his M-14 and tightened the mounting screws. When he finished, he sighted on a number of objects, just to get the feel of the weapon again.

Then he checked the magazine he and Fetterman had prepared. They had loaded the rounds themselves using 43.2 grains of 4064 powder. That was a little hotter than desirable, but was needed because of the range from which they were operating. They had also used a 168-grain boattail hollow-point slug. The magazine contained twelve of the special bullets.

Tyme would have preferred to take a practice shot or two, just to be on the safe side, but he would have one chance, possibly two if he could get the second shot off fast enough, and that would be it. He would have to trust his calculations made at the camp a week earlier and hope that nothing had jarred the scope sufficiently to throw off the precision of its rangings.

He looked back at Fetterman and said, "It's up to our Chinese guy now."

6

Fetterman lay in the short grass of the rise, hidden among the bushes and trees, his binoculars to his eyes as he scanned the enemy base a klick away.

Tyme, who had been observing the camp through the ART scope, whispered to Fetterman, "This is no good. The range is too great in this light. We're going to have to get closer."

"Sun'll burn off the haze quickly," responded Fetterman.

Tyme shook his head. "We need to get closer."

Fetterman crawled backward and found Krung, who was watching the downslope side of the rise. He formed Krung and the Tai into a rear guard and told Krung they were to move closer to the enemy camp. Krung's job was to make sure the jungle directly behind them was clear of VC.

That done, Fetterman eased forward again to find Tyme, and the two of them began to slowly work their way through the thick jungle undergrowth, careful not to disturb the birds and monkeys overhead in the trees.

It took them nearly three hours to move to within seven hundred meters of the camp before halting again. Fetterman used his binoculars to watch the activities slightly below them. From one of the small hootches on the north side of the camp near the long barracks, two men exited. One of them wore the bright-green uniform of an NVA officer, and the other wore the khaki of a Chinese officer.

As the two men walked slowly toward the two-story headquarters, Fetterman scanned the camp looking for other Chinese. He turned his attention back to the NVA and Chinese, who had stopped while the NVA officer picked up something that had been lying on the ground. He examined it momentarily and then tossed it with an underhand motion toward the wire.

Three men and a woman, all wearing the deep green of NVA enlisted personnel, left one of the square buildings as the two men passed it. There was a flurry of saluting as the two groups passed one another.

"That our man?" asked Tyme, who had been tracking the two men through his scope.

"I'm not sure," said Fetterman. "I only saw him the one time, and that was from the rear as he was running for Cambodia. Build seems to be right."

Tyme pointed to the right and said, "There's a slight depression over there. Be good cover for us."

Fetterman nodded his agreement, and the two men crawled to the new position. Tyme pulled a rotting log around slightly so that it would provide support for his weapon. With his combat knife he dug out some of the wood to give his rifle a firm base. He checked the markings on the scope and the rifle a final time to make sure they were still properly aligned and then settled down to wait.

For several hours they watched the enemy camp. The only Chinese officer they saw had left the headquarters building and walked toward a square structure that sat in a cluster of radio antennae. Fetterman studied the man as well as he could, convincing himself this was the Chinese officer they had come after. From the rear he looked the same. Broad, square shoulders and a long torso.

An hour later the man left the radio shack and began to walk slowly across the compound toward the barracks. There was no one with him.

The conditions were almost perfect. It was late in the afternoon, and the target was alone. Tyme asked, "Do we take him?"

Fetterman was staring through his binoculars, watching the man walk, trying to see something that he recognized from the brief glimpse he had had of the Chinese on the morning after they'd found the remains of the Vietnamese patrol. There was so much that he thought he recognized, but it was so little to go on.

"Yeah. Take him," said Fetterman finally.

Tyme slipped the safety on his weapon and worked the bolt, ejecting a good round. He wanted to make sure he had a round chambered properly. He set the cross hairs on the back of the Chinese officer, tracking him for a moment, trying to compute the speed the man was walking. He then shifted the weapon, leading the Chinese by nearly four feet because of the extreme range. He took a deep breath, let it out, took another and let it half out. He squeezed the trigger slowly, applying pressure until the weapon almost fired itself.

The crash of the shots was apparently unheard by anyone. For what seemed like several seconds the Chinese officer walked on toward his hootch. Tyme had already fired a second round and was now watching the scene below him although he knew he should be up and running.

The Chinese officer took the first shot in the shoulder. He staggered under the impact, but didn't fall. Stunned by the sudden pain, he reached back, as if trying to brush away an annoying insect.

Having seen the first round hit, Tyme should have gotten to his feet, but he stayed, mesmerized by what he saw. The second bullet hit the officer in the middle of his back. The 168-grain slug, slowed by the bone and tissue it hit, still had the power to pierce the man's chest and exit through one of his ribs. Blood and bone spattered the ground in front of him. With the muscle control suddenly gone from his legs, the Chinese crumpled to the ground, blood spreading under his shirt.

As soon as he saw the first round hit, Fetterman stored his binoculars and got to his knees. He waited for a moment, watching Tyme, and then said, ''Let's get the fuck out of here.''

They worked their way back up the hill toward the Tai, who were watching the VC base for signs of pursuit.

As soon as the patrol had put the hill between themselves and the camp, Fetterman grabbed the handset of the PRC-10 and keyed it long enough to announce, ''We have sighted Crinshaw's body.''

''Why aren't the VC responding? They should be after us by now,'' Tyme asked.

''They haven't figured it out yet,'' said Fetterman, pointing to the east so that Krung would take the point.

As they began their escape through the jungle, there was a wavering scream of a siren from the camp. Fetterman said, ''Now they've figured it out!''

FOUR KLICKS FROM the Cambodian border, Gerber and one hundred and five men from the Tai strike company were moving north to south on a preplanned course. They had been out for just over twenty-four hours, and during that time they had seen two NVA soldiers who had escaped into the jungle and one VC who hadn't. They had buried the body in a shallow grave, keeping the weapon as proof of the KIA for Crinshaw.

The first night they had set up a perimeter without any real trouble. Around midnight two mortar rounds had landed in the center of the laager, doing no damage and causing no casualties.

Gerber immediately ordered out a counter-mortar patrol, but they found nothing in their two-hour search. There were no more incoming rounds, and the men, on a half alert, passed the night quietly.

The next day they were awake early and had a fairly substantial field breakfast. Gerber allowed the men to have fires to heat their rations. The Tai boiled water for their rice. The Special Forces NCOs cooked the scrambled eggs and ham from C-ration boxes. Sam Anderson, the newest member of the team, had a perverse taste for the ham and lima beans, which no one else liked. All the Americans shared the canned bread and jam, and topped off the breakfast with canned pears.

As the sun climbed higher, heating the jungle, they began their patrol. The line of march was generally to the south, but angling toward the border. Twice American aircraft flew overhead, and one made a close pass, as if to identify the men in the column as friend or foe.

It was late afternoon when Gerber reached the first of the rendezvous points. He spread two platoons of the strike company along a trail through the trees in an L-shaped ambush. The third platoon was scattered behind it as perimeter security that could be quickly organized into a relief force. Then all he could do was wait for Fetterman and his patrol.

FOR MORE THAN TWO HOURS Fetterman and his men had been rushing through the jungle. They hadn't heard any VC or NVA behind them, but they would certainly be there. Now they were approaching the Ho Chi Minh Trail, and if they couldn't cross it quickly, the enemy would have a chance to close the gap between them.

Fetterman came up to Krung, who was lying on the ground at the edge of the trees looking out across the expanse of compressed earth and pea gravel. Crouching, Fetterman could see they were in trouble. The traffic was heavy for so late in the day.

Most of it was bicycles, but no one was riding them. They were all being pushed. The handlebars had a long pole tied to them so that the VC walking beside the bike could steer. Another pole stuck up where the seat should have been so the porter would have a way to balance the load. The frame supported huge sacks of supplies or equipment. Some of it was rice and some was mortar rounds; some of it couldn't be easily identified.

Surprisingly, there were two trucks. One of them was barely keeping up with the foot traffic. The other was weaving in and out of the bicycles.

There were also soldiers, both male and female, moving along the Trail. Each carried a personal weapon. Most of them had SKSs, but some carried the AK-47 assault rifle.

Fetterman eased forward so that he could look farther to the north. He couldn't see a break in the formation, and he cursed quietly to himself. There wasn't going to be an easy, quick way to cross, and he didn't like the idea of his patrol being trapped between the Trail and their pursuers.

Fetterman crawled away from Krung to where Tyme waited. He put his lips close to Tyme's ear and said, "We'll have to move to the south, paralleling the Trail, and hope that the traffic breaks soon."

"Is that likely?"

"Hell, I don't know. But right now it's all we have, and we don't have time to debate it."

Tyme nodded and turned so that he could alert the others. Once again Krung was sent out as the point. They moved quickly and quietly. Behind them there was no sign of their pursuit.

As the daylight faded, the traffic began to thin. Some of the men and women halted in the rest areas scattered along the Trail. Others dropped off to sit on the side, resting and eating their evening meal. Fetterman and his patrol kept edging along, looking for a place where they could cross without alerting Charlie. He knew the enemy from the camp had to be close, and now there was more enemy in front of him. Running to the south was gaining him almost nothing.

Fetterman scattered his men through the jungle, three of the Tai watching their rear in case the VC managed to catch up, while he, Tyme and Krung spread out to watch the Trail. For ten minutes no one new appeared. All he could see was three NVA soldiers who had stopped by the side to eat supper. If it hadn't been for them, crossing would have been almost simple.

Fetterman decided he couldn't wait any longer. He crawled to where Tyme was hiding under a large bush, watching a small green snake trying to sneak up on a rodent that was already dead.

Fetterman pointed at the ground in front of him, telling Tyme to stay still, then moved off to bring Krung over. When he had them together, he said, ''We're going to have to take out those three guys.''

Krung grinned at the American master sergeant.

''We're fortunate,'' said Fetterman, ''that all of them have taken up positions on our side of the Trail. We'll take ten minutes to get ready, then we'll hit the targets at the same time, using our knives. That done, we'll cross immediately, taking our rear guard with us. We'll do it in one mass gaggle. Questions?''

''Shouldn't we cross one at a time as the manual says?'' asked Tyme.

''Shit, Justin. Forget the fucking manual. It's more important to get us across,'' said Fetterman. ''Krung, you take the guy farthest from us. Tyme, you take the one closest, and I'll take the other. When you've killed your man, fall back to here. Anything else?'' When no one said anything, Fetterman added, ''Then we go ten minutes from right . . . now.''

Tyme was in position in less than seven. He had worked his way silently through the jungle behind his target, taking each step carefully, rolling his foot from heel to toe slowly so that he didn't snap a twig or rustle the decaying vegetation. He took each breath slowly, rhythmically, forcing himself to be calm. As he lowered himself to the jungle floor and crept closer to his target, he kept his mind on his task. All of his senses were working overtime watching the jungle so that he didn't disturb the animals that might be near.

When he was less than a yard away, he stopped and rocked back so that he was on the balls of his feet, ready to spring. He slowly pulled his Randall combat knife from its sheath, gently wiping the blade on the sleeve of his sweat-soaked jungle fatigues as he waited, his eyes shifting back and forth from his watch to his target.

When the second hand reached the twelve, Tyme leaned forward, reaching for the enemy soldier, who was hunched over his last meal. He stole a glance right and left, but saw neither Krung nor Fetterman.

Without waiting for any kind of sign, Tyme sprang ahead, grabbed the enemy's chin, lifted and sliced neatly through the throat. He heard the whisper of razor-sharp steel on the tender flesh of the neck and felt the warm blood gush over his hand.

As he pulled the head back, the soldier's helmet fell off, revealing long, jet-black hair. Tyme looked into the soldier's eyes with growing horror. He had just slit the throat of a young woman. His knife paused in midair before he delivered the thrust up under the breastbone so that he could pierce the woman's heart, finishing the job.

Her dark-brown eyes held his for just an instant, then clouded over. She kicked her legs out spasmodically, drumming her heels on the packed earth of the Ho Chi Minh Trail. She died a second later, Tyme's knife still hovering over her chest.

Tyme moved slowly, as if he had to think out each step before he took it. He dragged the body into the bush, picked up her pith helmet and tossed it in after her and then stood staring at the blood that stained the front of her uniform. He kept his eyes away from the gaping wound in her throat.

Fetterman touched his shoulder and asked, ''You okay?''

''It was a woman,'' Tyme said, shaking his head.

Fetterman thought for a moment before replying. Tyme was obviously upset, but there was no opportunity to worry about it now. ''So what?'' said Fetterman, shrugging his shoulders. ''She was an enemy soldier.''

Before either man could say anything more, Krung ran up and said, ''VC!''

Fetterman turned and saw a single enemy soldier approaching from the north. The VC saw them and grabbed for the stock of his weapon, trying to swing it around so that he could fire. Fetterman reacted quickly: he dropped to one knee, raised his M-1 carbine and squeezed off a single shot before the VC could fire. The round hit the enemy in the face, exploding out the back of his head, and he collapsed to the Trail.

''That tears it,'' said Fetterman, ''we have got to move now!''

7

NEAR THE CAMBODIAN
BORDER, SOUTH OF THE
PARROT'S BEAK

It was almost dusk when Gerber reached the last of the rendezvous points. He deployed the strikers in three platoons, each watching a section of the border. Gerber was in command of the center section so that he could take charge of either the right or left flank if he had to. Kepler headed up the unit closest to Cambodia. It was spread on-line just inside the trees and facing a series of rice fields that spread out into Cambodia, giving him a clear view for three or four klicks. Behind him, deeper in the trees, Sam Anderson commanded the third platoon. He guarded the left flank and the rear. The remainder of the force formed a circle inside the tree line that could be used as a reserve or blocking force, whatever the situation demanded.

All they had to do was wait until morning, hoping that Fetterman and his tiny group made it to them by then. If not, Gerber would begin to move back along his original line of march, holding at each of the previous rendezvous points. He would keep circling until Fetterman arrived, or until it became obvious that he wasn't going to make it.

When the evening meal had been eaten and the remains of the food and cans had been buried under three feet of jungle dirt and rotted vegetation, Gerber moved among the men quietly, advising them of their jobs for the night. He would leave one man in three awake until midnight, then two men in three. And they would wait.

FETTERMAN AND HIS PATROL dashed across the Ho Chi Minh Trail and nearly leaped into the jungle. There was a shout behind them and a burst of fire from an automatic weapon. But they plunged onward, heading east, trying to run away from the Trail and the men who were now chasing them.

Krung sprinted ahead, taking the point without being told, but in the fading light of the setting sun he had to slow down. The spreading blackness was beginning to mask the pitfalls.

There was more shouting in Vietnamese and more firing. Fetterman dived for cover, nearly tripping over one of the Tai. Tyme was crouched beside a large palm, his scoped M-14 pointing back the way they had come.

"On your feet," Fetterman ordered. "Krung, get back on the point. Move it! We stay here, we die!"

As they got up and began to run again, firing erupted all around them, but it seemed poorly directed. None of the rounds was hitting anything near them, and Fetterman figured the VC were trying a recon by fire to see if they could induce Fetterman and his patrol to shoot back.

Instead of shooting they ran. They ran as fast as the jungle would let them. One of the Tai stumbled and cried out, falling to his face. Fetterman grabbed him under the arm, jerking the man to his feet.

"You hurt?" he asked. When the man failed to respond, he ordered, "Move it. Run!"

But Fetterman knew that headlong flight wasn't the best way for a military unit to retreat. It might put distance between the enemy and the patrol, but it gained nothing in the long run. He knew they had to do something to slow the enemy's pursuit, but at the moment there wasn't much he could do. His patrol was getting scattered throughout the jungle, the gaps among the men widening as they fled the VC.

He caught up to Krung on the bank of a shallow stream. Tyme was leaning against the trunk of a palm, breathing rapidly and watching the trail behind them.

"What now?" he said, gasping.

"Ambush," said Fetterman. "We cross the stream and ambush them."

With that he stepped into the center of the stream and leaped up on the other bank. He disappeared into the jungle as the men of the patrol followed him. He pointed out positions to each soldier, telling him to fire only when he had a good target and warning that no one was to shoot until Sergeant Tyme did. He set them in two lines, one behind the other. The first, with Tyme in the middle, was to surprise the enemy with a fusillade and then fall back, allowing the VC to cross the stream. Then the second would open fire, causing more casualties and therefore making the VC more cautious in their pursuit.

The men waited tensely, oblivious to the staggering humidity and the clouds of mosquitoes that descended on them when they stopped moving. For a moment everything around them was quiet, and then they heard a faint sound coming from the jungle in front of them, the noise of a branch sweeping across the canvas of a VC backpack.

Fetterman wanted to whisper to the men to be patient, to wait for the enemy. But he didn't dare move. All he could do was sit tight, letting the sweat drip from under his helmet and run down his face, making his skin itch.

The VC appeared suddenly, rising out of the trees on the other side of the stream. Tyme tossed the grenade he had been clutching, and when it exploded, the Tai with him opened fire. Two of the enemy fell, one into the stream, but the others did not retreat. They attacked, leaping the creek to land among Tyme and his men.

Tyme got to his knees as one of the VC jumped up in front of him. The American swung the butt of his rifle upward in a low arc so that it hit the man in the crotch. There was a shriek like tires on concrete as the man collapsed. Tyme shot him in the face and turned in time to see another enemy soldier. He thrust with his rifle, trying a vertical butt stroke, but the VC countered, his AK connecting with the ART scope mounted on Tyme's rifle, shattering it.

Tyme ducked, kicking out with his foot and hitting the enemy in the knee, snapping it. As the man fell, Tyme fired twice.

Then the shooting all around him tapered, and over the noise he heard Fetterman shouting in English and French for them to fall back. Tyme glanced to the right and saw one of the Tai struggling with a VC. In a moment he was on them and hit the enemy in the back of the head with his rifle butt. As the Vietcong dropped, the Tai shot him. Then, backing up, firing into the trees near the stream, Tyme and the Tai retreated.

They passed Fetterman and Krung, who waited until their men were clear and then opened fire. Fetterman didn't have a target, and he just pumped out rounds to slow the enemy advance. He emptied a magazine, dropped it from the weapon and jammed a new one home, firing it single shot, almost as fast as he could pull the trigger.

Finally he turned to run, Krung right beside him. It was almost completely dark, and Fetterman could barely make out the shapes of Tyme and his men in front of him. He tried to close the distance, gaining a little.

They headed east, away from the Ho Chi Minh Trail and the enemy soldiers. They ran until their hearts pounded and their lungs ached. They ran until each step was a test of will. They would run a hundred steps and walk fifty and run a hundred more. They ran until they were sure they were out of Cambodia, until they could hear nothing but the sounds of their own breathing and the pounding of their own hearts in their chests.

Then they stopped. Stopped to rest because they could not go farther. And even then Fetterman put out security. Two men in front of the patrol to look for the enemy and two behind it in case the VC were closer than he suspected. Then Fetterman dropped to the ground and pulled his canteen, drinking deeply and spitting, trying to get the cotton out of his mouth. Finally he took a measured swallow and felt it spread in his stomach. He took another and waited, his breathing slowing.

Fetterman then took out his map, covered himself with the poncho liner, making sure the edges touched the ground all around, and pulled his flashlight. He studied the map for a few minutes, looking for landmarks he might have passed. Once he switched off the light, stood and studied the black landscape around him. He looked at the stream and the swamps on the far side of it. Behind him was the stretch of jungle they had just traveled through. He tried to think back, starting with the location of the second VC camp, their direction of travel, the point where they reached the Ho Chi Minh Trail and the stream where they had ambushed the VC.

He thought he knew where they were and believed he could find Gerber and the patrols, if Gerber had followed the schedule established in the camp. Just then he heard one of the men run up.

"VC. Beaucoup VC."

"Where?"

The man turned and pointed in the direction they had come from. "There. Close."

Fetterman's first instinct was to run again, just as they had earlier. Then he thought about it. An ambush was no good because it would allow the enemy to catch up. Gerber and his men should be only four or five klicks away to the north. He could try to lure the VC into an ambush there. But he had to be careful because he couldn't just run up to Gerber's patrol in the dark. He had to let the VC do that.

He rounded up his men and told Tyme to take the point. He told him to run north about three klicks and stop. Fetterman would have to identify their location more precisely then.

For forty minutes they ran, first through the jungle, then along paddy dikes. They crossed open fields, running even faster to get out of the clearings before the VC saw them. They ran by a farmer's hootch with a single lantern light in the window. As they entered the trees again, they heard a burst of fire from an automatic weapon. Fetterman figured it was the VC shooting at the light, and that put them about three minutes back.

Suddenly Tyme stopped. Fetterman, who had been the rear guard, slid to a halt, but didn't need to ask what the problem was. They were on the edge of a gigantic open area where the jungle gave way to paddies and swamp. A half klick away was another tree line, and Fetterman was sure that Gerber and the strikers were there.

Silently Fetterman moved his men along, keeping the cover of the trees near the edge of the rice fields. They came to a bend in the tree line so that they could look over open fields, back at the jungle where they had been. Fetterman stopped his men, using the available cover of bushes, palms and the eighteen-inch paddy dikes. He told each of the men to wait for him to fire first and then to crank out the rounds as fast as they could.

Once they were in position, Fetterman took the tiny earpiece from the PRC-10 he had been carrying and keyed the mike. "Zulu Six. Zulu Six. This is Zulu Rover, over."

A second later a voice boomed back, "Rover, this is Six. Go."

Fetterman turned down the volume and reported, "Six, be advised that we are in the vicinity."

"Acknowledged."

Then there was nothing to do but wait. Fetterman switched magazines in his M-1 carbine, substituting one that contained tracers. He wanted Gerber's men to see the source of his firing, and the ruby tracers would identify him and his people. The VC used white and green tracers.

Minutes slipped by and nothing happened. Fetterman had just begun to wonder if he'd lost the enemy with his rapid trip through the jungle when, outlined in the paddies in front of him, he saw something moving. A dark-gray shape was silhouetted against the lighter gray of the sky and the horizon. The lone shape was soon joined by a second and a third, until there were fifteen or twenty men in the open, all moving slowly forward.

Fetterman muttered, "Wait for it. Wait for it. Let them get away from the protection of the trees."

As the men of the enemy patrol pulled away from the trees, Fetterman set his chin on the butt of his rifle so that he was looking over the sights on the barrel in the best traditions of U.S. Army night-fire training. It allowed him to aim the weapon without restricting his vision in the sights.

When he had the M-1 lined up, he pulled the trigger and watched the tracer stream toward the enemy. The others with him opened fire on cue, until the night was filled with the rattle of small arms, the flashes of the muzzles and the bouncing tracers as they struck the ground.

Two of the VC went down quickly, and the others dived for cover behind the paddy dikes. One or two fired back, their rounds wide.

But that was enough to give away their position to Gerber's men, and they began raking the paddies with devastating fire. There was the pop of an M-79 grenade launcher, followed by an explosion in the paddy.

Slowly the shooting tapered off. Then, suddenly, five of the VC stood up and threw Chicom grenades. As they detonated, all the VC were up and running, trying to gain the safety of the jungle behind them.

Fetterman had been waiting for that. He opened fire again, pulling the trigger as fast as he could. The men with him joined in, shooting at the fleeing shapes, watching them fall. The jungle where Gerber's men hid seemed to erupt, the muzzle flashes sparkling in the dark. The red tracers danced across the paddies, some of them bouncing through the night.

At that moment a parachute exploded into brilliance, lighting the ground in a wavering yellowish glow that pinned the VC against the trees. With targets plainly visible, the machine gunners opened fire with their M-60s.

And then the targets were gone. Fading into the jungle or falling into the paddies. The firing ceased as the flare burned itself out. A second one went off, but it caught no one in the open. After that there were only a few random shots as someone fired at the shadows.

There was a crash of thunder overhead that sounded like someone had channeled it into a single, thin line. It rattled teeth before it blossomed into fire in the paddies in front of them, momentarily lighting the ground with mushrooming flame. A second shell exploded closer to the trees, and the third dropped in the jungle at the edge of the clearing.

Six quick explosions followed, flashing briefly as the rounds detonated, throwing shrapnel through the air like a thousand darts that could rip a man apart. There was a brief calm as another six rained in as the American artillerymen in one of the fire-support bases got the rhythm, and then silence.

When the firing stopped, Tyme crawled to Fetterman and asked, "What now?"

"We keep our eyes open and wait for morning. Then we join the captain."

At dawn Fetterman used the radio to announce that he was coming in and for the men to hold fire. He was told to throw smoke and then to come ahead. Gerber was standing with a small group of strikers when Fetterman appeared out of the trees and walked across a short section of the paddies.

Fetterman saw the captain, broke out of the group and said, "We've succeeded with Crinshaw's body. The man is down."

"Fine," responded Gerber. He wanted to say more, but it wasn't the time nor the place to get into a long conversation. It was possible that the VC would have left a sniper.

He turned to Anderson and said, "Cat, I'd like a patrol to sweep across the paddies and see what we might have hit last night."

"Excuse me, Captain," said Fetterman, "but I'd like to take that patrol."

"Any particular reason?"

"Yes, sir. Those guys chased my butt all the way from the Ho Chi Minh Trail, and I would like to get a look at them."

"Thought your guys would like a rest," said Gerber.

"I'll take part of the platoon here. And Boom-Boom."

"Take three squads. Hurry it up because we'll want to get out of here and head back to the camp."

"Yes, sir." Fetterman turned, saw two of the squad leaders and said to them, "Get your men up and on-line to sweep through the paddies." He spotted a third and gave him the same instructions so that he had thirty-six men standing side by side just inside the tree line. Fetterman took his position in the center and sent Tyme out to anchor the left side of the line. On his order they all stepped into the open, then spread out until there were five or six feet between each of them as they moved forward.

They stayed off the paddy dikes and walked through the paddies instead. Most were dry, having been drained after the farmers had harvested the crop.

As they approached the area the VC had defended the night before, they saw the first body. It was lying facedown, the helmet touching the dirt in front and hiding the head. There were no obvious signs of injury except for the ragged rust stain on the ground. As the men walked by, Fetterman stopped long enough to pick up the weapon and check the body. There was a single bullet hole in the face. A neat, round hole, the edges slightly bruised, just below the right eye. The helmet had hidden the real damage. The exit wound. A fist-sized chunk of the skull was gone. When Fetterman kicked the helmet out of the way, he could see the gray brain matter that had been jellied by the impact of the bullet.

Farther on they came to the area the artillery had hit. They couldn't tell how many of the VC had been killed there because they could only find tiny pieces of bodies. A finger on the side of a dike, a foot still in the boot, most of one arm and some of the shoulder muscle, a single undamaged lung. Adding all the pieces together would almost add up to one man, but Fetterman knew that the artillery had probably landed among nine or ten people to leave the evidence he was finding.

At the tree line they found another body that was nearly whole. The cloth of the uniform was burned by the white phosphorus of the marking rounds the artillery had used. Most of the equipment was gone, taken by the survivors.

In the forest they found a couple of blood trails, indicating there were some wounded who had managed to escape the artillery fire. Standard procedure was to follow the trails until a dead soldier was found or the blood vanished. Fetterman didn't have the time. He'd seen what he wanted to, and now he turned the men around and headed them back to the main body of the patrol. It was time to return to the camp.

The trip back to the base was uneventful. Rather than follow the patrol pattern that had been laid out days before, Gerber turned the patrol directly to the east, cutting across rice fields and through fingers of jungle that reached out to break up the open ground. Gerber had requested airlift support, but it was denied in Saigon because of other priorities. Since they were no longer in contact and had no casualties, they would have to walk.

By three o'clock that afternoon they were working their way through the perimeter wire. Bromhead and Bocker met them at the gate and helped organize the cleanup detail, weapon check, equipment inspection and storing of the extra ammo in the bunker. Then the strikers were released for the rest of the day.

As soon as he could get close to Bromhead, Gerber asked, "When did all our company leave?"

"Crinshaw and his boys left early this morning. The Vietnamese general decided that he didn't like the way we roughed it out here. No women. No good food. No women. No entertainment. And no women. He pulled out yesterday. His people found the dead rangers and worked it so that an Army Aviation shit hook flew the bodies out. I guess they were pretty ripe."

"What about Robin Morrow?"

"She's still looking for the story to end all stories. She got to Crinshaw at one point, and he made sure to tell me that she was to get anything she wanted. Within reason, of course."

Gerber shook his head. "I'm still surprised by that. You'd think Crinshaw would have a fit about a woman here."

"The media, Captain," Bromhead reminded him. "She has a public forum from which to relate our general's daring exploits. He's not about to do anything to piss her off. Especially since she conned him into signing that order authorizing her visit in the first place."

"Yeah, that's right." Gerber thought for a moment and then said, "I want you to take out a patrol, say ten, twelve men, and make a wide sweep south of the camp. Look for signs of the VC moving in close. But organize it so that you're back by dusk. I don't want anyone outside the wire tonight."

"Any reason you want me back by dusk?" he asked.

"Only that we've kept everyone up for a couple of days, and it's time to stand down for a day or two. If you don't find anything around us, that is."

"Yes, sir. I'd like to take Bocker with me. He seems to get stuck here all the time."

Gerber nodded. "Have Anderson take over the radio watch. Check with me before you move out."

As Bromhead headed for the commo bunker, Gerber spotted Fetterman sitting on the short sandbagged wall near the south gate unlacing his boot. As Gerber approached him, he said, "You and I should get together with Kepler and tell him about the patrol."

"I had the same thought, sir. Besides, I want to tell him about the Ho Chi Minh Trail. That thing is unbelievable. Twenty, thirty yards wide and damn near paved."

"Well," said Gerber slowly, "we'll want to be careful what we say about the Trail. The only way you could have seen it was by being somewhere you weren't supposed to be."

Fetterman finished unlacing his boot and took it off. He held it upside down and shook some red dirt out of it. "I'll think of something. Maybe one of Kepler's trusted agents can report it."

"When you've finished here, find Kepler and report to me in my hootch. We'll go over all this then."

GERBER WAS WAITING for them when Fetterman knocked on the door. After he'd invited them in and told them to sit down, he picked a bottle of Beam's off the littered desk, pulled the cork and took a deep swallow. Then he handed the bottle to Fetterman, who did the same and passed it on to Kepler. Kepler gave it back to Gerber, who took another drink, corked the bottle and said, "That's smooth."

"Why don't you fill us in on the mission now," Gerber said as he sat down.

Fetterman nodded and began telling them about the trip to Cambodia. He stopped once to spread a map on the desk so that he could show them his routes of march, locations of the enemy camps, and the point on the Ho Chi Minh Trail that he crossed. He speculated on a couple of the infiltration routes, the points where the Trail disintegrated as it crossed the Cambodian border into Vietnam.

Sitting down again, he told of the shooting of the Chinese officer, the loads they had used and the distance from which the kill was made.

At that point Kepler stopped him and asked, "Are you sure you got the right guy? We never really got a good look at him, and you said Tyme made the shot from over seven hundred meters."

Fetterman didn't reply right away. It was true he had never seen the Chinese officer up close. But he had seen him as he ran for Cambodia and had seen him from nearly the same angle as he walked through the camp. Fetterman nodded once and then said confidently, "Yeah, I'm sure. It was the right guy."

"Okay," said Gerber, "Tony, you and Derek get together and work out that report on the Ho Chi Minh Trail. We'll have to be very careful with it." He didn't tell them that he would have to go to Saigon the next day to report the success of the mission to the CIA.

THIRTY MINUTES LATER Bromhead found Gerber still sitting in his hootch, his feet propped on a table and a can of beer in his hand. Bromhead, now in full field pack and carrying a full load of ammo, walked in.

"We're ready."

"Who all are you taking?"

"I've Bocker as senior NCO. Lieutenant Bao is going out with a couple of the Tai. Sergeant Tam and six of the Viets are going, too."

"Remember to be back by dusk. And check in by radio every hour."

"Yes, sir. Anything else?"

"Just be careful out there. Don't do anything stupid."

"I'll be careful."

Bromhead had his patrol at the south gate when Robin Morrow ran up, carrying her camera bag and wearing a field harness with a canteen and large bowie knife on it. She was wearing khaki pants, a khaki bush shirt and a large Australian bush hat.

"Say, Lieutenant," she said, "mind if I go along? Captain Gerber said that it was all right with him, if you didn't mind."

Bromhead hesitated. It didn't sound right to him, not after some of the negative things Gerber had said about the press. How the media were always searching for a good story, one that was visual, exciting and who the hell cared for the facts. Damn the facts if they got in the way. Still, she had Crinshaw's ear and doing everything to please her probably wouldn't upset the general, and that would make the captain happy.

"You sure that Captain Gerber said it was okay?"

She pointed over her shoulder toward Gerber's hootch. "You can ask him if you want," she said.

Bromhead looked at Bocker, who shrugged slightly and glanced at his watch. "Okay," said Bromhead. "You stay close to Sergeant Bocker and do whatever he says. We're not going to slow down or go easy to suit you. You have to keep up and listen to everything I say."

"No problem. You won't know I'm here."

Once they were through the gate and into the deep elephant grass outside the last strand of the perimeter wire, Bromhead picked up the pace. The patrol moved rapidly to the south, down toward the river where the ground turned soggy and spongy and where the footing was dangerous. Since he wasn't particularly interested in sneaking through the area, Bromhead didn't mind the splashing or the sucking pop they made as they walked through the mud. And when Morrow lost her balance, falling sideways into a water-filled shell crater, he laughed. To make it funnier, Bocker had leaped toward her to keep her from falling, but had only saved her camera bag.

"Welcome to Vietnam, Miss Morrow," Bromhead said as she stood in water up to her knees.

Bromhead quickly deployed the men of his tiny force for security. Bocker lifted Morrow to her feet and even produced a large OD towel from his pack so that she could try to dry off. That done, she tucked her blond hair up under her bush hat and said she was ready to go.

They continued, weaving in and out of the trees, bending the patrol to the west along the northern bank of the river. They moved quietly and cautiously now, realizing the VC might be anywhere.

Morrow danced off the trail a couple of times, trying to get pictures of men at war. She tried for sunlight streaming through the branches of the trees, with the leaves obscuring some of the foreground. She caught the men, both American and Vietnamese, silhouetted by shafts of sunlight, their weapons held at the ready. She photographed their faces, young, determined, staring ahead warily, their eyes searching for the enemy. She wanted close-ups that showed the strain on the young faces, dark circles under the eyes, the dirt smeared on their skin as they hunted the VC. She tried to capture the moment. Young men engaged in the greatest adventure of all: the hunt for other young men.

She took dozens of pictures. She photographed Bromhead as he talked on the radio carried by one of the Vietnamese strikers, the antenna held in his hand so that it bent over the top of his head. He didn't want it sticking up to signal his location to the enemy.

She got a picture of Bocker as he reached out to help one of the Vietnamese over a fallen palm. And one of the point man as he crouched near a large bush, pointing forward, as if spotting the enemy for the men at his rear.

Finally she stepped close to Bromhead and asked, "Can we stop for a minute? I want to change a lens."

"Miss Morrow, we're on a military mission here and not a goddamned walk through the park," Bromhead said sternly. But he called for a ten-minute break anyway.

While sitting with·her back against a large teak tree, Bocker crouched near her and said, "Miss Morrow, I wouldn't go stepping off the trail and crashing through the jungle. Charlie has begun to booby-trap this area pretty heavily. You have to be careful or you'll blow yourself up."

She smiled up at him as she snapped her camera bag shut. "Don't worry about me, Sergeant. I'm being careful and I've been through that course on booby traps the Army gives its men when they arrive in Vietnam."

"Yes, ma'am. Except that class isn't as thorough as it could be. You'll find the VC are a little better at it than the Army gives them credit for. Thought I should say something because we don't want to lose you."

"I appreciate the concern," she said, getting to her feet. "But I do know what I'm doing."

Bocker didn't move. "I'm not sure that I know what I'm doing," he said, "and I've been here ten months. Charlie is tricky, and just when you think you've got it all figured out, he throws something new into the game. First he has small booby traps with trip wires across the trail. We learn to look for those, and he then begins to bury single bullets, their primers against a nail so that they detonate when you step on them, firing the round into your foot or, if you're unlucky, up the inside of your leg. You have to understand the nature of this war. It isn't just soldiers killing soldiers, but terrorists killing innocent people so that the government will capitulate."

"I understand that, Sergeant. I really do."

"Yes, ma'am," Bocker said, straightening. "Except that if you get hurt out here, it's going to cause the captain a great deal of trouble."

"Because I'm a woman?"

"No. Because you're a reporter."

Bromhead looked back at them. Seeing both of them on their feet, he said, "If you're ready, we'll get going."

There was only an hour of sunlight left when they found the VC. The point man stopped, dropped to the ground and waited for the rest of the patrol to catch up. Bromhead crawled forward and saw the solitary enemy soldier sitting with his back to a palm tree, his AK-47 leaning next to him.

Bocker, who had come up behind him, made a motion with his index finger across his throat, asking if they should kill the man.

Bromhead shook his head and pointed to the rear, indicating they should fall back the way they had come and then head straight for the camp. They had the information they wanted.

It was then they both heard the whirring pop of the motor-driven film advance of a 35 mm camera as it cranked through a dozen or more shots. Morrow had managed to get into a position where she could photograph the enemy, unconcerned about the noise her camera was making.

It looked, for an instant, as if they had gotten away with it. Then, springing suddenly to life, the VC rolled to his right, grabbed his rifle and started spraying bullets into the trees to the left of where Morrow was crouching.

Bromhead and the Tai striker who had been walking point both opened fire at the same time. The rounds from the striker hit the tree high, peeling bark and shredding leaves. Bromhead fired low, kicking dirt up in great brown splashes.

The VC rolled to his right, to the cover of a large bush. When he leaped to his feet, Bromhead hit him with rounds in the shoulder, the back and the hip. The Tai striker added to the damage, scoring hits in the lower back and both legs. The enemy dropped to the ground, rolled over a couple of times and then was still. There was a spray of blood where one bullet had exited his chest, severing an artery. A second spray, not as high as the first, followed and then a third that was little more than a bubbling. The VC was dead.

Bocker and two of the strikers ran forward, one of them grabbing the AK-47. Bocker checked the body and then pointed to the north and pumped his arm twice, telling the striker to hurry to the flank in case there were other VC.

Bromhead was on his feet immediately, and in three running strides was right in front of Morrow. She was looking more than a little shaken, but he was unable to stop himself from teeing off on her.

"You stupid, goddamned bitch," he yelled. "Just what the hell did you think you were doing?"

"I was just—"

"I don't give a fuck," interrupted Bromhead. "Of all the stupid stunts! We're out here trying to find the enemy and work around him, and you've got to go advertise that we're here. That guy could be the point for a whole company of VC for all we know. We've got to get out of here because of all the shooting. When Bocker returns, you stay with him. You stick to him like glue. You don't get more than three feet from him, and you keep your goddamned camera in the fucking case. You got that?"

Before she could answer, Bocker appeared at Bromhead's elbow. "He was alone, sir."

"Okay. Put someone on point and head them to the camp via direct. You take charge of Miss Morrow and see that she doesn't cause us any more trouble."

8

U.S. SPECIAL FORCES
CAMP A-555

As the returning patrol moved through the gate, Bromhead didn't suspect anything was wrong. He saw Gerber standing near the command bunker on the south wall only thirty feet away, but Gerber was often there when a patrol came in.

Just inside the gate Bromhead turned to face the patrol and gave the order for the men to clean their weapons. Then he looked back at Gerber.

"I'll want to see you in my hootch just as soon as you're free," Gerber said as he walked up to Bromhead.

Since it was said casually, Bromhead didn't think much about it. Gerber liked to hold a debriefing session after a patrol had returned. Then he looked into Gerber's eyes and saw that they were cold. He also noticed Gerber's mouth was set in a hard line, and suddenly Bromhead knew he had been wrong in letting Morrow go on the patrol. It took a physical effort to keep from moaning.

He turned the job of checking the patrol's weapons over to Bocker, and as soon as he entered Gerber's hootch he saw that he was in trouble. Gerber was sitting behind his desk, a stack of papers in front of him. "Just come in and close the door," was all he said.

As soon as Bromhead closed the door, Gerber was on his feet shouting, "What the fuck is going on in your mind?"

"Sir?" said Bromhead, sure now about why he was there.

"Don't play dumb with me," cautioned Gerber. "What kind of stupid play was that? Who told you to take a reporter on patrol? A female reporter at that."

"She said that she'd checked with you and that you'd said it was up to me."

Gerber collapsed into his chair, rubbed a hand through his hair and stared at his subordinate. "Oh, come on, Johnny. Don't be naive."

Bromhead unbuckled his web gear and sat down. The sweat stains on his jungle jacket and around his waist were apparent. "I guess I should have known that you didn't give her permission, but she did say for me to check it out with you and knew where you were. Besides, since she has Crinshaw's ear, I thought you might have figured it would be good for us. Crinshaw would appreciate us doing all we can for her."

"Just use your head. We don't need having a reporter killed, especially a woman." Gerber stopped and waved a hand through the air, as if to erase a slate. "Now, suppose you tell me what happened out there?"

ACROSS THE CAMP Fetterman and Tyme were in Fetterman's room, seeing just how fast they could empty a case of Coors beer. Tyme had just taken a large swig out of his and slammed the can on the tabletop.

Fetterman, showing the first signs of becoming drunk, was speaking with a precision that he normally ignored. "It was a damned good mission, Boom-Boom. A damned good one."

Tyme nodded, bobbing his head up and down in an exaggerated movement. His face was getting numb. "It's nice when things work out as well as they did."

Finally Fetterman said, "How are you doing?"

Tyme stared at the older man and then asked, "What do you mean?"

"I mean, how are you doing now that the mission is over? After what happened on the Ho Chi Minh Trail?"

Tyme stood up, drained his beer and walked over to the table where a half dozen full cans waited. He opened one with a bayonet, took a deep drink and then turned back to face Fetterman. Tyme wasn't sure how he felt about it. He hadn't really thought about it, and at the moment he wasn't sure he wanted to think about it.

"I thought we had gotten beyond worrying about what happened there," said Tyme.

"I don't think you have," responded Fetterman. "I saw the look on your face. We didn't have time to talk about it then, but we do now. And we've both had enough to drink to be able to talk about it."

"There's nothing to talk about, really."

"Come on, Boom-Boom. This is your old master sergeant. I know better than that."

"I was just surprised that it was a woman. That's all. I hadn't expected it."

"Justin. Talk to me."

Tyme took a deep breath. "Shit, she was so young."

"And carrying a weapon, along with supplies for the VC, so they could go on killing our people."

"But she thought she was safe. She wasn't paying any attention to what was happening. She didn't have a chance."

Fetterman finished his beer and crushed the tin can effortlessly with one hand. He tossed the remains into the corner of his hootch.

"Okay. I see we're not going to get anywhere on this, so I'll just throw out a few comments for general consumption.

"First of all, I know that you wouldn't have been greatly upset if the enemy soldier had been male. Even if he had been young. I suppose you can make a case for the woman not being on the Ho Chi Minh Trail because she wanted to be there. She was probably drafted and ordered to be there. But that's the same as it is for a lot of men who fight wars. If it were left to choice, very few men would ask to fight in a war. But no one ever gives you a choice.

"So we can ignore that argument. She was there, in the wrong place at the wrong time, and it's too bad that she had to die. But it was better than your dying in her place. Tough on Co Cong is just tough on Co Cong. The VC use lots of women. We've killed them before. We've seen their bodies lying on the—''

"That's not the point," said Tyme, interrupting.

"That's precisely the point, my boy," said Fetterman. "She was an enemy soldier doing a job for the enemy."

"But I came up behind her and cut her throat."

"As we have a number of times."

"But those were men."

"So what?" Fetterman nearly roared. "There is no difference between a man and a woman when she is wearing the enemy's uniform and carrying the enemy's rifle. You think she would hesitate if she had the chance to stick the knife into you?"

"No, but—"

"There are no buts about it. Killing an enemy soldier is killing an enemy soldier. If you're going to fight a war, people are going to die. If you're going to fight a war, you've got to be prepared to kill people. There is no other way to do it. If you're not prepared to kill people, then you have no business being here."

Tyme nodded, sipping his beer. "I know you're right. It still bothers me."

"Let me ask you a question," said Fetterman. "Are you bothered by the other people you've killed? Did you enjoy any of it?"

Tyme remembered the first man he had killed in hand-to-hand fighting. There had been an exhilaration about it. Not the killing, but the fact that he had been in a death struggle, and Tyme had won the fight. He didn't enjoy the act of killing. It was the contest. The fight to the death.

He regretted taking the human life. It was such a permanent act, something that, once done, could never be undone. But he had chosen to be a soldier, and with that choice came the territory. He wasn't sure that he had the right to take a human life, but somehow, by risking his own, it became almost right. If he were willing to put his own life on the line, then it became right for him to take the enemy's, and if he lost his, he had no complaints. He understood the rules.

Fetterman had been watching Tyme. Finally he said, "Justin, if you weren't bothered by this, I would worry about you. If you get to the point where you live for the killing, I'll transfer you out of here immediately. And if you hesitate to use your knife when you have to, I'll have you out of here on the next flight.

"We walk a fine line, and we have to stay on it. If we fall off, to either side, then we stop the game and go home. Sometimes in a box."

The private party of Fetterman and Tyme continued until 2:00 A.M. when Tyme, trying to stand up as he announced that he was going to his room to sleep, fell flat on his face. Fetterman nearly laughed himself sick, picked Tyme up to make sure he wasn't hurt, then went out to take a shower.

The water in the fifty-five-gallon drum perched on the roof of the shower had been refilled after sundown and was probably cold. It was a gravity-fed system and never got too warm with only the sun to heat it. But it was a shower, and that made it better than bathing in the river or in one of the water-filled shell craters. Fetterman didn't mind. He got wet, soaped and rinsed in less than three minutes. Then, feeling better than he had since he arrived in Vietnam, he went to bed.

It took only four minutes for him to fall asleep. But in that short time he felt the elation of a well-planned, well-executed mission. He couldn't ask for anything better. No one killed or wounded on his side, and the enemy had suffered.

IT WAS JUST AFTER TWO when Gerber walked into the team house. Morrow was sitting at one of the tables, her notebook in front of her next to a can of beer. Her eyes were closed and she was tapping her chin with a yellow pencil. Her damp hair hung straight down, and there was sweat on her forehead and upper lip. She had unbuttoned her khaki shirt to her navel.

"Thought everyone was asleep," said Gerber to announce himself.

Morrow jumped, as if she had been jabbed, and snapped, "Don't do that. You scared me to death."

"Sorry," he said. He turned to the coffeepot, but it was empty. He stepped to the refrigerator and pulled it open. A lone can of beer sat in it, but when he picked it up, he discovered it had already been opened. He gave up looking for something to drink and sat down opposite Morrow at the table.

"I thought maybe we should talk," said Gerber.

Morrow took a deep swallow from her can of beer, as if steeling herself. "Talk about what?"

"You conning my exec into letting you go on his patrol."

"Nothing to talk about. I wanted to go along, and I knew that you would never allow it if I asked you, so I short-circuited the system and got to go. Simple as that."

"Simple as that," repeated Gerber. "Jesus, Robin! What the hell were you thinking of? Nothing is as simple as that."

"Well, listen to the hypocrite," she said. "Nice job, Robin. Way to con Crinshaw, Robin. But when it's you who gets conned, it's a different story."

"Okay," said Gerber, holding up a hand to stop her. "I deserve that. I haven't been fair. But you could have done some real damage if anything had happened to you."

"Don't worry about it, Gerber," she said, suddenly angry. "I was just doing my job."

Gerber watched her, wondering when he had lost control of the situation. He had thought it would be a good chance to talk to her about conning her way onto the patrol, and suddenly he was on the defensive, as if he had done something wrong.

As he stared at her, he saw she was an attractive woman. She looked a little the worse for wear, away from the luxuries of hot showers, air conditioning and good food, but still damned attractive. If she didn't look so much like her sister, he would have made the effort to talk to her, to be with her sooner. Now he had gotten off on the wrong foot.

He smiled at her and said, "Can we start this again? I don't think I handled it quite right."

"Okay, Captain, we can start again."

"Let me put it this way," he began and then stopped, wondering why he was trying so hard not to insult the woman. She had duped one of his men into taking her on a patrol when she should have been in the camp. "Next time you want to do something like go on patrol, have the courtesy to ask me. I'm responsible for everything that happens here, and I'd like to know what's going on."

"All right, Captain," she said. "I apologize." She stood and walked around the table so that she was facing Gerber. She pulled a chair out and sat down, slowly crossing her bare legs.

Gerber tried not to stare at her, but he couldn't help himself. He wanted to keep the relationship on a professional level. Camp commander and military officer to journalist. But then he said, "I thought we had gotten beyond that captain nonsense."

"I'm always formal when I'm chewed out."

"I wasn't chewing you out. I was merely asking for a little courtesy."

"I stand corrected," she said, leaning forward slightly so that the edges of her shirt pulled apart, revealing the sides of her breasts.

Gerber wanted to reach out and touch her, but restrained himself. He didn't want to get involved with a woman, any woman, at the moment. Especially one named Morrow. He had done a good job of forgetting about Karen in the past few days, even with an almost exact replica of her in the camp.

Morrow reached down and scratched her knee and then drew her fingers along the inside of her thigh, her nails leaving light-red marks on her flesh. She glanced at her leg and then looked back at Gerber.

"So, Mack Gerber, how did a nice guy like you get stuck in a hole like this?" she asked, not realizing it was nearly the same thing she'd said to Bromhead a couple of days earlier.

"I don't see it as being stuck," he said automatically. "I'm doing an important job here."

Morrow edged closer to him. She touched his knee and repeated, "An important job?"

"Yes," he said and then realized she didn't want to hear about the mission of the Special Forces in Vietnam. She had left her notebook and pencil behind and was now talking to him on a personal level. The professionalism he was trying to maintain was slipping away fast.

Something seemed to shift in the team house, and the heat and humidity of the Vietnamese night slipped away forgotten. The journalist was gone, replaced by a desirable woman in sweat-stained clothes.

Gerber wanted to touch her, to kiss her. He wanted to ease the shirt from her shoulders and the shorts from her hips. But he didn't move. He sat there looking at her as the thoughts swirled through his head and the memories of her sister intruded.

Morrow seemed to feel it, too, because she took Gerber's hand in hers, lifting it from the table.

"This isn't the right time," he said quietly, "or the right place." There were too many other people around. Not in the team house itself but in the camp, and there were almost no doors that locked. But it went beyond the inconvenience of the location. It had to do with Karen and the way she had left.

"You sure?" she asked.

He didn't want to hurt her, but he wasn't going to be forced into something that he didn't want. He withdrew his hand and said, "For now, I'm sure. But just for now."

She stood. "Okay," she said, "I can be patient, too."

AT 0600 Anderson, who was guarding the radio, got a call from Big Green announcing that he, along with two additional helicopters, would be landing in less than ten minutes. Big Green expected Gerber to meet him at the pad.

Anderson acknowledged the call, told the young Vietnamese NCO there to stay alert and then hurried out to find Gerber.

Gerber was on the helipad before the helicopters were in sight. He asked Anderson if there had been any more to Crinshaw's message.

The big sergeant shook his head. "No, sir. Just that he was coming in with three ships and that you should be there."

"Okay. Why don't you go get Sergeant Fetterman and Lieutenant Bromhead up here, too. And find Minh and tell him that Crinshaw is inbound."

As Anderson disappeared, Bromhead walked up, buttoning his fatigue shirt and carrying his rifle. "What's happening?"

"Damned if I know. Crinshaw is inbound with another fleet of helicopters."

Gerber turned and saw that Fetterman was heading toward the pad. Behind him were Smith, Bocker and Tyme. When Bocker was in earshot, Gerber said, "What are you people doing out here?"

Bocker shrugged. "Don't know, Captain. Just seemed like we should be."

Gerber noticed they all were carrying their weapons. Then, behind them, Minh and a squad of the Vietnamese appeared, and near the commo bunker a group of Tai, led by Bao and Krung, was forming.

"I don't like this," said Gerber to Bromhead, indicating the armed men who were beginning to surround the helipad. "I don't like this one bit."

The popping of rotor blades interrupted him. All heads turned so that they could watch the aircraft dropping toward them. Anderson tossed a yellow smoke grenade onto the center of the pad, and the lead aircraft shot its approach to the smoke, then hovered beyond it, giving the helicopters behind room to land. As its skids touched down, the cargo door slid open and two big sergeants dressed in freshly starched jungle fatigues leaped out, each carrying an M-16.

As the other helicopters landed, a squad of military policemen, each man wearing a ceremonial black helmet polished to a high gloss with a large white MP painted on it, jumped to the ground and spread out.

Behind him Gerber heard rather than saw his men doing the same. Tension filled the air like electricity just before a thunderstorm. There was no reason to suspect any trouble, but apparently everyone did. Gerber didn't like this one bit.

The whine of the Huey turbines seemed to die as one, as the pilots of each of the aircraft shut down the engines. For a moment the three groups of men stood staring at each other as opponents at an armed camp. Gerber's Green Berets stood around the forward edge of the pad, while the MPs filled the sides and rear. All around them were the Vietnamese and Tai. Everyone was armed.

Crinshaw appeared in the doorway of the lead helicopter and stood, bent at the waist, looking out. Then he stepped down slowly, glanced around and moved to Gerber.

Gerber saluted and said, "Welcome to the camp, General."

"Cut the shit, Gerber."

"General?"

"What are all these men doing here?" demanded Crinshaw.

"Part of the welcoming committee," said Gerber.

"Well, get them out of here!"

Gerber looked at Bromhead, who had taken a step to the rear. Then he turned to Fetterman and saw the hard look on his face.

"What's this all about?" asked Gerber, turning back to Crinshaw.

"Don't go asking me questions, boy. You get these men out of the area and we'll talk."

Behind Crinshaw the MP lieutenant had drawn his .45, but was holding it with the barrel pointed downward.

Gerber looked at Minh and said, "Captain, why don't you get your people some breakfast." He raised his voice and repeated the instruction for Lieutenant Bao.

Slowly the Vietnamese and Tai began to drift away. Only Minh and two of his NCOs remained behind. None of the Green Berets made any move to depart.

When all the Vietnamese were gone, Crinshaw waved to another officer who had been standing near the lead helicopter. The man wore clean fatigues and held an attaché case. He had short dark hair trimmed so closely around the ears that it looked like the whitewall haircuts given recruits prior to basic training. He was badly sunburned, as if he had only recently arrived in Vietnam, and wore wire-rimmed glasses. Gerber saw no signs of weapons or field gear.

The man stepped forward, stopping one pace behind Crinshaw, who nodded to him and said, "Read it!"

"Yes, General." The man set his case on the ground and unfolded a sheet of paper. He looked at Gerber and said, "I am informing you, as camp commander and commander of this A-Team, that charges of murder have been filed against two of your men."

For just an instant Gerber felt like laughing. But Crinshaw was not known for his sense of humor; this couldn't be a joke.

"They will also be charged with violation of various other military regulations and Vietnamese and international laws."

Gerber ignored the man with the attaché case and looked directly at Crinshaw. "What kind of crap is this?"

"No crap, Captain. Fact. Your Sergeant Fetterman and Sergeant Tyme are going to be arrested for the murder of a foreign national in a neutral country. I told you that you would go too far and I'd be there to hang your butt. Now here I am."

Abruptly Crinshaw stopped talking. He saw Robin Morrow coming around the corner of a hootch. He pointed at her and demanded, "What the fuck is that civilian still doing here?"

"Looking for a story," said Gerber, almost smiling.

"Have her look somewhere else," Crinshaw shouted hoarsely. "Now you get Fetterman and Tyme here. Tell them to bring their gear because they'll be staying at Long Binh for a while."

Suddenly something changed. The situation that had only seconds before seemed tense now escalated beyond that. Then Gerber identified the triggering element. He heard the slide of a .45 being pulled back so that a round could be chambered. Somewhere behind him he heard one of his men jack a round into his weapon. There was a rattling of weapons as others, on both sides, followed suit.

A couple of the MPs stepped back to take cover behind the helicopters. Some dropped to one knee. The Green Berets did the same, each one of them taking whatever cover was available, some near the pile of sandbags that were used for the ammo bunker, one behind the fifty-five-gallon drum used for burning trash for an emergency light on the helipad and one falling back to the commo bunker entrance. As it now stood, a wrong word would set off a fire fight between the Green Berets and the MPs.

"Captain, you had better do something before you are all in trouble."

Gerber turned, taking it all in. His men crouching around the pad, the MPs near the helicopters and Morrow near the corner of a hootch, her camera out, taking pictures as fast as the automatic advance could feed the film. All this because he had allowed Fetterman to pursue the war a little more enthusiastically than Crinshaw thought it should be done. All this because politicians and civilians didn't understand the nature of war and thought you could limit it by putting restrictions on your own side that the enemy wouldn't follow.

Gerber turned and looked at his team sergeant. Fetterman was standing where he'd been when Crinshaw had gotten out of his helicopter. He had his weapon pointing at the general. The safety was off.

Quietly Gerber said, "Tony, you think you could get your gear together?"

"Certainly, Captain. No problem. And Boom-Boom?"

"Him, too. Make it snappy."

"Yes, sir."

Gerber turned to Bromhead, who was crouched near a pile of sandbags that were going to be used to reinforce the ammo bunker. "Johnny, take the rest of the men to the team house."

"Sir?"

"Do it."

"Yes, sir." Bromhead moved off toward Sully Smith and Sam Anderson. He spoke to them and they reluctantly stood. Together they walked to a couple of the other men.

"You might want to have your MPs relax," Gerber said to Crinshaw.

Crinshaw nodded to one of the NCOs, who in turn went off to talk to the MPs.

Ten minutes later Fetterman and Tyme returned to the helipad, each carrying a duffel bag full of extra clothes, shaving kit and other personal items. Fetterman had hidden a bottle of Beam's disguised as shaving lotion deep in the bottom of his. He wasn't sure he could sneak it by the guards at the stockade, but he was sure as hell going to try.

At the aircraft Crinshaw was sitting in the cargo compartment smoking a pipe. The MPs were standing at ease, waiting.

Fetterman whispered to Gerber, "Captain, you get us out of this. We're counting on you to get us out."

"I'll get you out," Gerber replied. "Don't worry." If he had to, he'd testify he had issued the orders to the two men. That way they couldn't be held ultimately responsible.

Four of the MPs came forward, two of them carrying handcuffs. Crinshaw jumped down from the helicopter to follow.

With one hand in the air, Gerber stopped them. "You have no need for those," he said, pointing to the handcuffs.

"Regulations, Captain," said the MP lieutenant.

"Not on my men."

"We have your word they won't try to escape?" asked Crinshaw.

"Of course you do," snapped Gerber.

The general waved off the MPs. "Let's get out of here," he ordered.

The MPs separated Fetterman and Tyme, putting one on the second aircraft and the other on the third. Crinshaw turned and waved a hand over his head, telling the pilot of the lead aircraft to start his engine.

Just before he boarded, Crinshaw leaned close to Gerber and said, "Don't think you're in the clear on this deal, Captain. I suspect that once we start taking testimony, you'll be coming in to keep your men company."

Before Gerber could respond, Crinshaw climbed on board. Gerber stepped back as the pilots wound the helicopters up to full operating RPM. The noise increased to a steady roar from the turbines that was replaced by the popping of the rotor blades as they began to lift off. The wind from the rotors swirled around the pad, threatening to blow away everything that wasn't tied down. Gerber put a hand on his beret to keep it from blowing away and turned his back to the red dust that had begun to sandblast him. A moment later he felt the hot blast from the turbines as the helicopters maneuvered before taking off to the south.

Gerber watched as they climbed out, gaining altitude rapidly and then turning to the east toward Saigon.

"What are you going to do now?" a soft voice asked.

Gerber turned to look at Morrow. She had her camera clutched in one hand and held the other to her eyes to shield them from the bright sun.

"I'm not sure. But I'm going to have to do it fast."

9

LONG BINH JAIL, LONG BINH, REPUBLIC OF VIETNAM

The helicopters didn't fly to Saigon and Hotel Three, but diverted to the north to land at the airfield at Long Binh, where they were met by a convoy of jeeps and three-quarter-ton trucks. Crinshaw got into one of the jeeps and was driven from the field toward the headquarters building at Bien Hoa situated to the west. Fetterman and Tyme were put into the covered back of one of the three-quarter-ton trucks with two MPs sitting near the tailgate.

The thick canvas that covered the framework behind the cab absorbed the heat and held it in, making it uncomfortably hot in the back. Tyme sat on a fixed low bench on one side of the truck, with his head bowed and his hands clasped around his knees.

Fetterman sat on the opposite side, watching the two MPs, who were looking out the back. He used the sleeve of his fatigues to wipe the sweat from his forehead and hoped the ride to LBJ would be short.

They bumped along in silence for a while, the fumes from the truck's exhaust blowing back into the bed, where it mixed with the damp tropical air making it hard to breathe. Fetterman slid along the bench to get closer to the opening where the air wasn't quite as foul.

He looked at Tyme and said, "Hey, Boom-Boom, take it easy. It could be worse."

Tyme turned so that he could see Fetterman and said, "I don't understand why the captain let them arrest us."

Fetterman glanced at the MPs, as if to tell Tyme that it wasn't the place to discuss the matter. He then sat back and closed his eyes, waiting for the ride to end.

But he wasn't nearly as relaxed as he wanted Tyme to believe. He knew exactly how serious the charges were and wasn't sure that Gerber would be able to do anything to get them out. Crinshaw's information was right on one point. They certainly had crossed the border and Army regulations and international law prohibited it. A case could be made for smoking the Chinese officer since he was helping the enemy. A strong case. If the man had been in South Vietnam when he had been shot.

The fly in the ointment was that the man had been in Cambodia, where technically he wasn't fair game. Fetterman smiled to himself when he realized Crinshaw had missed on a couple of charges. He had forgotten conspiracy. They all had conspired to kill the man. And he had forgotten about being out of uniform, a fairly minor charge when compared to the rest of them.

Still, he had faith in the Army system. They couldn't find him guilty of murder if he'd only been doing his job. And then he realized he was guilty. The difference between doing his job and murder was an imaginary line, and Fetterman had crossed it.

Tyme stood a chance of getting off since he was the junior NCO on the mission, except that he had pulled the trigger. Their only defense was that they had been following orders, and that defense had not worked for the Nazis after World War II. If there had been an officer on the patrol, then that ploy might have worked, but not the way the thing developed. When it came right down to it, they were guilty as hell.

The truck rumbled to a halt in a clatter of grinding gears and squealing brakes. The driver came around to drop the tailgate, and as it fell away, the two MPs stood up.

"Let's move it," said the larger, darker of the two.

Fetterman stood and dropped to the ground, blinking in the bright sunlight of midday. Even with the temperature hovering at about ninety, Fetterman found it cool compared to the stifling interior of the Army truck.

Tyme appeared and handed down his duffel bag and then Fetterman's. He stooped, put a hand on the bed of the truck and dropped to the ground.

"You men leave your bags here," said a third MP who had appeared from inside the stockade. "Someone will pick them up later so they can be searched. Follow me."

Fetterman turned and stared at the building surrounded by a twelve-foot-high double chain-link fence that was topped with concertina wire. There was a gate in front of them, flanked by a white guard hut where an MP armed with an M-16 watched without interest the activity outside the fence.

The main building was a flat, white, two-story structure that reflected the bright sunlight. The windows of the upper story, where the prisoners were kept, were barred, but the ones on the bottom, where the administration offices and storage were housed, were not.

The MP who had spoken led them past the guard and through the gate to the double doors that led into the building. There they were met by an MP lieutenant who was six feet tall and extremely thin. He had very short blond hair and a long nose. He held a clipboard in his hands, a sheet of paper folded over the top.

"Fetterman, Anthony B.," he read from the clipboard.

"Yes, sir."

"Tyme, Justin."

"Yes, sir."

"You will follow me into the holding room until someone can be freed to take your fingerprints and finish the processing. Cause any trouble and you might just disappear into the jungle around here." He flipped the paper back and turned, entering the dim recesses of the building.

The inside was incredibly clean. The floors showed no sign that anyone ever walked on them. The bulletin board beside one of the doors had several documents posted on it, but all were new. One demanded that soldiers wear their ribbons proudly.

They walked past a Coke machine to an office that was divided in half by a waist-high wooden counter. The counter was painted a bright green that rivaled the verdant jungle. Two MPs sat at desks behind it while a man wearing gray clothes with a big white P on the back of the shirt pushed a broom lazily around the floor.

The lieutenant stopped long enough to request the key for holding room two, and one of the seated MPs pulled it from a lockbox mounted on the wall.

The lieutenant ushered them out a second door and into another hallway. He stopped in front of a metal door, unlocked it and reached inside to turn on the lights. "You men will wait here until someone comes for you," he said as he stepped back out of the way.

Fetterman entered first. The room was brightly lighted and contained a single fixture recessed in the ceiling and protected by a metal cage. Fetterman looked at the chairs carefully and saw they were made of metal and bolted to the floor. There was nothing else in the room.

When Tyme had entered, the lieutenant shut the door with a dull metallic clang and locked it from the outside.

Within five minutes the door was unlocked and opened. A staff sergeant wearing the black armband of an MP told them they were to follow him. In the hallway were three more MPs.

Fetterman and Tyme were taken to a small room where they were photographed, front and profile. Next they were fingerprinted. As they were cleaning the ink from their fingers, another MP arrived and asked Fetterman to follow him. Tyme was to be taken back to the holding room to await the arrival of his defense counsel.

Fetterman was escorted to a room on the second floor. Inside, a man in rumpled jungle fatigues was waiting. He had silver captain's bars pinned to the collar of his uniform, but wore no other insignia or patches. He had longish brown hair, blue eyes behind black, horn-rimmed glasses and skin that was fairly tanned. Although he was slim, he didn't seem to be thin. He was tall and had large, bony hands. He put a large black briefcase on the table and pulled a large bundle of papers out of it. He read them over for a moment and then turned to Fetterman.

"You're in a shit load of trouble," said the man.

"Thank you," said Fetterman. "Would you be good enough to tell me who you are?"

"Oh, of course." The man set the papers down and held out a hand. "I'm Dennis Wilson. I've been appointed to act as your defense counsel."

"You're a lawyer, then?" asked Fetterman, shaking Wilson's hand.

"I'm assigned to the Adjutant General's Office and have had a year of law school."

"Great!" said Fetterman. He hadn't expected Clarence Darrow, but this kid probably didn't have enough qualifications to be a law clerk, let alone a defense attorney. "You want to tell me a little more about what's been happening here?"

Wilson dug through his stack of papers. He grabbed a file folder, opened it and said, "According to this, on or about the twelfth of this month, you led a patrol consisting of yourself, Sergeant First Class Tyme and a couple of the indigenous personnel on a border-crossing expedition that violated a dozen international agreements. While on that illegal patrol you did conspire to murder an individual of another nation not engaged in the conflict in South Vietnam. Having completed that assignment in the foreign country, you did return to South Vietnam."

Fetterman sat back in his chair and laughed. "Well, that about sums it up. If all that is true, then why didn't they arrest Captain Gerber? He would have had to approve our operation."

"As of now there is no proof that Captain Gerber knew that you were going to cross the border and murder a foreign national. If testimony or evidence show that Captain Gerber knew of this mission, then I suppose his arrest will be forthcoming. Now, would you like to tell me your side of the story?"

"You mean somebody is actually interested in that?"

"You're not helping yourself with that attitude, Sergeant."

"And what do you expect? Yesterday I'm in the field fighting the Communists, and today I'm arrested for doing that job a little better than someone thinks I should. Besides, I don't know you, who you work for or how much of what I tell you will remain privileged. You could be setting me up for someone."

Wilson took off the horn-rimmed glasses and began to polish the lenses with an OD handkerchief he pulled from the top pocket of his fatigues. "I can understand your reluctance to talk to me, but I assure you that anything you tell me will not go beyond this room. My job is to help. That's the only reason I'm here."

"You know," said Fetterman, smiling, "that 'I'm here to help you' is one of the three great lies, like 'the check is in the mail' and 'I won't come in your mouth.'"

"I could give you a written pledge," Wilson said with a touch of exasperation.

"What good would that do me when this is over and I'm in jail because you violated that trust?"

"As I said, I can understand your reluctance. All I can say is that Sergeant Tyme is currently with his counsel."

"If Boom-Boom is telling that man anything, I'll be extremely surprised."

"Then you refuse to cooperate?"

"Did I say that? All I said was that I had no guarantee that anything you say is true, or that anything I tell you will stay in this room. If you're going to get me out of this, however, I suppose you need to know what happened."

Wilson brought a large yellow legal pad and a ballpoint pen out of his briefcase. "Yes, I do. We have the Article 32 hearing tomorrow afternoon, so I'll have to know everything."

GERBER WASN'T WORRIED. He didn't like having his men arrested by MPs and spirited to Long Binh Jail, but he wasn't worried. Jerry Maxwell had told him not to get caught, but he didn't think the CIA would let Fetterman and Tyme go down in flames. He would speak to Maxwell, who would speak to his boss, who would talk to someone in Washington, who would then order someone in the Pentagon to tell Crinshaw to quietly drop the charges. That would be that. No problem at all.

As he had done too many times in the past few days, he packed his knapsack with a change of clothes and got ready to leave for Saigon. He left the knapsack sitting on his cot and headed for the commo bunker, where Bocker and his Vietnamese counterpart were sitting at the chart table playing cards.

"Have we got anything scheduled in here this afternoon, Galvin?" asked Gerber.

"Resupply chopper from Tay Ninh should be here in thirty or forty minutes. Nothing else. Why?"

"I need to make a trip into Saigon about a couple of things, and I'd like a ride."

Bocker tossed his cards facedown on the table and said, "I can rustle up something sooner if you would like, sir."

"That won't be necessary. I can wait for the resupply ship. Just don't let it get out of here without me."

"No, sir." He hesitated for a second and then asked, "What's going to happen to Tony and Justin?"

Gerber smiled. "Don't worry about them. I won't let anything happen to them." Without another word Gerber left, heading back to his hootch. Once there he opened his wall locker and took a bottle of Beam's from the bottom shelf. He pulled the cork and took a deep drink, breathing through his mouth after he swallowed to ease the fire in his throat.

"Mind if I join you?" asked a feminine voice from the doorway.

Gerber turned and saw Robin Morrow silhouetted against the light. She was dressed in much the same fashion as she had been the night before. Khaki shirt unbuttoned all the way, but now she had the tails knotted together. She wore khaki shorts and jungle boots. There was sweat on her forehead although her hair was pulled back into a ponytail. A camera hung around her neck.

Gerber held out the bottle and said, "It's warm and I don't have any mixers."

Morrow stepped inside and took the Beam's. "Why cut the effect with mixers?" She took a long drink, her throat working convulsively as she swallowed. She lowered the bottle, blinked her eyes rapidly and said, "Wow."

"You don't have to kill yourself with it," he said.

She handed the Beam's back and sat down in one of the lawn chairs. "What are you going to do about the men who were arrested?"

"Personal question or professional?" asked Gerber.

"A little of both."

"I plan to go to Saigon as soon as the resupply chopper arrives and talk to some people I know there. I think we can straighten this whole thing out before it goes to trial."

"Uh-huh," said Morrow. "Operations into Cambodia. Murder of foreign nationals. Quite a story as I see it."

"Alleged operations and murder," said Gerber quietly.

"Alleged doesn't mean shit," said Morrow. "Just how are you going to spring them from charges like that? Who are you going to talk to?"

Gerber was suddenly frightened. The one hope he had for getting Fetterman and Tyme out of LBJ was to keep everything quiet. To keep the press out of it. But Crinshaw, spouting off about cross-border operations while Morrow stood there and took pictures, might have sunk the whole deal. Gerber corked the bottle and sat down on his cot. "What are you going to do?" he asked.

"I'd like a ride into Saigon with you to talk to a few people of my own. Besides, I should check in at the bureau and file a couple of stories."

"But nothing about Fetterman and Tyme," said Gerber, a little too quickly.

"Not yet, anyway. I don't have all the facts. You going to give me a lift or not?"

Gerber hesitated before replying. Hell, if he didn't give her the ride, she would find another way to Saigon. He couldn't keep her prisoner in the camp. Too many people knew where she was.

"Sure," he said.

"Good," she said as she stood. "I'll buy you dinner."

He watched her leave, wondering if it might not be too late to save Fetterman and Tyme. Too many people seemed to be in on this one. As he thought that, he suddenly realized Crinshaw shouldn't have had any idea of what had happened. No one on his team would have told Crinshaw a damned thing about it. And Crinshaw hated the Vietnamese so it didn't seem likely that he heard it from them. Besides, other than Minh, none of the Vietnamese actually knew anything other than that Fetterman and Tyme had gone out on a mission.

Yet Crinshaw did know something; otherwise he couldn't have arrested Fetterman and Tyme. One of the first things he would have to do when he got back to camp was find out who had been talking out of turn and stop them.

He retrieved the Beam's and poured a healthy slug into his canteen cup. Then he sat on his cot and leaned back against the wall and slowly drank the bourbon. The nature of war was different than what he had read in history books. No masses of brightly dressed men marching to save king and country. Here there were only tired, dirty men who were arrested for fighting the war a little too effectively.

Several minutes later he heard the sound of the approaching chopper and downed the remainder of the Beam's in a single swallow. He set his canteen cup on the papers piled in the center of his desk, picked up his knapsack and reached for his M-14. Then he put it down, deciding it was too much trouble to carry the weapon to Saigon. Instead, he stuffed his M-3 grease gun into the bottom of his knapsack. Next he stripped off his fatigue jacket and strapped on a shoulder holster containing a .45 automatic. He put his jacket back on and walked toward the helipad.

Morrow was already there, standing well back so that the chopper would have room to land and she wouldn't be in the rotor wash. She had changed into jungle fatigues and had a suitcase and her camera bag at her feet.

Gerber was nearly to the pad when Bocker ran out of the commo bunker and tossed a green smoke grenade onto the center of it so the pilots would have a landing point. He saw Gerber, waved and ran back.

Gerber stepped next to Morrow and yelled over the noise of the landing chopper, "You taking all your clothes with you? That mean you're not coming back?"

"I'll be back," she shouted at him. She turned to watch as the helicopter flared to stop its forward motion and then settled to the center of the pad, sucking the green smoke up in the rotor wash and swirling it toward her.

The crew chief leaped from behind his M-60 machine gun in the well of the Huey and trotted to Gerber. He pushed the boom mike of his flight helmet out of the way and yelled, "We've got some supplies to leave here."

Gerber turned to look at the commo bunker, wondering if Bocker had arranged for someone to assist the helicopter crew with the unloading, then saw Anderson approaching from the direction of the team house. Gerber pointed at Anderson, and then the crew chief nodded his understanding. He asked, "You the passenger for Saigon?"

"That's right." He indicated Morrow. "She needs a lift, too."

"No problem, Captain."

Anderson stopped beside Gerber, leaned close and said, "Are you going to help Fetterman and Tyme?"

"I'm going to try, Cat," said Gerber.

He nodded and moved to the cargo compartment of the helicopter. The crew chief slid two boxes containing batteries for the night-ranging weapons, sniperscopes and PRC-10s across the deck of the helicopter. On top of that he tossed a bright-orange bag containing the personal mail for the Americans. Anderson picked it up and, lifting it clear of the chopper, stepped back.

"Good luck, Captain," he yelled as Gerber helped Morrow into the chopper.

Gerber held a thumb up to acknowledge Anderson's remark as the crew chief set Morrow's luggage in the cargo compartment, sliding it under the troop seat. Gerber sat down on the red canvas troop seat that was next to the housing for the transmission and buckled his seat belt. He glanced at Morrow, who sat right next to him, leaning against his arm.

The engine noise increased, and the chopper lifted to a hover, hanging in the air three or four feet above the pad. It turned slightly toward the runway, then the nose dropped and the helicopter raced along the ground without climbing. Suddenly the nose came up and the chopper shot into the air, leaving Gerber feeling as though his stomach remained behind on the ground.

They reached altitude and turned toward Saigon. Gerber glanced to his left and could see the top two buttons on Morrow's shirt were unfastened. He watched the rise and fall of her breasts as she breathed.

She turned and looked at him and smiled. She leaned against him so that her lips were next to his ear and her breast was pressed against his arm. Over the whine of the turbine, she yelled, "How long is the flight?"

He turned his head and put his lips against her ear. "Should take about forty minutes."

She nodded, but didn't move away from him.

They flew on in silence for a couple of minutes, Gerber aware of the pressure of her breast on his arm. He wondered if she knew that he could feel it and decided she had to be able to. He also felt the warmth of her hip as it pressed against him. He thought about shifting his weight to see if she would move with him, but decided to let her play out the game the way she wanted to.

As they neared Go Dau Ha, she grabbed his arm, pressing closer and pointing out the cargo-compartment door. She yelled in his ear, "What's that?"

He liked the feeling of her warm breath on his ear. He said, "Bridge at Go Dau Ha or, as we call it, Go To Hell. Every time we get it built, the VC drop it back into the water. That's why it looks like a cement triangle sticking out of the river and not like a bridge."

"I thought it was some kind of religious structure."

As they continued, Gerber realized she hadn't let go of his arm. She kept the conversation going by asking him about the hamlets they flew over or the military bases they passed. He pointed out the big swamp area south of Highway 1 that was a free fire zone.

He wondered what the flight crew thought of the attention she was paying him, but when he looked, both pilots were staring ahead, watching their instruments and the sky in front of them. There were a lot of other aircraft in the friendly sky—flights of helicopters circling, single ships popping up and dropping down, small propeller-driven airplanes buzzing by and squadrons of jets going to and coming from missions.

The crew chief, hidden in his well on one side of the helicopter, and the door gunner on the opposite side kept watch of the sides and rear. No one had time to worry about the Army captain they had picked up. Gerber was surprised they didn't pay more attention to Morrow.

Gerber sat back to enjoy the flight, realizing it was the best one he had been on. Morrow was making all the difference. She was trying so hard to make him aware of her that Gerber had to smile to himself. Maybe that was why the flight crew seemed to ignore her. They didn't want to be frustrated because she was so obviously trying to attract Gerber's attention. And she was having a great deal of luck doing it.

It was late in the day when they landed at Hotel Three. The crew chief helped Morrow from the chopper and then handed down her suitcase and camera bag. He smiled at her and she yelled her thanks over the engine and rotor noise.

Gerber grabbed his knapsack and leaped to the ground. He took Morrow's suitcase from her, and she shouldered her camera case. They walked across the grass of the heliport to the terminal building.

As they entered, Morrow said, "What's the plan?"

"I've got a number of calls to make and some people to see," answered Gerber.

"Mind if I tag along?"

"Yes. Besides, it's going to be very boring. Nothing that great stories are made of."

''That makes me suspicious,'' said Morrow. ''Anytime I'm assured there's nothing interesting happening, I figure that there is.''

''You still can't go with me,'' Gerber replied. ''Where do you want to eat this dinner that you promised to buy?''

''Nice try, Mack, but I know you're trying to change the subject.'' She smiled at him.

''You're still not going with me,'' he said.

''I'll let you win this one,'' she responded. ''Besides, I can ask you at dinner tonight.''

''Which will be where?''

''The Caravelle, downtown. Help me get a taxi,'' she said.

Finding a taxi outside the air base was no problem. They got in the back of a beat-up old Ford that might have been blue once. The driver shot off into the traffic before he even knew the destination, weaving in and out of the bicycles and motor scooters. But the palm-lined streets were wide, and the driver knew the best route to the Caravelle after Gerber had shouted the name to him.

When they pulled up in front of the hotel, Gerber said, ''Get me a room when you check in. I shouldn't be more than an hour or so.''

''I hope you brought some civilian clothes,'' said Morrow.

''I brought a clean uniform and I'm afraid that's it.''

She got out, lifted her suitcase and camera bag out of the cab and shut the door. She leaned back in the window and said, ''I'll get the reservations. Hurry back because I want to eat.''

He smiled and said to the driver, ''Let's go.''

They took off in a squeal of tires and blaring of horns. As soon as they were away from the hotel, Gerber said, ''MACV compound, and when we get there, I'll want you to wait.''

They pulled up in front of the MACV HQ, and Gerber got out. He flashed his ID at the MPs stationed at the doors and went inside. He walked down the nearly deserted corridors, located the stairwell and descended to the basement level. He told the guard at the bottom that he wanted to see Jerry Maxwell.

''Sorry, sir, he's checked out for the day.''

"Did he say where he was going?" asked Gerber, trying not to sound irritated. In fact, he was mad as hell.

"No, sir. Would you care to leave a message?"

"Yes. Tell him that Mack Gerber would like him to call tonight. I'm at the . . . No, that's not such a hot idea. Tell him I'll see him at nine tomorrow."

The guard nodded. "Mack Gerber. Nine tomorrow."

Gerber went back upstairs and left the building. As he got into the cab, he instructed the driver to take him back to the Caravelle, and once in front of the hotel, he paid the driver, grabbed his knapsack and went inside. At the desk he asked for his room key and went upstairs, found the room and went in. He dropped his knapsack on the double bed and looked in the bathroom.

The telephone rang, and Gerber picked up the receiver.

"Hi, Mack. You ready to eat?" said an exuberant voice at the other end.

"I'll assume that it's Robin," Gerber said with a laugh. "No, I'm not ready. I just got in. Give me about twenty minutes."

"I'm in the rooftop bar and way ahead of you on the booze. You'd better hurry or I'll be too drunk to eat and too good to resist."

"Sounds like you want me to slow down," he said.

"Suit yourself," she responded. "See you in a few minutes."

Gerber hung up and looked around the room. Lamps on bedside tables flanked a large bed, and there was a tall wood wardrobe in the corner instead of a closet. A ceiling fan spun lazily overhead while a small air conditioner stuck in the room's only window wheezed faintly as it fought a losing battle to cool the room. Gerber dropped into the one chair to take off his boots. It was better than his hootch, he decided, and certainly cooler.

Opening his knapsack, he set out his shaving kit on the side of the bathroom sink. He tested the taps that hung over an old Victorian bathtub and rejoiced at the feel of hot and cold running water.

He shaved quickly and went back to change into his clean fatigues.

Gerber took the elevator to the rooftop bar and restaurant. The doors opened on a crowded bar and a wall of loud music. Most of the people inside were in civilian clothes, with just enough military uniforms sprinkled around to remind everyone of where they were. Gerber was the only one in fatigues, though. He pushed his way in toward the bar at the far side of the room, weaving among the tables, looking for Robin Morrow. To his right were a couple of steps that led to French doors and a rooftop terrace that overlooked Saigon. The doors were open, letting in the humidity that the air conditioners on the lower floors were trying to keep out.

To the left was a wall of windows, the blinds partially drawn to obscure the sun sitting on the horizon. A gigantic crystal chandelier that contained a hundred light bulbs threw a soft but bright light over the room.

At first Gerber couldn't find Morrow. She was lost in the crowd of diplomats, embassy workers, journalists and civilian contractors. Then, in a corner near one end of the French doors, he saw her stand and wave. He ducked around a massive man in an Air Force uniform wearing the eagles of a colonel.

"I thought you'd never get here," she said as he approached.

"I didn't think I'd find you when I saw the number of people in here. You sure you want to eat here?"

"It has passable food, and besides, anywhere else would be just as crowded," she answered.

Gerber sat down and looked across the table. Morrow was wearing a white silk dress that was cut low in the front. She had washed her hair and then brushed it until it reflected the light from the chandelier and sparkled with the oranges and reds of the setting sun.

She leaned forward slightly, her elbows on the table, and reached for Gerber's hand. He saw a bead of sweat between her breasts and noticed that her hair was damp where her bangs brushed her forehead.

"Not terribly cool in here," he said.

She smiled at him, showing her white teeth. "No. Not very." She locked her eyes on his and held them there, staring intensely at him. She held his hand in both of hers.

There was something about the look that Gerber didn't at first understand. When he did understand it, he wanted to break the eye contact, but found he couldn't. He felt himself respond to the look. His mind raced, and he knew everything that he wanted to say, but could not find the words.

Robin didn't move. She stuck the tip of her tongue between her teeth and slowly licked her lips. She squeezed Gerber's hand in hers. Gerber knew he was no match for her.

"Would you care to order?" asked a waiter who had appeared at their table.

Gerber exhaled as if he had suddenly just remembered how to breathe. With a physical effort he tore his eyes away from Robin's. "What?" he asked. Then added, "Not yet. We'll order in a minute."

As the waiter left, Morrow said, "We don't have to eat, you know."

"I thought you said you were starving," Gerber replied. But he knew exactly what she was talking about. Now, however, with the mood broken he could see only trouble on the horizon with her. She was a journalist who was looking for a story. She was a woman who could leave Vietnam and him the minute she felt like it. She wasn't trapped by Army regulations and orders. And to top it off, she was Karen Morrow's sister.

Gerber wondered if his reluctance to have anything to do with Robin was because of Karen. Was it the lies that Karen had told, or was it just that he didn't want a woman to complicate his life?

Suddenly he asked, "Are you married?"

She laughed at that. "Not even going steady. Yet."

He opened his mouth to ask her to go to his room and instead asked, "You care to dance? Some people are dancing."

"Anything you say. Anything at all."

He stood and came around the table, holding out his hand. He saw a flash of her thigh as she swung her legs out from under the table. The tight skirt that kissed her knees had a long slit up the side.

On the dance floor he held her loosely, carefully, as if she might break. He had his left hand on her bare back, and her skin was damp with a light coat of perspiration.

She moved with him for a moment and then pulled him close, holding him tightly. She rubbed herself against him, slipping a leg between his. When she looked up, she put her lips to his ear and said in a low voice, "You really want to stay here?"

"No," he said. "Not at all. Let's go to my room."

She took his hand and pulled him toward the elevator. Gerber asked, "Your purse?"

"I've nothing at the table."

As soon as the elevator doors closed on them and they were alone, Morrow turned and kissed him, forcing her tongue into his mouth, probing quickly, hungrily.

When the bell rang signaling they had arrived on the right floor, Morrow broke the kiss. "We're here," she said breathlessly.

At the door to his room, Gerber fumbled for the key, found it and opened up. Morrow pushed past him and then nearly dragged him in as she kicked the door shut. She kissed him again savagely. Gerber brought his hand up until he could feel her erect nipples beneath the cool silk of her dress.

She stepped back, staring straight into his eyes. Then she reached behind her and drew the zipper on her dress down slowly. She smiled and let her hand fall away. The dress slipped from her shoulders, revealing her to the waist.

Gerber moved to her and kissed her throat. Then he kissed her shoulder and chest, finally licking away the sweat that beaded between her breasts. At the same time he slipped the dress from her hips so that it pooled around her feet.

Her breath was coming in short bursts, as if she couldn't get enough air and had forgotten how to breathe. She clung to him.

Gerber lifted her up and carried her to the bed. He set her down and smiled. Under her dress she had only worn panties. No bra or stockings.

She reached up and unbuttoned his fatigue jacket. When she saw the shoulder holster, she said nothing; she just tugged on it until he helped her remove it. He took off his T-shirt and tossed it to the floor.

Morrow sighed and kissed his stomach as she tried to unfasten the waistband on his fatigue pants. She slipped her hand inside and squeezed gently.

"Will you make love to me?" she asked quietly.

"I'm not sure that I'm ready for this," he whispered. "I'm not ready to love someone."

"Doesn't matter. You will be."

For a moment he hesitated, letting his emotions run wild as he considered everything. Suddenly he realized that she was right. It didn't matter. He pushed his thumbs under the waistband of her panties, and as she lifted her hips, he slid them to her knees. Now he bent over her so that he could kiss her, his tongue deep in her mouth.

She laid back, her blond hair spread on the pillow, and said, "I love you, Mack."

10

MACV HEADQUARTERS, SAIGON

Gerber arrived at the headquarters building shortly before nine and went immediately downstairs, where the MP on duty logged him in and opened the gate. The door to Maxwell's office opened before Gerber could reach it, and Maxwell stepped out long enough to grab Gerber by the arm and haul him inside. Maxwell then looked out the door to see if anyone other than the MP was standing there.

"I don't have a lot of time this morning," Maxwell said. "I've got to brief the commander in an hour and a half, and I still don't know what I'm going to say."

Gerber fell into the chair beside the littered desk and noticed there were more Coke cans on it. There were also more manila folders, but none of them were stamped Secret. For his part, Jerry Maxwell didn't look very good. He was pale as if the blood had drained from his face. The dark circles under his eyes stood out in vivid contrast to his skin color. Gerber wondered if the man were going to fall over.

"I won't take much of your time," said Gerber.

"That's good." Maxwell took off his suit coat and hung it on the back of his chair. He took his pistol, a Swenson .45 Auto Custom, from his shoulder holster and put it in the middle drawer of his desk. Then he sat down and tried to look calm.

"Now, what can I do for you?" Maxwell asked.

"You remember that problem we discussed the last time I was here?" Gerber said.

Maxwell looked startled, but quickly covered it up. "What problem?" he replied.

"We talked about a Red Chinese operating out of Cambodia and how he was hurting our operations."

"Now hold it right there," interrupted Maxwell. "There are no Red Chinese in Cambodia. You never mentioned that."

"What the hell do you mean I never mentioned that?" Gerber spoke in a cold voice. "We sat right here and talked about Phoenix and the elimination of the top cadre on the enemy's side."

"Mack, I just don't know what you're talking about. You were never here. I never heard of this Phoenix." Maxwell picked up one of the Coke cans, shook it and said, "Damn!"

Gerber opened his mouth to respond, then changed his mind. It suddenly dawned on him what was happening. Maxwell and the CIA had stepped into something, and everyone was denying they knew anything about it. And he and his men were caught in the middle.

"I've got two men at LBJ charged with murder," said Gerber quietly. "They went on the mission that you and I discussed here because you said that such an operation was within the new guidelines issued by MACV."

Maxwell slammed a hand to the desktop. "You just won't get it, will you? You sit here pretending that you don't understand. There was no conversation in this room about any mission into Cambodia. There was no conversation about Phoenix. Nothing."

"There are logs proving I was here," said Gerber. Even in the air conditioning of the basement he was beginning to sweat. He felt it under his arms and trickling down his sides, but it wasn't the temperature that was causing it.

"There are no logs. You're on your own on this one. There is nothing that I can do and very little that you can do."

Gerber looked at the floor in front of his feet and then turned his gaze on Maxwell. "You bastard. You're going to sit there and let my men go down? You're going to do nothing to help?"

"I told you then that a nice quiet mission into Cambodia would be overlooked," said Maxwell. "I said *quiet* and if there was trouble you were on your own. Now there's trouble. More than I care to think about. Your boys weren't quiet. There's a stink all over Saigon, and you're going to have to live with it. You make too much noise in the wrong place, and you're going down, too."

"But—"

"There are no buts, Gerber. I'm giving you the facts of life, which, I might add, I shouldn't be doing." Maxwell opened one of the file folders that was lying in front of him. "Now, if you're through, I have work to do."

"Then you plan to do nothing?"

"About what?" asked Maxwell. "I have no idea what you're talking about. Now, don't take this personally, but would you kindly get the fuck out of here? I have work to do."

Gerber got to his feet and stared down at the CIA agent. Maxwell didn't meet his gaze. He felt sorry for the man. Felt sorry for him because he had to cave in to the pressure and had to do things that he might not like. Gerber could tell this game they were playing was eating him up, but he knew Maxwell well enough to know he wouldn't jeopardize his own career to save Fetterman and Tyme.

"There is one thing you might do," said Gerber. "Get two passports made out. One for Fetterman and one for Tyme, but don't use their real names."

Maxwell snapped the folder shut and sat staring at the wall. "You're asking for trouble. Now get out."

Outside, Gerber caught a ride back to the Caravelle with an Air Force major who was on his way to Tan Son Nhut, but didn't mind the detour. Robin was not in his room when he got there, and when he tried to find her, he discovered that she hadn't even registered in the hotel.

"That's just great," he said aloud. Maxwell wouldn't help get Fetterman and Tyme out of LBJ, and now Morrow had deserted him. He walked into the bathroom, jammed his shaving gear into the kit and then stuffed it into his knapsack. He took a quick look around the room and then went to the door. When he got to the front desk downstairs to pay his bill, he learned that Robin had taken care of it.

On the street Gerber waited for a taxi, passing up the chance to ride in a lambretta that contained two old women and a young man. He didn't feel like riding in the open air. He wanted the solitude of the back seat of a taxi.

The doorman finally got him one, and Gerber took it to the gate at Tan Son Nhut. He paid the driver, giving him a large tip for not talking, and headed toward Hotel Three. Then he had a better idea and changed direction so that he could see Bates before he went back to camp.

When Gerber got to the outer office of Bates's domain, a Spec Four told him to cool his heels while he checked with the colonel. Gerber sat down in one of the metal chairs that lined the perimeter of the room. There was a potted plant stuck in one corner and a table littered with back issues of *Stars and Stripes* and the *Army Times*. The wood floor was bare, and there was nothing hanging on the walls. The room was, however, air-conditioned, and a ceiling fan revolved slowly, trying vainly to stir up the air.

The Spec Four reappeared quickly and said, "Colonel Bates will see you."

Gerber got to his feet and entered the inner sanctum. It wasn't as fancy as Crinshaw's nor as severe as Gerber's. Somewhere in between. The desk was wood and recently polished. There was a blue couch along one wall and two blue armchairs in front of the desk. A rug that was little more than a bamboo mat was spread between the armchairs and the desk. Blinds on the window would kill the rays of the late-afternoon sun, but had nothing to do in the morning. Out the window Gerber could see part of the street and another building. He could hear the aircraft on the airfield, but it was a quiet sound, deadened by the distance.

"Morning, Colonel," he said.

"Have a chair, Mack." Bates leaned to his right as if to look around Gerber and raised his voice. "Petersen, I don't want to be interrupted. And close the damned door." He turned back to Gerber and said, "What's on your mind?"

"Simple question. How much do you know about what's happening?"

"Probably more than you think. General Crinshaw advised me of the arrests of your boys and the charges. He didn't bother filling in all the details. I was going to fly out this morning and see what I could do."

"Crinshaw briefed you?" asked Gerber, surprised.

"Somewhat. He didn't tell me all that much. You want to go over it now?"

For a moment Gerber hesitated. The mission that Fetterman had led was supposed to have been quiet. Now, it seemed, everyone was aware of what had gone on. Gerber couldn't see how telling Bates could make anything worse. Besides, he needed an ally. One who had access to the inner circles of Army politics in Saigon.

Quickly Gerber outlined what had happened, starting with the ambush of the Vietnamese ranger patrol, and continued right up to his most recent meeting with Maxwell. He left nothing out.

When Gerber finished, Bates said, "I'm not surprised."

"Now what the hell does that mean?"

"Think about it, Mack. Yours is not the only A-Team I have in the field and not the only one that works with the CIA. Who else do you think they sent out on Phoenix? You just happen to be the only one with your tit in the wringer."

"Why is that?"

Bates leaned forward and clasped his hands. "I would guess because of the target. Everyone else took out Vietcong and NVA cadre. Not Chinese, and not in Cambodia."

"So what do we do?"

Bates looked at his watch. "I think that maybe we should sit in on the Article 32 hearing. That might give us an idea of how much Crinshaw and his people know. Although, from what you've told me and what I've seen from Crinshaw's office, there doesn't seem to be much that they don't know. All the sessions are going to be classified, but I don't think we'll be excluded since we already know what's going on."

"And then what?"

"Then we can plan a strategy." Bates got up and walked around his desk. "I've got my jeep outside. We can drive it over. It's getting too hot to walk."

As he stood, Gerber said, "Where's this being held?"

Bates opened the door. "In Crinshaw's new building. He's emptied one of the conference rooms and set it up for the trial board. He's treating it as an unimportant case, and he's trying to keep the journalists from showing up."

Outside, they climbed into the jeep that Bates had signed out of the motor pool and rode across the base in silence. Outside Crinshaw's blue, two-story building, they pulled into a parking slot reserved for visitors. There were four MPs flanking the double doors of the entrance, but Bates and Gerber had no trouble getting by them. On the second floor there were two more guards stationed outside the trial room, and they wouldn't let either Bates or Gerber through without additional clearances.

"I would suggest, then," Bates told the MP staff sergeant, "that you get your boss over here, and I mean right now."

The sergeant stared at Bates for a second, wondering what he should do. Bates was a lieutenant colonel and seemed to know what he was doing. The sergeant turned to the corporal with him and said, "Go get the lieutenant."

The corporal ran off and returned a few minutes later with an officer carrying a clipboard. "What's the problem here?" he asked.

"No problem," said Bates. "Just tell your people to open up and let us go in."

"Ah, yes, sir," said the lieutenant. He read the names off both Bates's and Gerber's fatigues and flipped through the papers on the clipboard. "You're not on the list, sir."

"Then you had better get your list updated because we are going in there," said Bates.

The MP lieutenant folded the sheets over the top of his clipboard and read through the names a second time and then said, "If you'll wait here for just a moment, I'll make a call." He turned and trotted down the hall to a room near the stairway. A minute later he reappeared and said, "Let them in."

The staff sergeant stepped aside and opened the door. He said unnecessarily, "You may go right in, sir."

Gerber stopped just inside the room. On the far wall was a single window letting in the bright light of the early-afternoon sun. On either side of it stood flags, one the American stars and stripes and the other the South Vietnamese flag. In front of the window were five high-backed chairs for the members of the trial board, and in front of them was a long table of polished mahogany.

On the left side of the room, off by itself, was a small table and a single chair. There was a closed book on the table, and Gerber could see that it was a copy of the *Uniform Code of Military Justice*. The trial officer, the man who was supposed to make sure that military regulations weren't violated and that the law was followed, would sit there.

In front of the table for the trial board was the chair to be used for the witnesses. Farther into the room were two more tables separated by six or seven feet. Behind one were two chairs and behind the other were three. These would be used by the prosecutor and the defense. It wasn't quite what you'd find in *Perry Mason*, but it was a courtroom nonetheless.

Separated from the rest of the room by a flimsy wooden rail that looked as if it had just been erected was a group of chairs meant for the observers. There weren't many chairs, and with all the trouble he and Bates had had getting in, Gerber wondered who Crinshaw was expecting.

Bates and Gerber took seats in the back and waited. In a couple of minutes people began arriving . First there was an enlisted man who checked the trial officer's table and then set manila folders in front of each of the chairs of the trial board. The trial officer, a major wearing a dress green uniform, entered and sat down at his table. He glanced around quickly and then opened the book sitting in front of him.

Moments later Fetterman and Tyme entered, each escorted by two MPs. Fetterman stopped and leaned toward Gerber. "Glad to see you, Captain. How are things?"

"I should be asking you that," said Gerber. "They treating you all right?"

"Just fine," said Fetterman.

Gerber turned his attention to Tyme. "Anything you need, Justin?"

"Just get us out of here," he said.

Just before they moved off, Fetterman said, "Thanks for coming."

The defense counsel followed a moment later, and the prosecutor after that. Gerber recognized the prosecutor as the major who had been with Crinshaw when Fetterman and Tyme had been arrested.

After they all had found their seats, the door opened again and one of the MPs announced, "Gentlemen. General Crinsnaw."

Crinshaw, with four other officers, all colonels and all unknown to Gerber, swept into the room and headed for the trial-board table. Crinshaw took his place at the center, picked up the gavel and banged it once.

"This is a preliminary hearing and is now in session," he said.

"Can he do that?" asked Gerber.

"If you mean start the hearing, yes," said Bates quietly. "If you mean act as senior officer, I think that technically he can. That is, if he didn't bring the charges. He may have directed that someone else do it so that he could preside."

"Hardly the impartial judge we would have wanted," grumbled Gerber.

Crinshaw looked at Gerber and Bates and said, "You have no authority to be here, and if you insist on disrupting this hearing, I will have you ejected."

When he had everyone's attention, Crinshaw said, "This is an Article 32 hearing to determine whether there is sufficient evidence to charge either or both of the accused men. It will be conducted in a manner set forth in the *Uniform Code of Military Justice*. All questions about procedure will be directed to Major Winston, who will act as the trial officer. Now, Major McKowen, would you care to proceed?"

Major James McKowen, the prosecution officer, stood and said, "I would like to call Lieutenant Le Phouc Khai."

Fetterman turned in his chair and shot a glance at Gerber.

Gerber shrugged in answer and leaned close to Bates. "Well, that explains part of it," he said. "It's one of Minh's strike company commanders trying to make a name for himself. He can't know too much."

Khai, wearing a new tailored uniform that displayed all of his various badges, ribbons and insignia, entered the hearing room looking straight ahead. He was tall for a Vietnamese, about five-foot-eight or -nine, thin and had short black hair. Like most Vietnamese he had a rounded face, dark-brown eyes and a small nose. He moved straight to the witness chair and was sworn in.

The trial officer, Winston, came from behind his table and asked, "Would you like a translator?"

"No, sir. I am fluent in English, as well as French and Spanish," said Khai in an accented voice that was almost impossible to understand.

"All right, Lieutenant," McKowen began as Winston returned to his seat. "For the record, would you please give us your name, rank and your current assignment."

"Yes, sir. I am First Lieutenant Le Phouc Khai, and I am Strike Company A commander and at the Special Forces camp designated A five, five, five."

"How long have you held that position?"

Khai looked at the prosecutor and then at the trial board. "Six months," he said. "I replaced Captain Minh, who was elevated on the death of Captain Trang."

"You said that you are the A Company commander. Would you tell us exactly what that entails?"

"I am responsible for the command and control of the company. My duties include assigning the men to details, overseeing the supply function, paying the men, coordinating the training and the patrols."

McKowen smiled and asked, "So you are aware of all the patrols?"

"Yes, sir."

"And you work closely with the Americans?"

"Yes. I act as a liaison between them and the Vietnamese assigned to me."

"All right," said McKowen, summing up. "Then it would be fair to say that in your capacity as company commander, you know what is happening in the camp on a day-to-day basis. You know who is detailed to accomplish what. You might say that there are no missions, no patrols, no operations accomplished without assistance from you."

"That is correct."

"All right, Lieutenant. Would you please tell us what prompted your report?"

Wilson jumped to his feet. "Objection. We have no knowledge of a report."

Crinshaw glanced at the trial officer, who nodded and said, "Counsel is correct. Major McKowen, you seem to have leaped over some ground here."

"I was trying to save a little time," he responded.

"Don't save it," snapped Wilson. "These men aren't going anywhere, and we all have plenty of time."

"That will be enough from you," said Crinshaw. "Watch your mouth, boy."

McKowen returned to his table and picked up his legal pad as if to check it for instructions. He said, "You recently became aware of some unusual activity near your camp?"

"Yes, sir. I knew that the Americans had run a cross-border operation."

"Objection!" shouted Wilson.

"Overruled," said Winston before Crinshaw could get a word in. When Wilson made no move to stand down, the trial officer added, "You can object to everything the prosecutor says when introducing his evidence, but we must assume that a report was made. Otherwise, none of us would be here. Therefore, the question stands."

"Thank you," said McKowen. He looked back at Khai. "The Americans were running an operation across the Cambodian border?"

"Objection," said Wilson. "A leading question. It hasn't been established as the Cambodian border."

Before the trial officer could respond, McKowen asked, "Which border?"

"The Cambodian border," Khai replied.

Crinshaw spoke up. "You see, boy? All your objecting is just drawing this thing out. We all know what border he was talking about. Now you just watch what you're doing."

Wilson didn't say a word.

McKowen proceeded to get Khai to talk about his knowledge of the operation that Fetterman had run into Cambodia and of the VC base he found there. Gerber was stunned as Khai talked about the mission as if he had an intimate knowledge of it, describing some things about it he couldn't possibly have known.

During the questioning Bates leaned close to Gerber and asked, "How could he know all this? Somebody on your team talking out of turn?"

"No one," whispered Gerber. "I can't figure it out. Nobody on my team would have told him this, and ne won't talk to the Tai."

And then Gerber did know how Khai could have such detailed information. There was one source other than Fetterman and his patrol. The enemy. The VC at the Cambodian camp knew exactly what had happened and knew when it had happened. Khai would have seen Fetterman and Tyme leave, he might have seen them zeroing the weapon or loading the special ammo for it, and he had seen them return. He could have put two and two together and figured it out. That is, if the VC intelligence system was good enough to get the information to Khai, and Gerber knew that it was. The conclusion was obvious to Gerber. Khai, one of Minh's strike company commanders, was a VC. The trouble was, how was he going to prove it?

The questioning went on for nearly two hours, and when it was finished, Crinshaw asked if the defense had any questions for the witness. Wilson stood up, moved to the witness chair and stared down at Khai.

"Lieutenant," he said, "were you on the operation that you just described in such detail?"

"No."

"Then how do you know so much about it?"

"I saw Sergeant Fetterman and Sergeant Tyme leave the compound. I saw Captain Gerber and a strike company leave, and I saw them all return. I heard from many people exactly what the mission was. There is no doubt."

"Who are these many people? Were they on the mission?"

"I have names."

"Would you share some of them with us?" asked Wilson.

Now it was McKowen's turn. "Objection."

The trial officer flipped through his book rapidly and then said, "The names do not have to be introduced at this time. The defense, however, has a right to those names outside of this proceeding."

Wilson nodded and then asked, "You didn't see any of the mission that you described."

"No, sir. But I talked to people who did."

"Then what we have is heresy evidence. You can't actually testify that—"

"Objection," McKowen said loudly. "The witness has answered the question. His position gives him knowledge of the activities of the unit and allows him to testify about the activities of the unit."

"That is not entirely true," snapped Wilson. "Many military operations take place without large numbers of people knowing about them, especially company commanders who are not directly involved. Just because he was on the Special Forces camp doesn't mean that he knows what was happening."

"Don't be naive," snorted McKowen.

There was a sharp bang as Crinshaw rapped his gavel for order. "That will be enough of that. Captain Wilson," he said, "you have asked your question, and it has been answered. Is there anything else that you want to talk about?"

Wilson stood staring, first at Crinshaw, then at McKowen and finally at Khai. At last he walked back to his seat and said, "No further questions."

"Major McKowen, do you have anything more?" asked Crinshaw.

"No, sir."

"You may step down, Lieutenant," said Winston.

"Major Winston," said Crinshaw, "what is the next step?"

"You have to ask if defense has anyone they want to put on the stand. I might remind counsel that this is not a court-martial, merely a hearing to determine if there will be one."

Gerber watched as Wilson quietly discussed something with Fetterman and Tyme. Gerber stood up and stretched, realizing that he had missed lunch. He sat down again and waited.

As Wilson got to his feet, he said, "The defense has nothing to present at this time."

Crinshaw smiled and glanced at Winston, who asked, "Do either of the men wish to make a statement?"

"Not at this time," said Wilson.

Crinshaw rapped the table with his gavel and said, "We will adjourn for a few minutes to deliberate."

"General," said Winston, "I believe you wish to call a recess."

Crinshaw waved a hand. "Whatever. You just keep everyone in here while we go talk about this."

As soon as Crinshaw was out of the hearing room, Gerber asked Bates, "What the hell kind of kangaroo court was that?"

"I think it was supposed to be some kind of arraignment hearing. I'm not sure myself."

"They'll never get away with it. A bunch of kids playing trial could have done a better job. It will never stand up on appeal. There were so many violations of Fetterman's and Tyme's rights and trial procedures that it'll get thrown out. Hell, even I can see that."

"I think," said Bates, "what the general has in mind is not so much legally proving that Fetterman and Tyme are guilty. He seems content with destroying their military careers. Even if everything is thrown out on appeal, there will always be the stink of it in their records. Everyone will know they were cleared on a technicality. Actually, it's a brilliant maneuver. He doesn't have enough to convict them, so he rigs it to get a conviction that is thrown out. It wouldn't matter if they were innocent. All that matters is they were arrested and tried.''

Gerber ran a hand through his hair. ''That doesn't make sense.''

''Sure it does. Lizzie Borden was acquitted in the ax murder of her parents, but look at the schoolchildren's rhyme. It says she was guilty, and nearly everyone believes it. Hell, even Fetterman's record can't save him. The people at his new post will figure he's some kind of rogue that can't be trusted in a peacetime assignment. And Tyme is through immediately, no matter what.''

''Okay,'' admitted Gerber grudgingly. ''It's a brilliant maneuver. But what does it gain him?''

''First, it removes your team sergeant and a damned good weapons expert. Next, he brings you up on charges because you're the commander. If you didn't know they went to Cambodia, then you're incompetent. If you did know, then you're as guilty as they are. In the end you're destroyed, too.''

''That's all providing that Crinshaw has a trial. It might end here and now.''

''Mack, don't you be naive, too.''

They lapsed into silence. Gerber watched Fetterman and Tyme talking together quietly. Wilson had gone over to Winston and was talking to him. McKowen was at the window, his hands on the frame as he stared into the bright afternoon sun.

A few minutes later the door opened again and Crinshaw reappeared. He went immediately to his seat. The other four officers followed and sat down. None of them looked at either Fetterman or Tyme.

Crinshaw banged his gavel for attention and said, ''After a careful review of what we have heard today, and taking into account that Lieutenant Khai's testimony is open to some question, we find that we do have reason to proceed to trial.''

Wilson was on his feet immediately, but before he could speak, Crinshaw shouted, ''The decision has been made, Captain!''

Tyme turned toward Gerber with a scared look in his eyes and said, ''Captain?''

"Sergeant Tyme, let's have your attention up here," demanded Crinshaw.

"I didn't think he'd actually go through with it," said Gerber. "I thought this would be enough for him."

Crinshaw started giving instructions. He told Fetterman and Tyme that they would be returned to LBJ to await their court-martial. The defense would have two days to prepare the case.

Gerber sat there feeling as badly as he'd felt since he'd arrived in Vietnam. A half dozen irrational plans flashed through his mind, but none of them stood a chance of working. He had to get out of the room and into the field where there might be something he could accomplish. He got to his feet and walked over to Fetterman and Tyme. "Don't worry," he said. "We're working to get you out of this."

Then Crinshaw began banging his gavel and shouting for order.

Bates stepped close to Gerber and said, "Let's get out of here. There's nothing more to be done."

"Yeah," said Gerber. "I know." As Bates left, he hesitated long enough to say to Fetterman and Tyme, "If there is anything you need, you let me know." With that he turned and walked out of the room.

Gerber caught up to Bates in the hallway, and together they walked to the first floor and stepped out into the blast furnace of the afternoon.

"Well, that was just fucking great," said Gerber.

"What are you plans now?"

Gerber climbed into the jeep and stared through the cracked windshield. "Head back to camp."

Bates started the jeep. "I think he has you boxed on this one, Mack. I can't see a way out, and he's holding all the cards."

Gerber smiled at that and said, "Then we've got to find a new deck." He remembered a couple of things that had been said in the hearing and what he had been told by Maxwell. All of it led to one point, and Gerber was beginning to see that point. It wasn't a full-blown idea yet, but the details were beginning to fill in. His head swirled with them, and it was now only a question of sorting them all out.

11

HOTEL THREE, TAN SON NHUT AIR FORCE BASE, SAIGON

Gerber lifted his knapsack out of the back of the jeep and said, "Thanks for the lift. I'll be in touch."

"Mack," said Bates, "be careful on this one. Crinshaw is looking to hang you, too. Don't go off half-cocked."

"I won't. I think I know what I have to do, but I'll check it out carefully before I act. You watch out for my boys."

"I will. Just be careful." Bates shifted into first, turned the wheel and stepped on the gas.

When he was gone, Gerber entered the terminal building to check on the flights out toward Tay Ninh and his camp. He was halfway to the wooden counter when he heard someone call his name. He stopped and looked around. Finally he said, "Robin. What the hell are you doing here?"

"Nice greeting, Gerber. What the hell do you think I'm doing here? I'm waiting for you."

"I thought you'd found another assignment," he said. After the empty room at the hotel, he had assumed she had split for something else. Besides, he'd had other things on his mind. He was happy to see her now, but what could he tell her about his troubles? Hell, she was a journalist, and this was a big-time story. A Pulitzer prize story if ever there was one.

"Are you crazy?" she demanded. "The big story is going on with you."

"Suppose I say you can't go back to the camp."

She stared at him, looking straight into his eyes. She smiled and said, "All you can do is keep me off the aircraft that you take back. I'll grab the next one. They'll let me fly out of here because I still have the letter of authorization from General Crinshaw. I suppose that you could put me bodily on a helicopter to return me, but I'd just come back."

"There are people I could call. People at MACV headquarters and at the embassy."

"And I could tell Crinshaw that you refuse to cooperate. I could ask him what's going on because you refuse to cooperate," she said harshly.

Gerber glanced around the terminal building. This late in the day there weren't more than two dozen people in it. A couple of very young sergeants in old, faded jungle fatigues wanting a flight back to their unit caught his eye, as did an Army nurse with first lieutenant bars pinned to the front of her fatigue jacket, scissors stuck in the pocket and black hair piled on top of her head.

Gerber took Morrow's arm and led her to the corner where there were a couple of beat-up chairs for the passengers to use while they waited. He sat down with her and leaned close so that he could speak softly. "I really wish that you'd reconsider your decision."

"Which decision is that?" she asked.

He looked at her closely. She was dressed in a khaki bush jacket and pants. She wore jungle boots, the new ones that had a green nylon panel on them that let the feet breathe. A camera was hung around her neck.

He thought about the night they had spent together and wondered why he was trying so hard to send her away. Anyone else in the Army would probably be trying to convince her to come with him. It was just that the timing was so lousy, and timing was turning out to be everything.

"Which decision?" she asked again.

"Coming out to the camp. There's no story there."

"This is probably the biggest story I've ever come into contact with out there."

"But you can't use it," said Gerber sternly.

"Why the hell not?" she demanded.

"Let's talk about this later," said Gerber. "I've got to check in at the counter to see what's scheduled through. I'll put your name down, too."

"Don't bother," she said. "I already took care of that. If something comes in that's headed in the right direction, they'll let me know."

Gerber dropped back into his chair. He took off his beret and set it on the table next to him. He wiped a hand across his forehead and then rubbed it against his chest.

When he didn't say anything, Morrow asked again, "Why can't I use the story?"

"Because there isn't one."

"You have two men arrested for crossing into—"

"Robin, will you shut up," interrupted Gerber. "This is not the time or the place to go into this. There are too many people around who could hear too much. All right?"

"We're not through with this discussion yet," she warned him.

"We'll take it up at the camp when we have the chance," he said.

Just at that moment the clerk who had been working behind the counter approached and said, "Ma'am, I've an aircraft from Tay Ninh that's going back now, if you'd still like a lift."

She smiled and said, "Yes, thank you. Captain Gerber will be going, too."

"That's fine." He leaned down so that he could point through the window. "It's the one with the knight's shield on the nose sitting on Pad Five."

They landed at the camp about an hour later, having had to stop in Cu Chi to pick up another passenger. They also touched down outside of Go Dau Ha to drop off mail. At the camp Morrow grabbed her suitcase and camera bag and headed to her hootch without talking to anyone.

Bocker pretended not to notice. Gerber told Bocker that he wanted to see Kepler right away and that he needed to talk to Captain Minh. With that he went to his hootch to wait.

Minh was the first to arrive. He knocked once and entered when Gerber yelled for him to come in. Minh sat down in one of the lawn chairs and said, "Welcome back, old boy."

"I'm afraid you won't think that way after I tell you what I've learned." Gerber took the chair behind his desk and leaned forward.

"Yes?" said Minh.

"Your Lieutenant Khai is a VC," he said abruptly.

"What? How do you know?" Minh was surprised, but unflappable.

"He knows too much about Fetterman's last mission. If you didn't tell him and I didn't, there is only one source he could have used. The VC."

"Can you prove that?"

"No. No, damn it, I can't."

Minh stood up and walked around his chair. He stopped and faced Gerber. "But you are sure? No mistake?"

"No mistake. What are you going to do about it?"

"Don't worry, Captain, I'll handle it quickly and quietly."

"I must warn you that Khai has an important role in the upcoming trial. You'll have to allow for that."

Minh nodded. "So there will be a trial, after all. What do you plan to do about Fetterman and Tyme?"

"I'm not sure yet. I have a couple of ideas." He looked up at the knock on his door. "Enter," he called.

Kepler stood there wearing dirty fatigues that were badly stained with sweat. "You wanted to see me, sir?" he asked.

"I've some things to do," said Minh. "I'll meet with you later, Captain, to finish our discussion."

When Minh was gone, Gerber said, "Have a seat, Derek. I've got a couple of questions to ask you."

"Yes, sir."

"First, do you have any information about the Red Chinese in Cambodia?"

"You mean officially?"

"Exactly."

"Nothing officially. There seems to be a tacit agreement among all the combatants to ignore the Red Chinese. No one wants to admit that the Chinese are helping the North and the VC. I think that if we had a body dressed in a Red Chinese uniform hanging in the wire, no one would take notice of it." Kepler smiled at that.

"Which means?" asked Gerber.

"Which means there are no Red Chinese in Cambodia. In other words, the man smoked by Fetterman and Tyme must have been a civilian."

"Oh, for Christ's sake."

"Yes, sir. Exactly," said Kepler. "If we were to obtain hard evidence of the Red Chinese in Cambodia, there will be a real effort to bury it."

"Okay. Second," continued Gerber, "what is the extent of the Ho Chi Minh Trail? How far south does it go?"

"The latest evidence I have suggests that it turns to the east just north of Highway 1, and, in fact, might incorporate portions of the highway," answered Kepler.

"Then if Sergeant Fetterman had gone far enough to the south, he could have avoided crossing the Trail?"

Kepler rubbed his chin. "I'm not sure, sir. Our information on it is sketchy at best. It may run all the way to the Gulf of Siam. I'm just giving you the latest that I have."

Just then there was another knock on the door. Gerber opened it and found Sergeant Bocker holding up a small package. "This arrived with the afternoon supplies, Captain," he said. "I thought you might want it."

"Thanks, Galvin," said Gerber. He took the package and turned it over to look at the return address. It had come from Maxwell in Saigon, according to the coded return address. "I'll want you back here in about an hour. Spread the word. Find Lieutenant Bromhead and have him meet me in thirty minutes." Gerber turned to Kepler. "You be here, too."

"BEFORE WE START this briefing," said Gerber, "I thought you would all want to know that Sergeant Fetterman and Sergeant Tyme are going to face a court-martial murder. Crinshaw and his kangaroo court decided that this afternoon.''

''Jesus!'' said Bocker.

''Exactly,'' said Gerber. ''The purpose of this meeting is to determine what we can do to get them out of LBJ. I've made a few preliminary plans and want to get some feedback from you people on this.''

Gerber crossed the room to the map he had tacked to the wall. He pulled the cloth that covered it free and said, ''Our mission is to return to the VC camp that Sergeants Fetterman and Tyme discovered and gather evidence that the Red Chinese are there.''

Bromhead nodded as he studied the map. He said slowly, as if formulating a plan as he spoke, ''To prove Fetterman's innocence, we have to show that he was chasing an enemy soldier into Cambodia. But I can't see where this is going to help us.''

''Ah, Johnny, my boy,'' said Gerber, almost mocking the way Fetterman sometimes talked to Tyme, ''it can't do anything but help us, even if Fetterman is not innocent. He, or rather Sergeant Tyme, did shoot the man. And they did cross the border. The important question is, what had our Chinese friend done just prior to crossing the border back into Cambodia?''

A smile spread across Tyme's face. ''The South Vietnamese rangers.''

''Exactly!''

''And suddenly,'' said Bromhead, ''Crinshaw begins to get pressure from all over to end the trial. Fetterman and Tyme were avenging the deaths of the South Vietnamese. They showed poor judgment crossing the border, but who could blame them after what they had just seen.''

''And,'' added Gerber, ''we have our government wanting the trial to end because the victim was a Red Chinese, and that is going to come out. The last thing anyone wants is for the Red Chinese to have an excuse to get into the war on an overt level. Not with nearly a billion of them on the other side of the North Vietnamese border.''

"A masterstroke of intrigue," said Minh, "but for one flaw. What are you going to do to put pressure on the brigadier?"

Gerber turned and looked at the Vietnamese officer. "I'm not going to have to. That will come from above."

"You have all your ducks lined up, but for one," said Minh. "You waltz into Crinshaw's office and present this to him, but he has no incentive to let your Sergeants Fetterman and Tyme go. He still has them in jail."

"We tell him," said Gerber, "that we are prepared to go public with this. Give the information to the press. That is, as a final resort."

"You could go him one better," said Minh. "Take Miss Morrow with you."

"That's definitely out," said Gerber. "I'm not going to take a reporter, a woman no less, into Cambodia, for any reason."

"Oh, but you must," maintained Minh. "She can provide the one thing that you can't. She can go to her publisher with the evidence and be believed because she has no ax to grind. With her help you can tell Crinshaw that if Fetterman and Tyme don't get off free, the world will learn exactly who they shot."

"I said that was out. We can do this without bringing her into it."

"What's the plan, Captain?" asked Bromhead.

"The mission is simple. We go to Cambodia and gather evidence of the North Vietnamese, the VC and the Red Chinese. We establish the exact location and size of the camp and document it with photographs. We find out exactly who is using it. Remember that we need the evidence as a lever. It doesn't have to be proof that would stand up in court, only sufficient to raise questions.

"Johnny, I'm afraid that you're going to have to remain here in camp, covering our rear." He saw that Bromhead was going to protest and held up a hand. "I know. It stinks, but somebody has got to hold down the fort. If I stay, then I can be arrested. If I'm out on patrol, then Crinshaw can't arrest me until he can find me. I'll leave T.J. and Cat here with you, so you'll have someone to talk to."

Reluctantly Bromhead nodded.

"We don't want to engage the enemy," continued Gerber. "We are an intelligence-gathering operation. We are going to find the evidence of the involvement of the other Communist parties so that we can force Crinshaw to drop the charges.

"We leave in the morning. We'll spend the first day moving carefully toward the border, so that any surveillance of our activity won't tip our hand. We cross at night."

"Will this be a sterile mission?" asked Kepler.

"No. We're going in carrying our own equipment and as American soldiers. I'm getting a little tired of fighting the war as if it doesn't exist. The only important point to remember is that no one gets left behind."

"How long are we going to be out?" Kepler continued.

"It better be less than a week. We can't spend too much time screwing around out there, or Crinshaw is going to have the trial over and Fetterman and Tyme shipped to Leavenworth.

"If there are no other questions, then everyone is dismissed for now. Detailed briefing at 2200 hours."

MINH AND ROBIN MORROW CAUGHT Gerber outside the team house as he was heading there for dinner.

"I have taken the liberty of suggesting that Miss Morrow talk to you about the patrol coming up," Minh said.

"Captain Minh," said Gerber, "I don't like being put on the spot like this."

"I'm sorry, old boy, but I believe I'm right on this one. The only way you'll win is by having a helping hand from the local newspaper."

"And I don't understand," Morrow nearly shouted, "what the big deal is."

"The big deal," Gerber shouted right back, "is that you are a reporter and a woman."

"What difference does that make?"

Gerber took a deep breath. "I think you can figure it out."

"You worried about me getting killed?"

"That's the least of the problems. If you get killed, it will probably mean that the rest of us are dead, too, and there would be nothing Crinshaw could do to us. Although getting a reporter killed out here wouldn't do us a whole lot of good when the news was released back home."

Morrow ran a hand through her hair. "Then what's the big deal?"

For a moment Gerber hesitated, wondering how to phrase it. Finally he just blundered ahead. "What happens if you're captured? There would be no way that we could protect you, and you surely can figure out what that would mean."

"Are you talking about rape? Are you suggesting that I not be allowed to go along because I might be raped?"

"Well, that's one good reason," admitted Gerber.

"Look, Gerber," said Morrow, "I don't want to be put in the position of saying that rape isn't traumatic for women, but I will say there is nothing that the enemy can do to me that is any worse than what they can do to a man. My sex doesn't make me any more vulnerable to torture.

"I had this fight with my editors when I wanted to come over here. They told me about the hardships. Living out of a suitcase or a knapsack. A lack of privacy. That I could be killed, captured or raped.

"And my response was always the same: if a man is killed, is he any less dead? If a man is tortured, is he any less hurt? I think I could handle the trauma of rape. I might be wrong, but that's no reason to leave me behind. How well could you stand up to torture or homosexual rape? Huh?"

She stopped speaking because she could feel the anger swelling in her again. Anger because she was not allowed to do her job. Anger because men were holding her back, protecting her from imagined problems.

She felt a knot form in her stomach and her knees shaking. She took several deep breaths trying to rein in her emotions so that she could tell them all what she thought of their reason for holding her back.

She turned to Gerber and said, "I've been through some of the training that you had to go through to get here. I stomped through swamps full of snakes and alligators. I went without food because we couldn't find any, and when we captured the cute little bunny, I made the men let me cut its throat to prove to them that I had the stomach to do it. Some of the training I had to take to prove to my editors that I could do it, and some of it I took because I wanted to know what it was like to be in the Army.

"So I won't fall down because we've walked a long way. I won't cry because of the horror I see out there. At least I won't until I get back here. I won't endanger your patrol by slowing you down or stepping on twigs, or even slapping an insect that is crawling on my neck."

"Or letting the motor of the film advance on your camera announce our presence."

"I learned my lesson there," she said, her face coloring slightly. "And I want to know where it says that men are somehow better able to handle combat. I want to know why anything that happens to me will be that much worse than anything that happens to the men. If you could tell me that men somehow held up better, and you could prove it, I would pick up my camera bag and go home. But you can't."

Gerber held up a hand, trying to stop her.

Morrow kept right on talking. "In Korea ten percent of the prisoners couldn't handle being captured and just rolled over and died. They didn't deal with it very well."

Minh, who had been standing by watching and listening to the entire tirade with an amused smile, said, "You know, some of the best armies ever seen have included women. Even in combat roles. May I remind you, Captain, that the Vietcong are an equal-opportunity army?"

"Damn it, you're supposed to be helping me," said Gerber.

"Why?" demanded Morrow. "You should listen to him."

"Now, old boy," continued Minh, "the reason for taking Miss Morrow with you is to document everything. She has a forum for publication if your plans fail. And I will tell you right now that anything you get is going to be buried by either your government or mine. Robin will be able to get it released, which is the only threat that is going to work."

"I don't know," said Gerber. He had to admit that Minh's arguments made sense. But that still didn't get Morrow on the patrol. Even if he could logically understand what was being said, emotionally he couldn't handle it. It just wasn't...what? Normal? Right?

"Captain Minh is right," Morrow said. "Suppose you gather your information and give it to Crinshaw and he classifies it all by claiming national security. Then what do you do? If I'm there, I can go to the network."

"Let's, for the minute, say that you're right," Gerber said. "There's still a problem. This is a hell of a story. What's to stop you from printing it, anyway? We help you gather it, and then you stab us in the back by using it even if it's not needed. The only reason for this mission is to get Sergeant Fetterman and Sergeant Tyme out of jail."

"Captain," said Morrow, her voice softening slightly, "I'm as interested in freeing your men as you are. Sergeant Fetterman never treated me as anything but an equal. He helped me when I needed it. He doesn't deserve what has happened to him, and I'll pledge to you that anything I see out there will not be used by me while it can still hurt any of you, or until you tell me that I should go to the network with it. Besides, after last night I thought you knew me better than that. I just didn't fully understand what was going on here. Captain Minh made it clear."

Gerber looked at Minh. He didn't want Morrow on the patrol for a number of reasons, a couple of them personal, but all the arguments made sense. Especially the one about needing the extra leverage to spring Fetterman and Tyme.

Reluctantly he said, "Okay. You go. But we can't compromise anything for your convenience. You have to hold up your end."

"Did you hear me ask for a compromise? Did you hear me say that I couldn't hack it?"

"There'll be a briefing tonight at 2200 hours. You be there. Without your notebook or tape recorder. We don't want anything written down that would suggest we planned this out."

"Understood, Captain," said Morrow "You won't regret this '

At 2200 hours all the Americans left in the camp were in the team house. Bocker, who had left one of the Vietnamese on radio duty so that he could attend, was handing out beer from the tired old refrigerator. Anderson had taken two and given one of them to Kittredge. They sat together at one of the rear tables. Kepler had a map of his own and was sitting near the front so that he would be close to Gerber and could verify what the captain was saying. He had checked his intel files before coming to the meeting. McMillan and Washington, the two team medics, sat eating sandwiches at a table to the left, and Bromhead stood at the door watching. He was to make sure that no one approached too close once the briefing began.

Gerber stood at the front of the room with a large map of the immediate area tacked on the wall behind him. On it he had traced a route. He checked his watch once, saw that everyone was present and began.

"After talking to Krung and a couple of the other Tai, and coupling that information with the aerial recon photos that Sergeant Kepler reviewed, we have pretty well established the exact location of the new camp. If we leave here at 0600 hours tomorrow, we'll have all day to get to the border. We rest there, cross in the dark and keep moving until morning. Given the distances and the route we're going to use, it should take three days."

Gerber went on, detailing the plan over the next fifteen minutes. He showed them the route of march, outlining probable areas of danger based on the latest information that Kepler had gotten from Special Forces headquarters in Nha Trang. He talked about the supplies they would take, the weapons they would carry and then explained the necessity of taking Robin Morrow. There were a few raised eyebrows, but no one commented. When he finished, he answered questions and then explained in greater detail why it was necessary for Morrow to accompany them.

By 2300 hours they had finished the briefing. Gerber dismissed the men, telling them to get ready to move out at first light. Then he drew Bromhead off to one side.

"Johnny, there is one thing that you're going to have to do. I wouldn't ask you to do this except that there's no way I can lead the patrol and take care of it."

"Doesn't matter, Captain. I'll do what I have to do."

"You'll have to keep a watch on that trial in Long Binh. If it looks bad for Fetterman and Tyme, you'll have to get something to them. There's a package in my hootch containing new passports for both of them. You might have to deliver them."

"No problem, Captain."

"You might want to think about this for a couple of minutes before you agree. Do you fully understand what it means?"

"If I'm caught sneaking passports in to them, I'll be arrested."

"Exactly."

"Doesn't matter, Captain. I'll do what I have to do. If it comes to that, I'll get them out of there."

"I'm sorry to have to put you on the spot like this, Johnny, but someone has to be available to do it."

"It's all right. We're getting a little short for this shit, but I'm happy that you feel you can trust me to spring them."

12

SOUTH GATE OF U.S.
SPECIAL FORCES CAMP
A-555

The patrol had gathered at the gate just before six. Gerber set his pack down near a low sandbagged wall that was a second line of defense if the VC got that close, and pulled the map from his pocket. He folded it so that the area they would be marching through would be on top and showed it to Krung and the three Tai who would be going on the mission with them.

Morrow stood to one side, watching. She was dressed in a camouflaged jungle suit borrowed from Minh. She didn't have a steel pot, but wore a boonie hat pulled down low to hide her blond hair. She had a pistol belt around her waist that held two canteens, a large bowie knife and a small first-aid kit. She had a small pack containing her C-rats, a poncho liner and a roll of toilet paper scrounged from the team house. And she had a small camera bag for the single 35 mm that she carried.

The other Americans on the patrol—Smith, Kepler, Bocker, Kittredge and Ian McMillan, the team senior medic—all carried three canteens. They also carried a pistol each, extra ammo, grenades, combat knives and flares. Bocker had the additional duty of carrying the PRC-10, and McMillan had his medical kit. Kittredge was responsible for the M-60 machine gun and two belts of ammo for it. Smith had an M-79 grenade launcher strapped to his back. All that was in addition to their rifles. Each carried an M-14 because it used the same 7.62 mm ammo as the M-60.

Gerber sat down in front of his pack, eased the straps over his shoulders, buckled it and stood up, shifting the weight so that it rode high on his back. He leaned forward, moved the pack around and then stood straight. He reached up to where his Randall combat knife was taped upside down to the harness of his web gear, making sure it would come free in a hurry without hitting the other equipment he carried.

Gerber checked the sky and saw low-hanging black clouds swirling to the west, indicating the possibility of rain sometime soon. Back to the east the sun was climbing in the sky. It all meant that the day would be very humid. Gerber was already beginning to sweat, and all he had done was stand up.

"Sergeant Smith," he said, "take Sergeant Krung and walk point."

"Yes, sir."

"Johnny," said Gerber, turning his attention to the young lieutenant, "I'm counting on you in case things go bad for Fetterman and Tyme."

"I understand, Captain."

Before he could say more, T. J. Washington, the big black assistant medical NCO, appeared from between two of the hootches in the Tai area. He shouted, "Captain. Hold up."

"What's up?" asked Gerber as the man halted in front of him.

"Radio message out of Saigon. They've got someone coming out to talk to you this morning."

"No call sign?" asked Gerber.

"Came through the Operations section of one of the helicopter units down there. Didn't say who the passenger was, only that he would be out here this morning and that you should meet him at the pad."

Gerber shook his head. "I'm on patrol. You tell him that I wasn't here when the message came in."

"He's going to want to know why I didn't radio the information to you, sir," said Washington.

"Because we're on radio silence and you couldn't see any reason to break it. Once he gets here, if he insists, you ask Lieutenant Bromhead about it." Gerber glanced at Bromhead. "I trust that you'll deny him permission."

"Can't have people calling all over on the radio when we have a patrol out on an ambush assignment," said Bromhead, grinning. "Might tip our hand."

"Very good, Johnny. I'll see you again in about a week." He raised his voice. "Sully, let's move them out."

They wormed their way through the wire and into the elephant grass south of the camp. Once clear of the final defenses, the booby traps that Sully Smith had hidden as the first obstacle for attacking VC, they turned to the west, along the bank of one of the smaller canals. Trees and bushes provided them with some cover, but the vegetation wasn't too thick so the going wasn't tiring. They crossed the remnants of roads, one of them having been paved sometime in the past but now little more than broken chunks of concrete that were slowly disintegrating .

They passed a number of abandoned hamlets, the mud and thatch structures falling down. They skirted the edges, avoiding walking through them. Morrow took pictures of them as they went by, almost as if to document the route they had taken. They also crossed several streams, but since it was the end of the dry season, it hadn't been difficult.

At noon they halted in a stand of huge trees that had one time hidden a farmer's two-room hootch. The remains of a mud wall and fence that had been the pen for a water buffalo were evident. To one side was a short domed structure that was an outdoor oven. Gerber allowed the men to build a fire in it to heat their C-rations for lunch. He was surprised that the canned food tasted so much better if it was heated slightly. But to admit that was to admit that your taste buds were ruined for life.

Before they began the afternoon march, Gerber asked Morrow how she was doing.

She sat with her back against a large palm tree, the remains of her lunch scattered in front of her as she scraped at the ground so that she could bury the cans. Her hair was hanging around her face, damp with sweat. She was pale, as if she were about to pass out.

She smiled weakly and said, "I'm doing just fine. Just fine." She glanced at the others, who seemed not to have noticed how far they had walked. "What time do you plan to make camp this evening?"

"Depends."

"Mack, the worst thing is not knowing how long we're going to be moving. If I have a goal, I can make it, but if it is just some time in the future, I'm going to fold up. I have to have that goal."

"We've made good time this morning," said Gerber. He took his map from the side pocket on his fatigue pants and studied it for a moment. "It's maybe ten, twelve klicks to the border from here. That's a couple of hours away, unless we rest frequently."

"You don't have to go slow because of me," she snapped.

"I know that. I just don't want to get too close to Cambodia in the daylight. Anyway, I suspect we'll be camped by four or five this afternoon." Gerber looked at Morrow closely. She was sitting with her legs flat on the ground and her hands by her sides. Her head was slightly bowed. She looked totally exhausted. "You sure that you're all right?"

"Yes. Would you worry this much about one of the men?"

"Yeah, I would. Anyone having heat stroke is going to slow us down. Maybe cause us to cancel the mission if we have to call for a medevac. Did you take your salt tablets?"

Morrow shook her head. "I'm not convinced that salt tablets are a good thing."

"Neither am I," said Gerber, "but they do seem to prevent the heat from sapping all your strength. Take a couple of them. And drink some of your water. We're going to move out in about ten minutes."

Gerber got to his feet and walked over to where McMillan sat eating the Army's version of fruit cocktail. He crouched near the medic and said, "You want to keep an eye on Miss Morrow? The heat seems to be getting to her."

"No problem, Captain."

"If she gets into trouble, or you think she's getting sick, let me know, but don't let her know what you're doing."

"Understood. She going to slow us down?"

"I'm not sure that it matters today, Ian. We made good progress this morning, and we're not that far from where I want to cross the border. I was going to slow us down, anyway. You just keep an eye on her."

"Yes, sir."

Gerber then moved over to where Bocker was sitting, listening to the radio. "You hear anything on the radio from the camp?" he asked.

"No, sir. Well, not for us, anyway. Heard T.J. talking to someone a little while ago about resupply. Think it was an incoming chopper."

"We move out in a few minutes."

"I'll be ready."

After lunch Gerber avoided the fingers of jungle that meandered toward Cambodia, opting for a path that headed nearly due west. He followed the canal to the northwest of Long Khot, keeping on the edge of the swamp and staying in the paddies. The water in some of them was nearly knee-deep, and there were no young rice plants to walk on so the feet of the patrol were sucked at by the mud, making it tiring to walk and slowing them down. They arrived at the Cambodian border at a point about seven klicks due south of Svay Rieng. Gerber knew the enemy camp he wanted was north of there. By swinging this far south, he hoped to avoid the southern end of the Ho Chi Minh Trail.

Gerber scattered his men, making use of the little cover available. There was a clump of trees that provided a good field of fire for a hundred meters in all directions, and he put the majority of his tiny force there with Morrow in the middle of them. He set two men about fifty meters to the north, almost in Cambodia, hidden in a depression that had a large bush growing in the center. From there they would be able to see anyone approaching and could alert the others.

Once security was set, Gerber moved back to the stand of trees. The men and Morrow rested, a couple of them sleeping, even though it was the hottest part of the day. Sweat rolled off them, soaking their uniforms as completely as if the rain that had threatened in the morning had finally fallen. Morrow had collapsed near a tree, removed her pack and then rolled onto her side, her hands under her head. She seemed to be asleep, but her breathing was rapid and shallow. She seemed to be exhausted, and Gerber wondered if she was going to make it.

Gerber sat down and took out the canned bread that came with his C-ration meal. He opened the tin and used his knife to cut the bread into halves. Then he opened the can of grape jelly and spread it all on one half of the bread. He squeezed the two pieces together and ate it. The bread was dry and the jelly runny, but Gerber didn't care. Then, opening a can of boned chicken, which he salted heavily, he ate his dinner while studying his map, looking for landmarks that he would be able to spot in the dark. The most obvious were the large river on the east side of Svay Rieng, the bridge over that river and Svay Rieng itself. It seemed to be a large town compared to most of the hamlets in the area and would probably have lights that could be seen from a couple of klicks in the dark.

When he finished eating, Gerber went and briefed Kittredge and Krung on the route they would follow after dark. They could easily get north of Svay Rieng in the dark, and they could lay low for the day. That done, he went to check on Morrow. She was sitting up, her legs crossed Indian fashion, eating peaches from an OD can.

"You look a hundred percent better," Gerber told her.

"I feel better," she said with a smile. "Just needed a little nap." She held up her can. "You want some peaches?"

"No, thanks. I've eaten." Gerber sat down next to her. "We're going to be on the move most of the night," he warned her.

"It'll be cooler without the sun," she said. "It was the sun that was getting to me. I'll be all right."

Gerber nodded and got up, putting a hand on her shoulder. She looked up at him, and Gerber could see that she was afraid. He walked off to check on the rest of his men and make sure they all had eaten something. Then he sent two men out to relieve the men in the clump of bushes. When he'd finished all that, he sat down off by himself and carefully cleaned his rifle. He didn't think it was dirty, but it couldn't hurt to clean it. Besides, it was something to do.

BRIGADIER GENERAL BILLY JOE CRINSHAW stood in front of his ornate desk and stared at McKowen. He slammed his fist down hard on the desktop.

"I don't give a shit about your stupid rule book. I want everything moved up. I want the trial to start in the morning. You tell that defense puke that national security comes before the accuseds' rights, and if he has a real problem with that, we'll find someone who doesn't."

McKowen opened the briefcase sitting on his lap and flipped through the papers. He said, "That won't give us time to assemble all the witnesses and interview them."

"Look," shouted Crinshaw, "the men are guilty. All this legal maneuvering is designed to get them off. I want them nailed."

"It doesn't matter how guilty they are if we go on violating their rights. You're pushing this too hard, General. If we're not careful, they'll get off scot-free."

"I want this finished. We can bury it under national security. I don't want you telling me why something can't be done. I want you to find a way to do it. You got that, boy?"

McKowen flipped through more of his papers as he tried to think of something fast. Finally he muttered, "Yes, sir."

Crinshaw walked around his desk to the blinds on the window. He pulled them open and looked out, but saw nothing that interested him. Then he moved over to the air conditioner and turned it down a notch so that it was blowing more cold air.

"I'm telling you the truth, Major," said Crinshaw as he walked to his desk. "Somebody causes a stink, we tell them that it's national security. We wear that like a cloak, and we can do anything.''

McKowen stuffed the papers into his briefcase and stood up. "I can be ready tomorrow, but I'll tell you right now, General, the defense is going to ask for a continuance.''

"You let me worry about that. I'll see that they don't get it. Anything else you need, Major?''

"No, sir. That should be it. I'll be ready tomorrow at nine.''

IT HAD BEEN DARK for over an hour when a light rain began to fall. Gerber decided that the conditions for crossing into Cambodia would never be any better. They left the trees, worked their way slowly to the bushes that concealed the two security men and then headed straight for Cambodia. Kittredge, still on point, consulted his compass frequently to make sure they weren't diverting too far to the west. In the dark and rain the patrol was grouped closely together so that not more than a meter separated them from one another.

They were moving over open ground, through paddies and clear fields, and since they were now in Cambodia, it gave them a feeling of being naked. But the jungle had shriveled to scraggly tree lines that were broken frequently by streams.

To the left was a tree line that ran almost north-south, and Gerber had Kittredge veer toward it. He wanted the cover it would provide, and it would give them an opportunity to take a break. Besides, Gerber was tired of the feeling at the base of his spine where he imagined an enemy sniper was aiming. He knew there were no snipers behind him, but he couldn't shake the feeling. He wondered if he ever would.

They were nearly to the trees when there was a stuttering burst from a machine gun, and in the mist of the falling drizzle, two men went down. There was a piercing scream from one of them, but nothing from the other. Gerber dived to his right, rolling in the mud, and aimed his M-14 over the paddy dike at the muzzle-flash of the enemy RPD machine gun. He glanced right and left, but in the dark and falling rain could see no one nearby.

All at once a dozen new weapons joined the machine gun, the green-and-white tracers from the VC positions slashing through the air overhead, or kicking up dirt and splattering mud in the paddies and along the dikes. Rather than use his M-14, which would only pinpoint his location for the enemy gunners, Gerber reached for one of the grenades he carried. He raised his voice and said, "On three, we toss the grenades before we attack the trees. McMillan, you stay here with Morrow and keep her head down."

Gerber didn't wait for any of his men to acknowledge as he began counting off, shouting over the rattling of the enemy weapons. As he shouted the last number, he lobbed the grenade as far as he could. He knew that he wasn't following the Army standard of throwing it like a baseball, but in Army training he'd never been pinned down by Russian RPDs and AK-47s.

As the grenades detonated in a flaming burst of light like the flashbulbs of a camera, Gerber was on his feet shouting at the top of his voice, "Let's go! Let's go!" He ran forward, dodging right and then left, firing five-shot bursts from the hip, watching his tracers disappear into the blackness of the tree line.

Then he was in the trees among the VC. Out of the corner of his eye, he saw movement and turned to fire. Just as he pulled the trigger, something snapped down on the barrel of his rifle and the ruby tracers buried themselves in the jungle floor. Gerber didn't try to see what knocked his weapon aside, he just kicked sideways with his foot, but connected with nothing. He then dived forward, rolling to his back so that he was suddenly facing the VC who had struck his rifle. The man turned and lunged with his bayonet, but Gerber blocked the blow with his own weapon, forcing the blade to the side. At the same time he kicked out, snapping the enemy's legs out from under him so that the man fell to his side. Gerber pulled the trigger on his M-14, but nothing happened.

He rolled to the right toward the enemy soldier and grabbed the barrel of the AK-47, twisting it away from him. As the man tried to stand, Gerber jerked the knife from his harness and slashed at the enemy. The VC screamed in pain, and Gerber felt himself splashed with blood. He thrust again, driving the knife to the hilt in the man's side. The VC went into a spasm, jerking the blade from Gerber's hand.

As Gerber got to his hands and knees, someone leaped on his back and an arm circled his throat, lifting his head. Gerber reached for the VC's elbow, dropped his shoulders and flipped the enemy to the ground. He grabbed the steel pot from his own head and used it to club the man, hitting him three times rapidly, hearing the sickening crunch of breaking bone as the VC's skull splintered.

As Gerber got to his feet, he heard the rattling of weapons around him as the two sides searched for each other in the dark. Gerber pulled his pistol from the holster and moved to the right. Charlie seemed to rise out of the ground in front of him, and Gerber jammed his weapon into the man's stomach and fired twice. He turned quickly and saw another VC running in the trees. Dropping to one knee, he emptied his .45 at the fleeing shape.

Suddenly the American force began taking heavy fire from the left flank. Gerber fell to the ground, rolled to his left and reached for a grenade. There was an explosion far in front of him, twenty or thirty meters away, the flash outlining the enemy machine gunners. Gerber threw a grenade, but it was long, detonating behind the enemy. Before he could try again, there was another explosion right in front of the enemy machine gun that bent the barrel upward toward the sky. The firing from that position ended abruptly.

The shooting tapered off to an occasional bang, but all of it from American-made weapons. Gerber couldn't hear any firing from AKs or SKSs. He eased back, out of the trees and away from the dead men, pausing long enough to retrieve his M-14. He worked the bolt and dislodged the round that had jammed it.

"Cease fire! Fall back!" he yelled.

In the paddies he found McMillan crouched over one of the Tai who had been hit in the initial burst. Morrow was beside him, shaking out a field dressing so that she could give it to McMillan.

"Wounded?" asked Gerber.

"Just him. Other one's dead. Took a round through the chest. Right in the heart. He had to be dead before he hit the ground."

"Who was it?"

"Le Khan."

"You okay, Robin?" he asked.

"Fine. A little shaky, but fine."

Kepler appeared at Gerber's side and said, "Sir, we've got three prisoners."

"What? Prisoners?"

"Yes, sir. Three of them surrendered as Kittredge blew up the machine gun. Just stood up, threw down their weapons and started yelling in Vietnamese. I'm afraid we killed the fourth before we realized what was happening. I've got the men sweeping through the trees to see what else they can find."

"Any of the others hurt?"

"Not really. I think Kittredge has a nasty cut on the arm, but he did it to himself with his own knife. He's more pissed than hurt."

Gerber stood up and took Kepler off to the side. "The last thing we need is prisoners. There's no way we can head deeper into Cambodia with a bunch of VC prisoners."

"You don't understand, sir. One of them's Chinese. A Chinese NCO, I think."

Gerber felt a tickle of excitement as his adrenaline began to pump. He tried to keep his voice calm as he asked, "Chinese? You're sure?"

"Yes, sir. Doesn't seem to understand Vietnamese, and he's definitely wearing the uniform of a Chinese." Kepler wiped the rain from his face with his arm.

"Christ, I don't believe it." Gerber turned and looked at the tree line, but could see nothing moving in it. "Get the men recalled," he ordered. "Get the prisoners subdued, collect the weapons."

"Yes, sir," Kepler replied.

Gerber turned back to McMillan. "Ian, can we move the wounded man?"

"I've got the bleeding stopped and given him a shot of morphine. The wound isn't that bad. Grazed the shoulder and went through the fleshy part of the upper arm."

"Derek, have your boys cut us some bamboo for poles to make stretchers. Let's snap it up. We've got to get out of here."

Gerber then got down and stretched out on the ground. He put a poncho over his head and used his flashlight to study his map. He saw that the shortest way out of Cambodia was the way they had come. The border near the Parrot's Beak whipped east and west before turning south again. He snapped off the light and folded up his map before he rolled up the poncho.

Kepler had returned with four lengths of bamboo. Gerber watched as Kepler laid two of the poles, separated by eighteen inches, in the center of a poncho. He then folded the excess material over top of the bamboo to create a stretcher, then repeated the exercise for the second stretcher. They put the wounded Tai on one of them and the dead man on the second after tying his body into a poncho liner.

When they were ready, Gerber said, "Steve, take the point. Keep Krung with you. Move due south and hurry it up. We want to get to the border as quickly as we can. And Galvin, you're going to have to guard the prisoners."

"No problem."

They moved out with Kittredge and Krung leading, followed by the two stretcher teams, Bocker and his prisoners and finally Morrow and Gerber. The pace was slower now because of the stretchers, and everyone was tired. The light rain that had aided them earlier finally stopped, and they could hear the sounds of the insects. The mosquitoes attacked them relentlessly. It was hard going, but they continued until they had recrossed the border and were in South Vietnam.

Gerber was tempted to stop in the clump of bamboo and palm trees they had used earlier, but knew that was the quickest way to get ambushed. Army training had taught him to not double back on his own trail except for an ambush or in very unusual circumstances, and not to use the same rest stops. He forced his team to the south, away from the border, until they reached Kinh Bay Thuoc. Then, as the first faint evidence of dawn began to appear, Gerber found a stand of trees that made an ideal camp.

As soon as he had the perimeter established, he looked at the prisoners. They sat huddled in the center with Bocker watching them warily. Kepler stood off to one side observing.

As Gerber approached his intel officer, he said, "Derek, what do you think?"

"I think we've got them dead to rights. There's no way to argue that he isn't here. We have the proof that the Red Chinese are here. I'll need some time to talk to them, but I think we've got it."

Next he went over to talk to McMillan about the wounded man. McMillan told him that a rest would probably be good for him, rather than undergoing the constant rocking movement of the stretcher. The man was in no danger.

He turned and saw Morrow sitting on the ground leaning on her pack, her eyes closed. He walked over to her and asked, "How are you doing?"

She opened her eyes and wiped the perspiration from her forehead. "Just fine."

"We're going to hold here for a while. I'm going to try to get us airlift out of here so we don't have to walk back to the camp."

"You think you'll have any luck with that?"

"Should. I have wounded and I have prisoners." He looked at her carefully and added, "You look a little flushed. You take your salt tablets?"

"Yes, sir," she said in a mocking voice.

Gerber sat down next to her and took off his helmet, setting it on the ground beside him. In the growing light of day, he could see it was stained with the blood of the man he had killed with it. He turned it so that he didn't have to look at the stain.

"Listen," he said, "I just wanted to say that you've held up your end just as you said you would. You've done a hell of a job."

Morrow turned so that she could see him better. She wasn't sure what to say. She brushed at the damp hair that clung to her forehead.

"You mean that?"

"Yeah. I just wanted you to know that anything I might have said was nothing personal. Hell, after the night in Saigon, you should know that. I'm just trying to do what's best for everyone."

She started to reach out to touch him, but stopped. She smiled and said, "I understand." She didn't speak for a moment and then, as if to change the subject, said, "You think we have what we need to spring Fetterman and Tyme?"

"Yeah, I think so. If I didn't, we'd still be in Cambodia. But I think the Chinese soldier is going to be the one thing we need to underscore this whole mess." Gerber looked at his watch. "Why don't you take a few pictures of our Chinese guest and then get some rest. It'll be a few hours before I can arrange airlift out of here."

13

TAN SON NHUT AIR FORCE BASE, SAIGON

It was shortly after nine when Fetterman and Tyme were brought into the trial room. The trial officer sat at his table, the *Uniform Code of Military Justice* sitting in front of him. McKowen sat behind his table, and two assistants, both young second lieutenants, sat just behind him on the other side of the rail. As soon as they were seated, the trial officer announced the entrance of the board. Everyone stood again while Crinshaw and the four other members of the board entered.

When everyone was settled, the trial officer, at the direction of the presiding officer, General Crinshaw, said, "Charges and specifications. One. That on or about Twelve June 1965, Master Sergeant Anthony B. Fetterman did willfully, and with malice aforethought, conspire to cause the death of a foreign national while operating illegally in a neutral country.

"Two. That Master Sergeant Anthony B. Fetterman did illegally enter said neutral country in violation of Army regulations, government policies and the law of the land."

He went on for another minute, outlining a list of minor charges and offenses, the worst of which seemed to be causing his subordinates to violate regulations. When he finished reading the charges against Fetterman, he read the ones against Tyme, which were virtually the same. When he finished, he sat down and waited, almost as if he expected applause for his performance.

Crinshaw banged his gavel unnecessarily and asked, "How do you plead?"

Wilson rose, repeated the charges against Fetterman and said not guilty after each one. He then went through the same routine with the charges against Tyme.

Again Crinshaw rapped his gavel on the table and said, "Is the prosecutor ready to proceed?"

"If it pleases the court," interrupted Wilson, "I have a motion."

Crinshaw looked immediately to the trial officer. "He has that prerogative," said Winston.

"Go ahead, then," said Crinshaw.

"Sir, I would like to move that the case be delayed by one week so that I may better prepare the defense."

"Denied."

"Sir, I would like to have Sergeant Tyme tried separately from Sergeant Fetterman because Sergeant Tyme is required by military regulations to obey the orders of his senior sergeant and is therefore not responsible for his actions. Had he failed to obey those orders, he could have been charged with making a mutiny."

"Denied."

"May I have a clarification?"

"National security," said Crinshaw, falling back to the position he'd planned to use. "We can't afford to have another trial after this one. It does not prejudice the case against Sergeant Tyme to have him tried at the same time. Anything else?"

Wilson looked at the yellow pad sitting on the table in front of him. He scratched out the motions that Crinshaw had denied. "That's all," he said.

"Is the prosecution ready?" asked Crinshaw.

McKowen stood and said, "I am prepared to proceed."

"Then please do."

McKowen checked his legal pad sitting on the table and said, "I would like to call Sergeant John Happel."

"Who's that?" asked Wilson, leaning close to Fetterman.

Fetterman shrugged. "I haven't the faintest idea."

Happel, a short, fat sergeant wearing an ill-fitting uniform that couldn't hide the massive gut hanging over his belt, walked into the trial room. He had black hair that had been cut short, thick eyebrows and a large nose that dominated his face. He was sworn in and sat down in the witness chair, facing Crinshaw and the four colonels of the trial board.

"All right, Sergeant," began McKowen, "for the record, please state your name, rank and unit of assignment."

Happel ducked his head twice instead of nodding and said, "John C. Happel, staff sergeant for the 205th Resupply Company here at Tan Son Nhut. I'm the supply sergeant."

"Have you had any dealings with either Sergeant Fetterman or Sergeant Tyme?"

"Yes, sir."

"Were all these official dealings?"

"Sir?" asked Happel.

"What I mean, Sergeant, were all your dealings with them in the proper channels with the proper forms?"

"Oh, no, sir. Lots of them were what you might call midnight requisitions. They would want something, come down to me and trade for it. They rarely had the proper supply forms."

"What sort of equipment were they obtaining?"

"Objection!" said Wilson, leaping to his feet. "This line of questioning is producing nothing."

"It is establishing that both Sergeant Fetterman and Sergeant Tyme are renegades who have no respect for the Army or the Army system," responded McKowen heatedly.

"What?" asked Wilson. "Because they sometimes went outside of official supply channels to obtain the equipment that they needed?"

"Exactly."

Wilson shook his head in disbelief. "In the interest of saving time," he said, "we are prepared to stipulate that both Sergeant Fetterman and Sergeant Tyme used unofficial channels to gather the material and information they needed to fulfill their duties." Out of the corner of his eye, Wilson saw McKowen open his mouth. Wilson added hastily, "On the condition that the prosecutor will stipulate that it is a common practice throughout the Army and not indicative of poor soldiers.''

''That's ridiculous,'' said McKowen.

''In that case I object again. And I plan to refute this testimony by bringing in other soldiers who are known for their abilities to gather material outside of normal supply channels. Every unit has one. They trade their surplus around so that everyone ends up with what they need. These talents are not those of bad soldiers, but of dedicated and loyal ones who are ingeniously completing their mission.''

''Counsel is summing up,'' protested McKowen.

''Mr. Trial Officer,'' interrupted Crinshaw.

''The objection is sustained unless the prosecutor can establish quickly the relevance of this line of questioning,'' Winston stated.

Fetterman looked at Crinshaw and could plainly see the general was not happy with the way Winston had ruled.

The prosecutor turned his attention to the fat sergeant sitting on the witness chair. ''I have no further questions in that case.''

''You may step down,'' said Crinshaw.

''Wait a minute, General,'' said Wilson. ''I have a couple of questions for this man.''

Crinshaw shot an icy glare at Wilson, but said nothing. Wilson turned and walked back to the defense table and picked up his legal pad. He read it for a moment while the tension built.

''I have only one question for the witness,'' he said. ''I want him to describe Sergeant Fetterman to me.''

The sergeant began to turn, his elbow on the back of the witness chair. Wilson jumped between him and the defense table. ''No, Sergeant,'' he said. ''I want you to describe him without looking at him. If you've had as many dealings with him as you claim, and if all of them were the under-the-table operations you've mentioned, you should know what he looks like.''

The sergeant stared at the trial board, as if he expected them to help him. He was quiet for a moment and then said, "I'm not very good at describing people."

"A general description will do. Nothing elaborate. Tall or short. Thin or fat. Blond hair or brown. Flattop? Just a general description."

"Well, I think he's on the tall side."

"That will be all," snapped Wilson. He went back to the defense table and sat down.

The prosecutor watched the fat sergeant leave the room. He sat there for a moment waiting. Then he shrugged and said, "I would like to call Lieutenant Khai to the stand."

The MP at the door opened it, spoke to someone outside and a minute later Khai entered. He was sworn in and then began describing the same things that he had talked about during the Article 32 hearing. He mentioned that a specific man seemed to have been the target and that Fetterman and Tyme had been bragging about killing the man who had engineered the deaths of the South Vietnamese rangers.

"I have never bragged about killing a man," Fetterman told Wilson.

"Don't worry about it," said Wilson. "We'll get our chance in a little while."

IT WAS NEARLY NOON before Gerber could arrange for airlift. Using the PRC-10, he contacted Crusader Operations in Tay Ninh, alerting them that he needed travel from his present location to his camp. He was told that airlift was not available and that all the aircraft were tied up in a mass combat assault into the Hobo Woods and Iron Triangle area.

"Roger," said Gerber, his voice harsh. "Be advised that I have wounded."

"Understand that you have wounded. Are they critical?"

"Negative, Crusader Ops. I say again, negative."

"Zulu Six, Crusader Six advises that he can supply three ships for airlift in approximately one hour."

"Understand. Advise Six that I have three POWs. And thank him for the lift."

"Roger, Zulu Six. Crusader Six will radio when flight is one five minutes from your location."

It was actually less than an hour. Gerber heard the call and told Bocker, "Acknowledge and throw smoke."

Bocker keyed the handset and said, "I will throw smoke."

"Roger Zulu Six."

Gerber found a smoke grenade and flipped it to Bocker, who pulled the pin and tossed it into the open. It billowed into a green cloud that drifted back to the west.

"ID green," said the voice on the radio.

"Roger green."

Gerber got to his feet and said, "Let's get into the field. Kittredge, I want you and Kepler on one aircraft with the prisoners. They try anything stupid, you shoot them. Ian, you get on one chopper with the wounded and the dead. You need to divert to Dau Tieng or Tay Ninh for the medical facilities, you do it. The rest of us will get on the last ship."

They filtered out of the trees into the open rice fields. Gerber spaced the loads so that they were thirty feet apart. The incoming aircraft would be able to land close to the group that it was to pick up.

He watched the helicopters approach from the north, dropping from the sky slowly as they got nearer. When they were a hundred meters from the LZ and still about thirty or forty feet in the air, they flared, slowing their forward momentum, one aircraft settling toward each group.

The patrol was hit by the rotor wash that threatened to knock them to the ground, and Morrow staggered a couple of steps. Gerber grabbed her arm, steadying her.

As the skids touched the ground, Gerber was moving, leaping into the cargo compartment, reaching out to lift Morrow in after him. Smith tossed some of the captured equipment in and then scrambled up after it. Gerber held a thumb up as Krung and Bocker climbed in, yelling to the pilot that he was ready.

They lifted off immediately, the nose of the chopper dropping suddenly as the pilot tried to increase his airspeed as they flashed across the paddies toward a tree line. He leveled off, and as they were about to collide with the trees, he pulled back on the cyclic, popping over them and then settling back so that they were flying only three or four feet above the ground, first to the south to gain speed and then turning to the east so that they were on the way back to the camp.

Gerber was fascinated as they climbed slightly to fly over tree lines, or farmers and their oxen in fields. He was grinning from ear to ear, enjoying the feeling of speed that he was getting from the flight. To the right, level with them, was another helicopter, and next to it the third, leading them. The door gunners and crew chiefs all sat behind their weapons, aviation-modified M-60 machine guns, ready to return any enemy fire they received.

He glanced to the left and saw Morrow gripping the edge of the troop seat in both hands, her knuckles white. She had her eyes closed and her lips were working as if she were praying silently.

Just beyond her, almost on a level with them but in the distance, he saw a rice farmer's hootch. He thought he saw someone jump inside, but couldn't be sure. A moment later there was a splash in the water of one of the paddies near them, as if someone had fired a single round at the flight. But none of the door gunners shot back, and Gerber wasn't sure that he had seen anything.

From the other side of the cargo compartment he heard a whoop and looked over. Smith was leaning forward, straining the seat belt, holding his steel pot with one hand as if the wind rushing through the open doors would be strong enough to tear it from his head. He turned, smiled at Gerber and gave him a thumbs-up sign.

The aircraft seemed to slow and began to gain altitude until they were at the normal cruising height of about fifteen hundred feet. Off in the distance Gerber could see the telltale square on top of the slight rise that was his camp. A cloud of bright yellow rose from the northern side of the camp where the helipad was.

They came screaming out of the sky, approaching faster than normal, and as they neared the ground, all three helicopters flared at the same time, stopping in a swirling cloud of red dust and yellow smoke.

Smith unfastened his seat belt, grabbed his equipment and leaped to the ground, rushing to the side of the pad. Gerber tapped Morrow on the shoulder, startling her. She snapped her eyes open and screamed, but the sound of her voice was lost in the whine of the turbines and the popping of the rotor blades. Gerber laughed and pointed to the ground. She nodded and reached down with a shaking hand to unbuckle her seat belt. Once out of the aircraft, she ran from the helipad toward her hootch without looking back.

Gerber got out and ran to the second chopper. McMillan was grinning as he helped unload the wounded man, who had been lying on the floor of the cargo compartment. The man was semiconscious as the morphine that McMillan had given him earlier began to wear off. McMillan held up a thumb to tell Gerber that the man was all right. He would be taken to the dispensary for treatment. The body of the dead striker was taken off, and two Tai carried it toward their area.

Kepler and Kittredge escorted the three prisoners from the lead helicopter. They moved rapidly from the pad toward the redoubt, heading straight for the team house. That would separate the prisoners from the rest of the compound and give them an extra barrier to cross if they had any escape plans.

Almost as the last of the patrol hit the ground, the choppers picked up to a hover, sending the people on the pad scrambling. They hovered to the west, to the runway, and then took off down it. They climbed out slightly so that they would clear the bunkers and wire on the south side of the camp. Once over them they dropped down, flying with their skids just above the elephant grass, the rotor wash clearly visible as it whipped through the vegetation.

As soon as the helicopters disappeared, Minh, who had been watching the show from the commo bunker, walked up. Gerber immediately said, "Where's Johnny?"

Minh waved the question aside and asked, "Who was wounded?"

Gerber explained about the ambush and then said, "I really should go tell Bao that one of his boys was killed before Sergeant Krung does. Where's Johnny?" he asked again.

"Don't really know, old boy. A Major Dumont arrived shortly after you departed and demanded, in no uncertain terms, that you be recalled from the field. Lieutenant Bromhead refused, following your instructions to the letter. After waiting most of the day, Dumont insisted that the lieutenant return with him to Saigon."

"Well, that's just fucking great!" Gerber said angrily.

"The lieutenant wanted to make sure I told you that he had the package that you had mentioned to him."

"Shit!" said Gerber. "I hope he doesn't do anything rash."

"Such as?" asked Minh.

"Just some special instructions I gave him." Gerber was worried. In his message Bromhead was obviously referring to the package containing the two false passports Maxwell had gotten for Fetterman and Tyme. Gerber was afraid that Bromhead might give them to Fetterman too soon.

"You heard anything about the trial?"

"Not really. Only that they moved everything up."

Gerber slapped a hand on Minh's shoulder. "I'll have to hope that Johnny can take care of himself in Saigon for a few hours. I'll find him tomorrow when I take the results of the patrol in to show Crinshaw."

"You think you found enough?"

"I'm not sure. I hope I can force Crinshaw's hand, but I just don't know."

Before they got away from the pad, Kepler and Robin Morrow returned. Morrow complained, "Sergeant Kepler doesn't want me with him while he interrogates the prisoners. I think he's afraid I'll see something he doesn't want me to see."

"It's not that at all, sir," Kepler said. "Psychologically I don't think it's such a good idea. Miss Morrow's presence might make them clam up."

"Sounds like bullshit to me," she said.

Gerber couldn't help himself. He burst out laughing. "You may be right, but let's let Sergeant Kepler have his way for now. I want you to get some pictures of the prisoners, but that will be later.''

An hour later Kepler found Gerber working in his hootch, his shirt hanging on the back of his chair as he sat at his desk. ''Something I think you should know, Captain,'' he said.

''What'd you get?''

''Well, the Chinese guy won't talk to me. I think he's claiming that he doesn't speak English, and the Vietnamese told me they couldn't speak Chinese.''

''I suppose we could have killed the interpreter.''

''Yes, sir. Anyway, I talked quite a bit to the VC. They told me something that I think might end our problem. I think they're telling me that Fetterman and Tyme dusted the wrong guy.''

''What?''

''From what I can gather, the officer who led the patrol that ambushed the Vietnamese is not the guy they shot.''

''Oh, shit!'' said Gerber. ''I don't believe it.''

''Well, sir,'' Kepler began, ''Fetterman never got a good look at the guy.''

''No. No,'' said Gerber. ''All this trouble and we hit the wrong guy.''

''How's this going to affect the trial?''

Gerber scrubbed at his face with both hands. ''That I don't know. I use that little gem right, and it might crush the case.''

FETTERMAN WAS SURPRISED when he received a visitor after his evening meal. He was surprised that Crinshaw would let him have a visitor and he was even more astonished when it turned out to be Bromhead. The young lieutenant stood at the far end of the second floor of the Long Binh Jail near an iron door with bars in the window, arguing with a corporal. The enlisted man finally nodded and backed away, allowing Bromhead to pass.

At the cell door Bromhead said, ''Well, Master Sergeant, I see that you've finally gotten yourself into a mess that you can't get yourself out of.''

"That's right, Lieutenant," responded Fetterman, "whatever that means."

"Corporal," Bromhead shouted, "open this door."

The man trotted over, took a large key ring holding two dozen keys from his pocket, selected one unerringly and unlocked the door. As he locked Bromhead in, he said, "Let me know when you're ready to go, sir."

When the corporal was gone, Fetterman said, "What's happened to the captain?" He thought about that and then said, "Which isn't to say that I'm not glad to see you, sir."

"Captain Gerber is out with a patrol, trying to find something to get you out of here."

"So, how are things at the camp?" asked Fetterman. He sat back on the single cot in the cell. There was a toilet stool a couple of feet away with a partially used roll of paper next to it. Only the back wall was solid. The rest were made of bars that ran from floor to ceiling. That allowed a guard at the door at the far end of the building to see into each of the cells.

"Things are fine. Listen, Sergeant, the captain asked me to come and see you if things got grim. I would have been here earlier, but I had to hang around with a major named Dumont. He finally went to talk to Crinshaw, and I came up here."

Bromhead looked around carefully. The corporal was at the far end of the room, out of easy earshot. There were a couple of privates sitting at a table, but they were more concerned with their card game.

"The captain gave me a final instruction before he left on patrol." Bromhead stopped talking and looked sheepish. "I don't really know how to phrase this, except to say if you, ah, would like a pistol and a passport, they're available."

"You got them with you?"

"Yes. If you want them."

"Lieutenant, I have been raked over the coals today. I've watched a court-martial that was more like a circus. I've watched a general officer subvert a system that was designed to protect the rights of the innocent. I'm tired of it all. I don't want to wait around to see if someone at a higher level is honest or not."

"What about Sergeant Tyme?"

"I'll take him with me. Can't leave Boom-Boom behind. He's like a babe in the woods."

"I've got a passport for him, too. Don't have a weapon for him, though."

Fetterman shook his head. "Just give me the passports, sir. If I have the pistol, I'll be tempted to use it, and I don't want to hurt any fellow GIs, even if they are MPs."

"Won't you need the pistol to get out?"

Fetterman grinned. "Really, Lieutenant, give me some credit. These rear-area jailers won't be hard to fool. They never make jailers out of the top-of-the-line troops. I'm as good as out of here."

After looking one last time to see where the MPs were, Bromhead reached into his jacket pocket and pulled out the two passports. "I don't know how the captain got them, but they're current and made out in false names."

Fetterman picked up one of the passports and opened it. It was a standard United States passport with a dark-green cover indicating that it wasn't issued to a government employee. It was the kind given to regular citizens. Inside were the proper entrance stamps showing that the passport holder had entered Vietnam legally four weeks earlier. It also contained the proper stamps for entering and leaving Japan. Fetterman read through his false travel itinerary in the fake document.

Bromhead stood. "I'd like to stay here, I mean in Long Binh or Saigon tonight, in case I could be of service to you. But I really should try to return to camp."

Now Fetterman stood and held out a hand. "Thanks for your help, Johnny. I enjoyed working with you."

"The same, Master Sergeant." Bromhead stood, his eyes locked on Fetterman's. He was remembering the first time he had talked to Fetterman, telling him to call him Johnny because everyone did. Fetterman had said to call him Master Sergeant because everyone did. But then it had been Fetterman who had bailed him out when the west wall had nearly collapsed as the VC tried to overrun the camp. They had shared some life together, but more important, they had defeated death together.

"It's a rotten deal, Master Sergeant. I wish there was something more I could do."

"You did what you could," he said. "Mrs. Fetterman and the kids would appreciate all that you've done."

That was Fetterman's highest praise.

14

U.S. SPECIAL FORCES
CAMP A-555

Gerber spent the night organizing his reports so that he would be prepared when he confronted Crinshaw in the morning. He asked Morrow to take more pictures of the prisoners and to develop them as soon as she could, and had Kepler continue his interrogation of the prisoners in case they had any more information that would be useful. Bocker arranged for a helicopter to take him to Saigon in the morning.

After a hasty breakfast of powdered eggs and reconstituted orange juice, he checked with Robin Morrow. She had been up all night developing the pictures. She told him that the hootches weren't completely lightproof and that her lab technique might leave something to be desired, but the pictures clearly showed all that they wanted shown. She said she would be ready when the chopper arrived at nine.

As Gerber stood in his hootch, his knapsack on his cot, he was interrupted by a quiet knock on the door. "Enter," he said.

Minh walked in, a grim look on his face. "Lieutenant Khai returned to camp last night," Minh reported. "He said that his part in the trial had been concluded and that he was reporting for duty."

Gerber sat down on his cot. Before he had gone on his patrol, he had been so sure that Khai was a VC. He knew many of the ARVN units were infiltrated by the Vietcong so to have one in a strike company on the camp wasn't totally unexpected. The evidence against him was circumstantial, but it seemed to be overwhelming. "You think we should talk about this now since he's back?"

"No, I don't think that will be necessary. I investigated the problem last night and regret to inform you that Lieutenant Khai took his own life when confronted with the accusation."

"My God!" exclaimed Gerber.

"It is of no consequence, old boy. The man was a traitor." Minh rubbed a hand over his face. "No, that is not fair. He was an enemy soldier and a spy, but I don't believe he was a traitor. He was loyal to his government. It just wasn't mine."

"Are there going to be any repercussions?" asked Gerber. He was suddenly aware of how tired he was. He wanted desperately for this to be over.

"I think not. My people in Saigon believe he was killed in action, and the men here know the truth. The situation is now resolved."

Gerber got to his feet and retrieved the bottle of Beam's from the bottom of his wall locker. He uncorked it and said, "I know there is nothing I can say to make this easier. To say that it is the nature of war is no help. I'm sorry for the way it turned out."

Minh took the Beam's and drank deeply, breathed and drank again. As he handed it back, he said, "It's not your fault. I'll get back to my duties. Good luck in Saigon."

Gerber sat down on his cot again when Minh left and took another drink of Beam's. At the moment there seemed to be nothing else to do.

Bocker looked in a moment later and said, "Chopper will be here in a few minutes, Captain."

"Thanks," said Gerber. "Please inform Miss Morrow."

"Yes, sir. Good luck, sir."

Within five minutes Gerber was at the pad with Morrow, watching the Huey approach from the distance. As it came in, he said to her, "This is it." He was echoing the words said by a million different soldiers before they entered a thousand different battles.

A little before noon they were in Crinshaw's outer office, facing the same old master sergeant who sat behind the same old desk. He stopped them before they could enter Crinshaw's inner office because they didn't have an appointment. The room was cooler than it had been the last time Gerber had been there. A new air conditioner had been built into the wall just under the window. The blinds were drawn so that there was no glare from outside, and that meant the lights had to be on. The walls of the office were made of dark stained paneling so even with the overhead lights and three lamps—one on each of the two end tables and the third on the old sergeant's desk— it was still dim inside. A coffeepot on a small table had been added, along with Styrofoam cups, sugar and creamer. The sergeant didn't offer any coffee to Gerber or Morrow. There were pictures scattered around the walls in wooden frames, watercolors of local scenes and one of F-4s sitting in sand-bagged revetments waiting to take off on new missions.

The sergeant reached for the field phone, spun the crank and spoke into it quietly for a moment. Then he gestured at the new beige couch. When he hung up, he said, "Please have a seat. The general will be ready to see you in a couple of minutes."

When they were seated, Gerber said, "Now you wait here while I start this. I may be able to get through it without having to bring you in."

"I don't understand your reluctance to go in with everything you have."

"It's simple. We're supposed to clean our own dirty laundry without having to resort to outside forces. The man who calls a senator because he feels he has been treated shabbily has his records flagged with a note that says there is Congressional influence. It's not a good career move. Likewise, someone who goes to the papers has his record marked. He's labeled as a maverick, a troublemaker."

"Then why do all this?"

"To get my people out of jail."

Before he could say more, there was a buzz from the field phone, and the sergeant pointed to the closed door. "The general will see you now, Captain," he said.

Gerber stood up. "It'll be a while before I need you, but if I holler, it's going to mean that I'm in a hole."

"Good luck, Mack."

"Thanks." He took a deep breath, hesitated for a second with his hand on the doorknob and then went in.

As usual, it was so cold in the office that Crinshaw was wearing a field jacket. Like the outer office, the curtains were drawn, giving the impression of late evening. The captured weapons were still mounted on the wall, and Gerber thought that a couple of new ones had been added. Gerber knew Crinshaw collected them by telling subordinates that trophy hunting was career suicide. The general sat behind his mammoth desk that was bare except for a green blotter, a couple of pens in a shiny brass holder and a single manila file. The file was open, and Crinshaw was reading the top page.

"Boy, you are in a heap of trouble," Crinshaw began. He held up a hand to stave off any protest that Gerber might want to make. "You are lucky that you came in before I sent out the military police to arrest you. I've already locked your lieutenant up in LBJ for helping Fetterman and Tyme escape. I should also tell you that you'll be arrested just as soon as I can get the MPs over here."

"Before you make any precipitative moves, General, I think you'd better hear what I have to say."

"Don't go telling me what I better do, boy. And before you open that smart mouth of yours again, let me remind you of your rights under Article—"

"Cut the shit, General. You don't intimidate me by reading my rights to me. You are not in possession of all the facts in this case. You had better hear what I have to say or you can kiss all our careers goodbye."

Gerber was going to say more, but Crinshaw had stood and was trying to speak. His face had gone a deep purple and his mouth was working, but there were no sounds coming out of it. He clutched his chest, and for a moment Gerber thought the older man was having a heart attack.

Finally Crinshaw got his breath back. His voice was strained, but quiet. "Talk to me," was all he said.

Gerber moved closer to the large desk. He handed a package of pictures across as Crinshaw collapsed into his chair and said, "First, maybe you'll want to look at these. They are proof that the North Vietnamese and the Red Chinese are operating both here in South Vietnam and in Cambodia."

Without a word Crinshaw grabbed the pictures and thumbed through them. He saw pictures of a couple of men in NVA uniforms sitting in Gerber's team house at the camp. He hesitated when he came to the one showing a man in a khaki uniform sitting at a table while Derek Kepler stood by, but all he said was, "So?"

"General, you have my men in jail for committing crimes in a neutral country. I'm showing you the country isn't all that neutral."

"Makes no difference what you have there. The entire army of the People's Republic of China could be in Cambodia, and it wouldn't matter. The Soviet Union could have giant bases there, and it wouldn't matter. Your people crossed the border illegally."

"All right, General," he said. "If you'll look at that last picture again, you'll see that it is of a man wearing the uniform of a Red Chinese NCO. You'll also notice that he is in the team house at my camp. In other words, he is currently a prisoner of war. Positive proof that the Chinese are assisting the North Vietnamese. He was captured after he participated in an ambush against one of my patrols. He was fighting the war.

"You'll further note," Gerber said conversationally, "that reports from all my operations in the last month have been appended to the photos. You'll note that there is an order signed by you stating that I am to allow one reporter, Robin Morrow, free access to everything I have, including participation on patrols—"

"I never said that she was to be allowed on patrols," countered Crinshaw.

Ignoring the interruption, Gerber continued, "And you will see a copy of an order, again signed by you, sending us out to look for a missing Vietnamese patrol and to do everything in our power to find it. That can be interpreted to mean we were to sweep into Cambodia if necessary. In other words, it's possible that my men were in Cambodia on your orders."

"That's really stretching things, Gerber," Crinshaw replied. "I never meant for you to violate Cambodia's neutrality and you know it. You're grasping at straws there. If that's the best you can do, I'll just call the MPs now and save us all some trouble."

"I have witnesses, both American and South Vietnamese, who can testify you hinted strongly that a recon into Cambodia would be permissible if the patrol was not found."

"That's not what I—"

"You wanted to convict Sergeants Fetterman and Tyme for the murder of a foreign national," Gerber continued, ignoring Crinshaw's protest. "Except that the foreign national was a soldier who had participated in a number of actions against us."

Now Crinshaw felt that he was on firmer ground. "Makes no difference. You can't go around smoking Red Chinese, especially when they are in Cambodia. All your arguments make no difference to me. That man you claim is a Red Chinese NCO does nothing for you or your men. You just don't get it, do you, boy. Fetterman and Tyme did cross the border into Cambodia, and they did shoot the man. We all know that."

"Then you admit that this case is about the killing of a specific Red Chinese," said Gerber.

"Among other things," admitted Crinshaw. He leaned back in his chair. He laced his fingers behind his head and looked at the ceiling.

"The man you are referring to," said Gerber, "the one supposedly dusted by Sergeant Tyme, is, in fact, still alive and well."

Crinshaw slammed his fist to the desktop with so much force that the penholder flew to the floor. "Now how in the hell can you know that?"

"Interrogation of one of our other prisoners, a North Vietnamese regular. We talked to him for quite a while. He told us that the Chinese officer who normally ran patrols into South Vietnam had been recalled to China three days after he eliminated the South Vietnamese ranger patrol."

Now Gerber held up his hand. "I know what you're thinking. But our prisoner told us all about it, including the story of a marvelous pistol the Chinese officer picked up as a trophy. I'm sure you'll be able to confirm that one of the South Vietnamese ranger officers was carrying a special weapon."

"Think you're pretty smart, don't you, boy? Think you boxed old Billy Joe pretty good with all your reports and pictures and interrogations and all, don't you? Well, you got one big problem. They still killed a Chinese, and they did it in Cambodia. I have them dead to rights, and they will be convicted the moment we catch them—and then we'll try them for desertion. When we're done with them, you'll be next. You sent them out to do that."

Gerber was suddenly tired of it all. He didn't like this one little bit. Vietnam was a war zone, although some of the newspapers liked to call it an undeclared war. But it was war nonetheless. Everyone was supposed to stick together with an eye on defeating the enemy. Personal hatreds and personality conflicts were supposed to wait until the enemy was defeated. Crinshaw wasn't interested in any of that. He wanted to destroy the Special Forces for some reason that Gerber just couldn't understand.

He sat down uninvited. It was something that his military training told him never to do. But now it didn't matter. He had already violated a dozen unwritten rules and about half that many that were written. Sitting down without permission certainly couldn't make things any worse than they already were.

Crinshaw was right on one point. Fetterman and Tyme were guilty of crossing the border and shooting a Red Chinese. They had done it because the CIA had said that other teams in other locations were eliminating Vietcong cadre and North Vietnamese leaders. The only real difference was that all the other activity was taking place in South Vietnam. Gerber's men had gone into Cambodia.

"Why don't you save us all some trouble, boy," said Crinshaw, "and meet the MPs outside. I don't want to look at you anymore."

"Because I don't think I'm going to jail," responded Gerber.

"One thing I should mention," said Crinshaw, rocking forward in his chair so that he could lean both his elbows on the desk. "None of what you have said will leave this room. This is national security and I've just classified it. You've got nothing. I'll give a call to MACV, and they'll pick up your prisoner and see that he gets back to the proper place. They'll keep it quiet, so that you don't even have that."

Gerber shook his head. He had used it all. He'd tried everything he had, and Crinshaw showed no signs of caving in. He had an answer for everything. Minh had been right about that. The fact that Fetterman and Tyme had shot the wrong man made no real difference. They had shot someone.

"The CIA at MACV headquarters is fully aware of the mission," said Gerber. "We discussed it before the men went into the field."

"The CIA and MACV deny all knowledge of such activities," Crinshaw shot back. "You just refuse to understand. You're all alone on this. Now why don't you just get out of here, you dirty son of a bitch."

Gerber stood, but made no move to leave the room. "If you continue to do this, I take you down with me."

For just an instant Crinshaw thought Gerber meant to kill him. His face drained of color, and he rocked back in his chair. Then he realized what Gerber meant. He said, "There is nothing you can do."

It was time to play the last card. The one that Minh had insisted would have to be used. Gerber was suddenly glad that he had allowed himself to be pushed into taking Morrow on the patrol. "A story has been written and is on its way back to the United States," he said softly. "It outlines everything that has happened. It points fingers at you for ordering the mission, for covering up and for obstructing justice. It proves that the Red Chinese are involved in Vietnam. It covers it all, every bit of it, and when it's published, we all go down."

Crinshaw burst into laughter. "That's old, boy. That's really old. It's got whiskers on it."

"It's not a bluff, General."

"You try something like that, you're going to be in jail for a long time."

"From what you've already said, General," countered Gerber, "I'm heading there for a long sentence, anyway. I've nothing to lose. You overplayed your hand."

"Why don't you just get the fuck out of here."

Gerber moved to the door and opened it. Robin Morrow was on her feet and inside before Crinshaw could say a word.

"She filed her story this morning before we came over here," he said. "A story that contains all the things that we've just talked about."

"I can stop the story, General," she said. "But without my word it gets printed and syndicated and broadcast. It's already on the plane heading home, with lots and lots of pictures."

"One call," said Crinshaw. "I can stop it with one call."

"It's too late," said Morrow. She looked to the right at the wing chair, walked over and sat down. "Far too late."

"I'm sure that I can convince your editors to withhold the story," said Crinshaw, smiling. "In the interests of national security, that is. They are reasonable people."

"I can stop it," said Morrow, "but you can't."

"Go ahead," blustered Crinshaw. "Print it. I'll get by, but you, Captain, you'll be court-martialed. And so will all of the men you're so damned proud of. Every last one of them. You'll all end up in jail or worse."

Morrow looked at Gerber, her eyes questioning, wondering if Crinshaw could make good his threat.

But Gerber knew he had won. Crinshaw had made his threat with no conviction in his voice. It was as hollow as a drain-pipe. He said, "Make your calls, General. I've got to get my people back to the camp. I've got my senior demolitions man in charge right now. There's not an American officer within fifty miles of the place.''

"There is still a regulation covering insubordination,'' said Crinshaw. "You're getting a little too smart in your tones. And I believe we have a directive covering who is to be left in command of units in the field.''

"Yes, sir,'' said Gerber. "But this is an extraordinary set of circumstances.''

Crinshaw slumped in his chair. He stared at the two people in front of him. The whirring of the air conditioner was the only sound as it continued to blast an icy breeze into the room.

"You say that you can stop the story,'' he finally said to Morrow. "It won't look suspicious to your people?''

She shook her head. "They won't even look at it without my say-so.''

"Everything stays in this room,'' said Crinshaw. "Everything.''

"Of course,'' said Gerber, suddenly wanting to laugh, to shout or scream.

Crinshaw turned to Morrow again. "I let you go out there and you do this to me.''

"I'm sorry about that, General, but—''

"Never mind,'' said Crinshaw harshly. "It all stays right here. You have no story. No pictures. Nothing.''

"Until you approve it for publication,'' she said.

"Don't hold your breath on that,'' he said. "It'll never see the light of day.'' He turned his attention to Gerber. "What do you need from me?'' asked Crinshaw, his voice subdued.

"First, call Long Binh and get my executive officer out of jail. Then call the judge advocate, or whoever, and order all copies of the trial proceedings brought here so you can destroy them. Then issue the appropriate orders so that neither Fetterman nor Tyme will be arrested for a jailbreak.''

Crinshaw nodded dumbly and sat staring at the bright-green blotter, as if in a trance. Then he shook himself. The color came back to his face and the anger flared in his eyes. "All right, Captain. You've made your point. Now get the hell out of here.''

"Yes, sir."

"One thing, General," said Morrow. "Just before I came in, two MPs arrived, and I think they wanted to arrest Captain Gerber."

Crinshaw picked up the phone. He grumbled into it and then said, "You're in the clear. Now get the hell out of here."

At the door Gerber stopped. He turned back and said, "One more thing, General. What do I do with the Chinese NCO?"

"That's your problem now, hotshot. You deal with it."

"Yes, sir."

Outside, the sergeant was telling the MPs to fade away. Morrow stopped at the couch to pick up her camera bag. She turned toward Gerber and broke into a smile, giggling almost helplessly. "You did it!"

"We did it," said Gerber, laughing. "Without you, it would never have worked. I had to have it all. If I had missed a single piece, Crinshaw might have been able to get out from under it. If it hadn't been for the threat of public exposure, Crinshaw still might have beaten it, but with the public in on the case, Crinshaw would have fallen, too. It had to be the whole package, or we would have lost." He laughed again, but more from relief than anything else.

"I do have just one question," said Robin. "What *are* you going to do with the Chinese guy?"

Gerber pushed a hand through his hair. "Hadn't thought that much about it. I suppose I'll turn him over to the CIA and let them worry about it."

"What will the CIA do to him?"

"I would imagine they'll question him and then send him home with a nasty-gram to the Chinese about keeping their people out of the war."

"You think that's fair?" asked Morrow. "After all, he helped you, even if he didn't mean to."

"Yeah, but he's also an enemy soldier. Besides, if the CIA sends him home, we'll get something in return."

"What about him?"

"What about him?" repeated Gerber.

"When he gets back to China, if the CIA sends him, won't they shoot him? Aren't you worried about that?"

"I doubt seriously that they would shoot him. But even if they did, why should I care? He's an enemy soldier, and if we met on the battlefield, I would be obligated to shoot him. For that matter, he would be obligated to shoot me. Hell, for all I know, he tried to. I'm not going to lose any sleep over an enemy soldier. I have too many friendly soldiers to worry about."

"Like Fetterman and Tyme?" she asked.

"And Bromhead."

15

It had taken less than an hour to get Bromhead out of Long
Binh Jail. Crinshaw's phone call had arranged it, and when
Gerber walked into the jail, he found the young lieutenant
waiting in a downstairs office, talking to the MPs about the war
in the field. They had then driven back to Saigon and the Tan
Son Nhut officers' club. Gerber had found a secluded table in
the back that was away from the late-afternoon diners. He had
asked for a bottle of Beam's and then ordered three drinks,
neat, to take to the table for Morrow, Bromhead and himself.

"You know," said Gerber, "you make me sorry for some of
the things I've said about journalists. You prove that there are
some who have a sense of responsibility, who won't violate
trust or human feelings, in search of the almighty story."

"I don't know whether I should thank you or stomp out of
here," Robin replied.

"I meant it as a compliment. I do appreciate all that you did
for us."

"Mack," she said quietly, "I think you know why I did it."

Bromhead looked from one to the other and said, "Did I
miss something?"

"You must have," said Gerber. "Jail will do that to you."

Robin picked up her drink and swirled it around. She had her eyes fixed on Gerber.

For a moment there was silence between them, but it was an easy silence with no pressure. Gerber sat there relishing it because it was the first time in several weeks he'd been able to relax. He didn't have to worry about patrols, or the disposition of troops, or where Bromhead was. In three or four hours he would have to get back to camp, but right now Minh would have to handle it. Smith was there to oversee it, and Charlie hadn't tried anything for a couple of months.

The only real problem was how to find Fetterman and tell him that everything had changed during the past twenty hours. He and Tyme could return to the unit with the charges against them dropped. Better than dropped. They had been erased. Gerber was sure Fetterman would check in, but figured he would receive the message while at the camp. Then he would tell him to bring Tyme home.

Morrow cut into his thoughts. "So now what? Is your general going to cause you any more problems?"

"That's going to be a very interesting situation. He could cause a lot of trouble for us, just by making us sign forms—in triplicate—for everything we need. Or by denying us air support and sending us the worst men for replacements. He could probably have the Vietnamese pull Minh and a couple of the top strike companies out and replace them with crooks. He could, but I don't think he will."

"Why not?"

"It would be like cutting his own throat. We've got a good record out there, and that makes him look good. No, I think he'll just look for ways to cut us down without hurting himself. We've made a real enemy, but not one who will let himself be destroyed to get us."

There was more to say, and more questions that Morrow wanted to ask, but it wasn't the time or the place for them. Now was the time to celebrate before they had to catch the flight back to the camp.

Gerber turned his attention to Bromhead. "I think you may have jumped the gun a little," he said, laughing. "Gave Fetterman the passports a little too soon, although it doesn't matter."

Bromhead had ordered another round of drinks when the waitress came by. "They were as good as convicted," he said in his own defense, "and the way the general was shoving everything through, I figured he'd have them on the way to Leavenworth by morning. I got them out as quickly as I could."

"I'm not criticizing you, Johnny, other than to say you shouldn't have let them catch you."

"I'll buy that," he said.

They were interrupted again, this time by the PA system in the bar. "Captain Mack Gerber, you have a call in the main office. Captain Gerber, telephone in the main office."

As he got up, Gerber said, "Just who in the hell could that be? If the waitress makes a swing past us again," he added, "get me a steak, rare, with a baked potato."

Gerber asked the bartender where he could take the call and was directed to a phone. He picked it up, listened for a second to the open line and said, "Gerber."

"Afternoon, Captain," said Fetterman. "How's the world treating you?"

"Tony! Where in the hell are you?"

"Bangkok, Captain. An aptly named little burg. Ol' Boom-Boom is living up to his name, too. Right now he is in the company of a young Oriental lass with the most beautiful black hair you could imagine. And, for contrast, he has found a blond lady. He's entertaining both of them with stories of derring-do that raise my hair."

Gerber laughed. "Bangkok! You old son of a bitch. How'd you get there?" He thought for a moment and then said, "More important, how'd you know to call me here?"

"Figured that after the young lieutenant sprung us, he'd get his ass in a sling and you'd have to rescue him. Then you'd head over to the club for a quick one before heading home. Besides, when you're a master sergeant, you have to know these things."

"I find that extremely difficult to believe."

"Yes, sir. Actually, I managed to get through to the camp, and they told me where you had gone. I called Colonel Bates and he suggested that I try the club."

"Speaking of which," said Gerber, "everything has been cleared at this end. The general has been convinced that a grave mistake was made, and the slate is now clean. You can return anytime you want."

"Well, now, Captain. That might be a problem. Me, I would be back immediately. Only get myself in trouble with Mrs. Fetterman and the kids by hanging around here. But Boom-Boom, he doesn't have such mundane worries. He wants to see the sights, entertain the ladies and have a good time. Figured that you might see your way clear to letting us have a couple of three-day passes, or maybe granting a little extra leave time."

"That's no problem, Tony."

"What about the escape, Captain? They can't be real happy about that."

"All I can tell you is that Lieutenant Bromhead is here in the club with me sucking down the Beam's like he was told that he'd better drink it fast or somebody else would get his share. Seriously, the theory here is: if there was no trial, then there was no arrest, and if there was no arrest, then there couldn't have been an escape. You're in, free and clear."

"Okay, Captain. We'll come on back in a couple of days. You might have to arrange for transport from Tan Son Nhut out to the camp."

"There is one other thing, Tony. We had some trouble with Crinshaw's body. They shipped the wrong one for burial. You understand what I'm telling you? We got the wrong body."

"Yes, sir. I get the message. Me and Boom-Boom will be there by 0900 tomorrow."

Gerber hung up the phone carefully. Two or three weeks would soon be wiped out. Totally gone. In the morning things would be back to normal, and he would be back at the camp. Tomorrow they would start the war again.

GLOSSARY

AC—An aircraft commander. The pilot in charge of the aircraft.

AK-47—Assault rifle normally used by the North Vietnamese and the Vietcong.

AO—Area of Operation.

AO DAI—A long dresslike garment, split up the sides and worn over pants.

AP ROUNDS—Armor-piercing ammunition.

ARVN—Army of the Republic of Vietnam. A South Vietnamese soldier. Also known as Marvin Arvin.

BAR—Browning Automatic Rifle.

BEAUCOUP—French for many. Boonie rats usually pronounced this word boo-coo.

BODY COUNT—The number of enemy killed, wounded or captured during an operation. Term used by Saigon and Washington as a means of measuring progress of the war.

BOOM-BOOM—Term used by the Vietnamese prostitutes in selling their product.

BOONDOGGLE—Any military operation that hasn't been completely thought out. An operation that is ridiculous.

BOONIE RAT—An infantryman or grunt.

C AND C—The Command and Control aircraft that circled overhead to direct the combined air and ground operations.

CARIBOU—Cargo transport plane.

CHICOM—Chinese Communist.

CHINOOK—Army Aviation twin-engine helicopter.

CH-47—Also known as a shit hook. See *Shit hook*.

CLAYMORE—An antipersonnel mine that fires 750 steel balls with a lethal range of 50 meters.

CO CONG—Term referring to the female Vietcong.

DAI UY—Vietnamese Army rank the equivalent of captain.

DCI—Director, Central Intelligence. The director of the Central Intelligence Agency or CIA.

DEROS—See *Short-timer*.

DONG—A unit of North Vietnamese money about equal to a penny.

FIVE—Radio call sign for the executive officer of a unit.

FNG—A fucking new guy.

FRENCH FORT—A distinctive triangular structure built by the hundreds by the French.

GARAND—The M-1 rifle that was replaced by the M-14. Issued to the Vietnamese early in the war.

GREENS—The Army Class A uniform.

HE—High explosive ammunition.

HOOTCH—Almost any shelter, from temporary to long-term.

HOTEL THREE—A helicopter landing area at Saigon's Tan Son Nhut Air Force Base.

HUEY—A Bell UH-1D, or its successor, the UH-1H, helicopter. Called a Huey because its original designation was HU, but later changed to UH. Also called a Slick.

IN-COUNTRY—Term used to refer to American troops operating in South Vietnam. They were all in-country.

KABAR—A type of military combat knife.

KIA—Killed In Action.

KLICK—A thousand meters. A kilometer. Roughly five-sixths of a mile.

LBJ—Long Binh Jail.

LEGS—Derogatory term used by airborne-qualified troops in talking about regular infantry.

LIMA LIMA—Land line. Refers to telephone communications between two points on the ground.

LLDB—Luc Luong Dac Biet. The South Vietnamese Special Forces.

LP—Listening Post. A position outside the perimeter manned by a couple of people to give advance warning of enemy activity.

LZ—Landing Zone.

M-14—Standard rifle of the U.S. Army, eventually replaced by the M-16. It fired the standard NATO 7.62 mm round.

M-16—Became the standard infantry weapon of the Vietnam War. It fired 5.56 mm ammunition.

M-79—A short-barreled, shoulder-fired weapon that fires a 40 mm grenade. These can be high explosive, white phosphorus or canister.

MACV—Military Assistance Command, Vietnam. Replaced MAAG in 1964.

MEDEVAC—Also called Dustoff. Medical evacuation by helicopter.

MP—Military Police.

MPC—Military Payment Certificates. GI play money.

NCO—A noncommissioned officer. A noncom. A sergeant.

NEXT—The man who said he was the next to be rotated home. See *Short*.

NINETEEN—The average age of the combat soldier in Vietnam. During World War II the average age was twenty-six.

NOUC-MAM—A foul-smelling (to the Americans at least) fermented fish sauce used by the Vietnamese as a condiment. GIs nicknamed it "armpit sauce."

NVA—The North Vietnamese Army. Also used to designate a soldier from North Vietnam.

OD—Olive drab.

P-38—Military designation for the small, one-piece can opener supplied with C-rations.

PRC-10—Portable radio.

PRC-25—Standard infantry radio used in Vietnam. Sometimes referred to as the "Prick-25," it was heavy and awkward.

PROGUES—A derogatory term used to describe the fat, lazy people who inhabited rear areas, taking all the best supplies for themselves and leaving the rest for the men in the field.

PULL PITCH—Term used by helicopter pilots that means they are going to take off.

PUNGI STAKE—Sharpened bamboo hidden to penetrate the foot, sometimes dipped in feces.

R AND R—Rest and Relaxation. The term came to mean a trip outside of Vietnam where the soldier could forget about the war.

RF STRIKERS—Local military forces recruited and employed inside a province. Known as Regional Forces.

RINGKNOCKER—A ringknocker is a graduate of a military academy. It refers to the ring worn by all graduates.

RPD—A 7.62 mm Soviet light machine gun.

RTO—Radio-Telephone Operator. The radio man of a unit.

RULES OF ENGAGEMENT—The rules that told the American troops when they could fire and when they couldn't. Full Suppression meant they could fire all the way in on a landing. Normal Rules meant they could return fire for fire received. Negative Suppression meant they weren't to shoot back.

SAPPER—An enemy soldier used in demolitions. Used explosives during attacks.

SIX—Radio call sign for a unit commander.

SHIT HOOK—Name applied by the troops to the Chinook helicopter because of all the "shit" stirred up by the massive rotors.

SHORT—Term used by everyone in Vietnam to tell all who would listen that his tour was almost over.

SHORT-TIMER—Person who had been in Vietnam for nearly a year and who would be rotated back to the World soon. When the DEROS (Date Of Estimated Return From Overseas) was the shortest in the unit, the person was said to be Next.

SKS—A Simonov 7.62 mm semiautomatic carbine.

SMG—Submachine gun.

SOI—Signal Operating Instructions. The booklet that contained the call signs and radio frequencies of the units in Vietnam.

STEEL POT—The standard U.S. Army helmet. The steel pot was the outer metal cover.

TAI—A Vietnamese ethnic group living in the mountainous regions.

THREE—Radio call sign of the operations officer.

THREE CORPS—The military area around Saigon. Vietnam was divided into four corps areas.

THE WORLD—The United States.

TWO—Radio call sign of the intelligence officer.

VC—Vietcong, called Victor Charlie (Phonetic alphabet), or just Charlie.

VIETCONG—A contraction of Vietnam Cong San (Vietnamese Communist.)

VIETCONG SAN—The Vietnamese communists. A term in use since 1956.

VNAF—South Vietnamese Air Force.

WILLIE PETE—WP, White Phosphorus. Called smoke rounds. Also used as antipersonnel weapons.

**A new thriller from a master
of psychological suspense!**

RAYMOND OBSTFELD

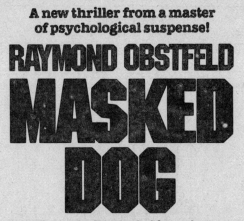

MASKED
DOG

A decade ago, the CIA searched for a volunteer to test a drug that would suppress fear in human beings, thereby changing the way war is fought, the way countries negotiate, the way the world works.

They found their guinea pig: Gifford S. Devane, a doctor sentenced to twenty-five years in jail for a brutal crime.

This imprisoned "volunteer" proved that the drug worked only too well. He became entirely fearless. He turned into a monster of superhuman strength. Only the jail's bars protected society from a terrifying menace.

Until Devane escaped.

**The Russians want him for his secret.
The CIA wants him dead.
And the Masked Dog
wants his revenge.**

MAS-2-R